There was a deep crater where there had been a large oak just minutes before. At the bottom of it the crystal ship was still glowing from the heat of re-entry. She felt the heat rush up into her nose, and without meaning to, she pulled back instinctively. She could feel her pulse beating, but she braced herself and started again. But a hand, strong and firm, pulled her back and she heard his voice. "No. Don't. It's too hot."

He was standing behind her, holding on to her. He was thinner than she had remembered and his face was drawn and pale. His knees began to buckle and she braced herself as he collapsed into her arms. They both tumbled to the ground. His lips, dry and parched, quivered as he struggled to say one word. "Mom."

Martha Kent felt his weight crushing into her, but, with tears streaming down her face, she held on to him for a long, long time.

Her son was home.

SUPERMAN
R E T U R N S™

NOVELIZATION BY MARV WOLFMAN

SCREENPLAY BY MICHAEL DOUGHERTY & DAN HARRIS

STORY BY BRYAN SINGER & MICHAEL DOUGHERTY & DAN HARRIS

SUPERMAN CREATED BY JERRY SIEGEL AND JOE SHUSTER

WARNER BOOKS

NEW YORK   BOSTON

Book design by Stratford Publishing Services

Warner Books
1271 Avenue of the Americas
New York, NY 10020
www.dccomics.com
Keyword: DC Comic on AOL

Printed in the United States of America

First Printing: June 2006

10 9 8 7 6 5 4 3 2 1

It must end as it begins;
with the crystal.

PART ONE

HOME

One

Kal-El was asleep when his world exploded. His only memories were of shifting back and forth in the soft, protective confines of his mother's womb, dreaming of the gentle sounds she made. They were encouraging songs and tender coos that let him know how much he was already loved. As she sang, he knew her hand would gently brush against her swollen abdomen then come to rest on his small, bulging stomach. He anxiously waited for that all-too-brief moment, hoping that very soon he would look into her eyes and let her know he loved her, too.

He was sixteen hours old when he opened his eyes to see her standing over him, a sweet proud smile on her lips. "You are so beautiful," she said, playing with the fringes of his already thick, black hair. "And you deserve so much more than what awaits you."

He recognized his mother's voice—it had comforted

him for as long as he could remember—and he returned her a small smile in response. Her fingers danced across his tummy again, tickling him. He giggled, the chubby flesh around his eyes wrinkled as he reached to touch her long dark hair. She was beautiful but her dark gray eyes were welling up with tears. He didn't understand what was wrong with her, but in the nine months he grew inside her he had learned to deal with her shifting moods.

A second figure entered the room. When he spoke Kal-El knew it was his father, a handsome white-haired man with piercing blue eyes. He had heard his soft voice, muffled and distant, many times before, but now there was an anger in it Kal-El had never known, and the words, which of course meant nothing to him, were spat out quickly, as if rushing through them would let his father get past the annoyance, whatever it was, and onto something more pleasurable.

"They won't listen no matter what I say and in spite of the proof I show them," Jor-El said. "They're fools, and the fools they are would let us all die." Kal-El watched his mother circle her arms around his father, comforting him. "We have our contingencies, Jor-El. We'll make this work. You know we will."

"I pray you're right, Lara, but you know how intractable they can be. You should have heard them. 'Krypton die? Oh, never, Jor-El. This is just another of your mistaken fantasies.' Fantasies?"

He paced the room angrily, slamming his fist against a bright white wall. "Those small-minded condescending buffoons don't know how close I came to . . ." Jor-El unclenched his fist and dropped his arm to his side. "Unfortunately, I didn't do anything, as much as I wanted to.

Korth-Or ended the meeting just in time, and I left without another word. Fantasies? After everything I've showed them, everything I've done, how could they treat me in this way?"

"They're frightened old men, Jor-El. They've spent their lives extolling the perfection of Krypton. How could they believe now that we will be victims of a cruel fate beyond our control?"

Kal-El suddenly laughed, wholly inappropriately, and Jor-El's anger faded. He turned to look at his handsome son, barely one day old. He'd been suddenly summoned by the Council from Lara's bedside, and this was his first opportunity to study his son closely. He looked so much like Lara; eyes steady but happy, lips curled into a wonderful, warm smile.

This should have been Jor-El's happiest day. This should have been a time for celebration.

His father was smiling back at him, but as with his mother, the infant could tell it was halfhearted. Jor-El's deep, reassuring voice had always given him hope, but he sensed trouble now, and he started to cry.

"Don't cry, Kal-El, everything is going to be so good for you." Jor-El nuzzled his cheek until Kal-El's tears sputtered out and were replaced with soft, happy giggles.

"Kal-El will never know another sunrise," Jor-El said, tickling the boy's stomach, working to keep him calm. "At least not ours. The sun that will one day warm him will be young and burn yellow, and it will be the source of his great strength. Lara, he'll come to cherish it, not ever knowing the star he was born under was red and old and dying."

They called him "Kal-El." That was his name. Jor-El was his father. And his mother was Lara. They were his family.

Jor-El carefully lifted him from the soft blankets and held him facing their wall-sized window to look out onto their beautiful world that, as far as he could understand, had always been there and always would. There was crystal as far as he could see, shining brightly, reflecting the growing red glow of Krypton's dying sun. Kal-El turned away and cried; it was all too bright and vivid for his still-innocent eyes.

Jor-El sat in the far corner of the room where Kal-El would be protected in the comforting cloak of shadows. He opened his eyes again and saw his father, his face drawn and tired, grimly looking at him.

"My son, although we failed more than we care to remember, you must know we were a great people once. Enlightened even. We yearned to touch the impossible, and more often than not we succeeded. You will take that greatness with you, my child, and it will comfort and guide you."

"The ship will hold?" Lara interrupted, taking the baby for his last feeding. "It is such a long journey."

He nodded, smiling thinly. "I harvested the crystals myself."

Lara kissed Kal-El's cheek, then made a sucking sound against it. He giggled again, and her tears, thought long ago spent, began anew. "It's not fair. We'll never see him crawl or learn to walk. Isn't there any hope?"

Jor-El shook his head; no matter how long one took to intellectualize what had to be done, there was no real preparing for the actual moment. "Not for us. But he will walk. He'll even talk. And when he gets *there*—he'll do so much more."

Kal-El cooed as his mother held him tightly, afraid to let him go. He heard her heartbeat quicken; it was not the same comforting, steady beat he had gotten so used to for all his short existence. Things were not right.

He wanted to cry, to bring their attention back to him, but instead he sputtered and gurgled some meaningless sounds.

Lara had worked alongside her husband for five years, three as his assistant before they were married, and two since, rechecking all of his calculations, then going over them again and again. For the past month she increased her efforts, all the while secretly hoping that they would learn the Council was right all along and that it was she and Jor-El who were wrong, that they had made some small, undetected error that somehow blossomed into his ridiculous theory.

Krypton's sun will go supernova? Impossible. Not in our lifetime or the lifetime of our grandchildren. Yes, it's a red giant, continuing to expand, and yes, it's been cooling for more than a generation, but it has eons to go before it explodes. Come, come, Jor-El. We'll all be long dead before that happens. Don't you understand, Jor-El, what you ignored is that Krypton is shifting in its orbit. That would explain the quakes we've been experiencing... They had a hundred excuses why Jor-El was wrong.

But Lara knew as much as she prayed to Rao that one day she would cradle Kal-El's own baby in her arms, tweaking its little nose, and gently pinching its soft, pillow cheeks, at some point in the next ten hours, when there was no longer any margin for error, she would wrap him securely in the brightly colored blanket she'd bought the previous month and kept boxed in the corner of the freshly painted bedroom next to theirs, then she would carefully tuck the blanket around him as she placed him gently into the crystal star they had kept hidden in a secret panel in their inner lab. They had practiced the routine at least a hundred times. Kal-El's father would activate the security protocols to protect him during his journey, place the father crystal in the pod next to him, and then, after delaying the inevitable for as long as they could, Lara would reluctantly nod her consent, and they would send him off to his destiny.

His dreams would begin as theirs ended.

Mount Argo rumbled, shaking their laboratory again, but this tremor was weaker than they had been for months. *Maybe we are wrong,* Lara prayed as she gazed at the vast city beyond their window. Maybe it is just earthquakes. Maybe they are finally subsiding. Of course she knew better; she had completed the calculations herself, but that didn't mean she couldn't hold out hope for some unexpected miracle. Perhaps Jor-El didn't believe in Rao, or in his mercy, but she always had.

She heard the baby cooing in her arms and kissed his warm cheek again. Jor-El always said Kal-El was destined for greatness. But destiny was a thing of faith, too, not much different from her own.

Lara turned again to look out into the city, still glowing with a strong, steady, internal light. As sure as she was of its fate, she couldn't bring herself to accept that its eternal greatness would, all too soon, simply cease to exist.

It had been a timeless city, strong and powerful. It survived the vast armies of three great nations waging war on its bloodied streets. It stood proud as the signing place of an everlasting peace. Since then, thousands of generations had lived here, and Lara, who was raised half a world away on the Crater Plains, and had spent her early years dreaming of living where Krypton's earliest founders had once walked, did not want to believe that this magnificence, and all it stood for, would soon be gone.

She had spent her first year out of the university touring the city and its outer regions, basking in its surprising history. She trekked out to the Valley of the Elders and camped there for over a month, living in the shadow of Krypton's greatest. She could feel the energy, raw and surging and still very much alive in the immense crystal monoliths that seemed to reach beyond the famed half dome whose vaulted roof protected the valley from the planet's temperature extremes.

At night she would huddle in her sleep cocoon, its warming fabrics giving her the courage to walk the next morning along the fabled roads that Sor-El, Kol-Ar, and Pol-Us, the chosen representatives from the three warring nations, must have taken when they created the original Laws of Humanity that governed Krypton since those troubled early days.

The Valley of the Elders was set in a deep, miles-wide canyon, and from the ground, those crystal monolith towers, constructed in a large circle, reflecting the full spectrum of light, looked to Lara like hands raised in reverential prayer, faceted fingers stretched to touch their enduring red sun if not Rao himself. The towers' exterior faces and interior walls were illuminated with the massive crests of the newly civilized Krypton's brave founders, each rune shape uniquely designed.

Lara remembered reading that the fabled three had argued against their inclusion here; with all humility they believed they had merely drafted a logical document of rules and order and did not deserve inclusion themselves in the circle of ancients. But when the grateful people of Krypton voted that they would have to be included, they begrudgingly accepted the honor. It was the people who followed the laws who deserved recognition, they said, not those who merely wrote them.

Kol-Ar's emblem was the open hand of truth and justice. Sor-El's crest was a diamond-shaped shield with a winding serpent inside, a warning not to return to the dishonesty and violence that once had plagued their planet. Pol-Us's sign was the open eye, to provide eternal vigilance against those who sought a return to the barbarous times.

These three, and the others who followed them, ushered in generations of peace. To Lara, being in their valley, breathing the air they breathed so long ago, gave her chills. She was sure the power she felt here would last forever. She could not know that in five years' time, in little more than the snap of her fingers, the valley, the towers, and everything around them, would be gone.

Kryptonopolis had been grown from a single crystal mount more than ten thousand years before, and it still showed no signs of decay. Other stones, resting atop the flat base, had been grown and shaped by the earliest Kryptonians into vast cities millions of buildings strong. The tall towers surrounding the great building that was home to Krypton's Science Council gleamed in the bright red sunlight.

Lara was happy they didn't live closer to the Council. When she first came to the city to work with Jor-El, she believed there was probably no greater honor than to be welcomed into those halls. But even before the Council's reaction to Jor-El's discovery, she had come to loathe that sanctimonious institution with every angry emotion she could summon.

Lara and Jor-El's home, larger than typical for Argo's south wall, had been cut into the mount's face by Sor-El himself. It looked out over Argo's cliffs into the wide expanse of the Xan Chasm and its rainbow falls. Even after five years she could not look into that cavernous gulf and not feel humbled by its majesty.

Krypton was a world of wonders she had just begun to explore, and she cursed the fates that demanded its destruction.

Jor-El reached for the baby. It was time. For a moment Lara's eyes glazed over. *No. I won't let you send him away. I want him to be with me for just one more day. One full day.* But Lara knew changing her mind now would condemn their son to the same fate awaiting them. She snuggled her face into Kal-El's, kissed him for the last time, then handed him to his father. "But why Earth, Jor-El? They're primitives. Thousands of years behind us."

"He will need that advantage." Jor-El gently drew his finger across Kal-El's forehead, down his nose, and came to rest on his tiny, red lips. "To survive he will need that and more."

Jor-El returned Kal-El to the crystal pod as Lara again tucked him into the blanket. "He will be odd. Different," she said, trying not to look into those large, innocent eyes for fear of changing her mind, this time for good. Jor-El briefly touched his son's hand, then ran his fingers over the pod's internal crystals. They flashed in the expected order as the star's power began to charge. "But he will be fast. Virtually invulnerable."

Kal-El's tiny hand patted the inside of the pod, mimicking his father's actions, not realizing this small, cramped space would soon become his new mother and father and home for more than two long years. The crystals would feed, nurture, and protect him. And even in his long sleep he would spend the time listening to Lara's and Jor-El's voices talking to him, teaching him all that the twenty-eight known galaxies had to offer.

"We should go with him," Lara said suddenly. "He's too young. He'll need us." Jor-El laid down the special white crystal he was programming and put his arms around his frightened wife. He pulled her close and held her until he felt her rigid body soften and melt into his. "I promised the Council we'd stay on Krypton, but I said nothing about Kal-El." His hands slowly moved down the curve of her back as he nuzzled her long, slender neck, enjoying again her sweet perfume smell and remembering why he had fallen in love with her so many years before.

She was supposed to be his lab assistant, but unlike the others who had applied for the job, she was not only smart but seemingly unaffected by his position in the Council. He wasn't used to not being fawned over.

He was, after all, Jor-El, perhaps Krypton's greatest scientist, or so he'd been told repeatedly by nearly everyone who wanted something from him, which was pretty much everyone at the Academy.

And, of course, he was also a direct descendant of Sor-El himself. *You're much too humble, Jor-El. Don't you realize how great you are? You discovered the Phantom Zone, for Rao's sake, the humane way of dealing with unrepentant criminals.*

Increasingly of late, however, as he thought more of his own mortality, he began to question that discovery. Perhaps eternal damnation in some nameless limbo was actually worse than a simple and swift death.

But Lara never treated him as one of Krypton's best and brightest. She had worked with many of the other so-called greats since leaving the university, and she had begun to think that though they might have once been good, maybe when they were young, fame and fortune had turned them into little more than, well, idiots. And lecherous ones at that.

At parties she entertained her friends with her deadly accurate impersonations—the meaner they were in tearing apart their professors, the more everyone laughed. She delighted in explaining exactly how she could take all these oh-so-brilliant men's ideas, mix them together, and convert them into a single energy source, and they still wouldn't produce enough power to operate a child's top. They were rude and arrogant, surviving on the glory of their past achievements as well as the diligent work of their young assistants, of whom they took merciless advantage. She would then take her bow, and her friends, all young assistants, of course, would wildly applaud her.

Lara graduated at the top of her class, and had done significant work since then while publishing numerous papers. She had agreed to apply for the job as Jor-El's assistant only after deciding she would accept nothing less than complete equality with him from day one. And he would have to credit all her work.

She was not going to assist him only to be forgotten and shoved aside. She was still fuming over what that fat fraud Bal-Do had done to her. The so-called great Jor-El would have to accept her on her own terms, she stubbornly decided.

Their first meeting took her aback somewhat. Initially, he seemed to be serious and somber, which she expected based on the sober tone of the papers he published. But as they spoke she saw he was able to laugh easily, even at himself, especially when she tried to explain why one of his early letters, which had been collected into a long-out-of-print holo, was not only based on a miscalculation, but pompous in its assumptions.

"I was young then," he explained, laughing. "Full of great ideas and so sure of myself. But you're right. I was pompous. But I think I'm better now." Lara felt ashamed she had even brought it up.

His eyes were warm and inviting, and though she didn't want to admit it at first, he was very easy on *her* eyes. His hair was white and plentiful, and his face was flawlessly smooth. He was a good fifteen years older than she, but he had the build of someone who had been athletic when he was younger and kept in shape even now. The feelings she was suddenly having were disconcerting, but she felt she went there with an agenda and swore she would stick to it, no matter what.

Unfortunately, the interview, which she carefully rehearsed so she could control it no matter what direction it took, never quite happened, at least not the way she expected.

Jor-El had read her papers, asked her a few insignificant questions—or so she thought—and then asked what she expected from this job, *if* she got it.

She was prepared.

"I want to work at your side as an equal."

"Which means . . . ?"

"I'm not an underling. I'm not an assistant. I'm not there to bring you food. And I'm certainly not there for *anything* not related to our work. I want that very clear."

He nodded, amused. "Understood."

"Also, whatever we work on, I want to be part of it. I want to share the effort and the glory."

"And . . . ?"

"And? And whatever papers we write, I want my name on them, too."

"Is that all?"

She calmly recited the rest of her rehearsed demands, fully expecting Jor-El to reveal the dark streak she knew he'd been hiding until then, folded her arms across her chest, stuck out her chin, and waited for him to say, "Thanks, but I'll keep looking."

Before the meeting she thought she'd be fine with that, but seeing the corner of those powerful eyes crinkle up in amusement, and watching him looking at her with a much more handsome face than she had assumed from his holos, she wasn't sure she still held that exact same feeling.

"No problem, Lara," he said, astonishingly. "Can you start the beginning of next week?"

"Uhhh, yes. I, um, just want to make sure. You heard what I said?"

He was checking out a research holo. He froze the image, paused, and looked up at her with a puzzled expression.

"My hearing's fine. I have no problems with anything you asked for. Pretty standard as far as I'm concerned. If you add anything to the work we're doing here, of course you should get credit. Doesn't make any difference to me where the ideas come from."

She kept staring at him. "That's it then?"

"Frankly, I was afraid you'd say the money wasn't good enough. So, are you trying to talk me out of hiring you, or are you taking the job?"

It was about an hour after she got back to her small apartment on the Helios Crevice, that she realized she hadn't even said "thank you." She sought to repair that mistake her first day at work, thanking him not once but nearly a dozen times.

That night, bundled up in her blankets, she cursed her excessive enthusiasm. "Take it easy, Lara. He's just a man," she told herself, although not quite believing it.

Within a week she was back to normal, questioning his work, his methods, and arguing nearly all of his conclusions. Although when she was still so impossibly young she was wrong more often than she was right, under Jor-El's patient tutelage she grew quickly.

They worked together for three years. And by the time

she couldn't deny that she was completely in love with him, he realized that he had already fallen for her.

Lara took Kal-El's tiny hand in hers and slowly massaged each pudgy finger. "I worry for him. Away from us he'll be isolated. Alone."

"No," Jor-El said, holding a long white crystal up to the sunlight filtering in through their living quarters window. The light refracted, painting an iridescent rainbow across the infant's face. "He will not be alone. He will never be alone."

The big quake took them by surprise. They watched helpless as the south wall of their home quivered, then splintered and shattered, taking half the room with it. They saw Mount Argo shrug off thousand-foot slices of its once-proud crystal face. The massive shards slid down the mountain, hugging it tightly, a child refusing to leave its mother's side, only to disappear into the mists of the Xan Chasm. Two million homes, carefully and delicately grown and carved into the crystal over many thousands of years, vanished into that abyss. More than three million lives were lost.

"Jor-El?" Lara was rushing to Kal-El's bed. The grinding roar outside had awakened him, and he was crying. She picked him up and held him close.

"It's happening, Lara. Sooner than we thought, but just as we said."

"I'll get the father crystal," she said.

They heard Krypton scream its helpless protest as

Argo's peak exploded. It took less than four minutes for the great mount, home of the planet's culture and science, to sink unseen into the darkness. Krypton was dying.

Jor-El leaned into the crystal ship and tenderly stroked his son's face. "You will travel far, my little Kal-El. We will never leave you."

Lara removed the father crystal from its compartment. It had accepted nearly 95 percent of its programming. "It's not complete. Some of the sciences are missing."

"There's no more time. It will have to do."

He was kneeling by his son, his voice strong and reassuring. Kal-El was smiling at him, listening attentively to his calm, steady tone.

"Even in the face of our deaths, the richness of our lives will be yours. All that I have, all that I have learned, everything I feel, all this and more I bequeath you, my son. You will carry me inside you all the days of your life. You will make my strength your own. See my life through your eyes as your life will be seen through mine. The son becomes the father, and the father, the son. This is all I can send you, Kal-El."

He felt another quake and placed the father crystal next to the child.

"It's time."

Lara kissed Kal-El, her face, trembling with tears, hovered just above his. "I love you, and I've hardly had a chance to show you how much. Keep my thoughts alive in you, my wonderful, special boy."

The star's hatch lowered onto the pod, and the crystals melted together in an impenetrable seal. Jor-El took his wife's hand, and they stepped back as the star began to rise.

Lara wanted to turn away, but her eyes never left the ship as it crashed through the ceiling, crystal rain cascading down.

"Kal-El, my son, you are all that remains of a once-proud people," Jor-El whispered, his voice breaking. "And in you Krypton's glory will live on."

Jor-El put his arm around his wife as they watched their son's ship fly into the night, a living comet beginning its long and dangerous journey. When it finally disappeared into the black, they kissed each other and waited for the end to take them.

The red giant knew its time had come. The nuclear fusion deep inside it had exhausted its last sources of fuel. Hydrogen fused with helium, then those into oxygen and carbon, then into silicon and sulfur and finally into iron, which could not fuse. Without the energy to push back against the massive crush of gravity, the collapse was beginning. Shock waves would soon blow the gaseous shells of the star into space in a supernova as bright as the entire galaxy.

As Kal-El slept, Krypton's red sun died. His new home began a slow crawl across the empty vastness, heading toward a tiny, nearly insignificant bit of matter on the rim of a faraway galactic spiral that received its meager light from a fragile yellow star barely out of its infancy.

The final fragments of his world, green and glowing like miniature suns, hungrily spread outward, beginning a fateful voyage of their own.

Even in his sleep, his eyes tightly closed, the Last Son of Krypton saw the blinding brightness. *What is that?* he asked himself. *Why is it so cold? Why am I afraid? I was never afraid before.*

Jor-El knew there could be no mistakes now, not at his son's expense. He carefully grew and nurtured the crystals himself, starting with a specially cultivated seed, layering in molecule after molecule. And, as it grew, building on top of itself, he shaped each section to its very specific need.

Jor-El had spent the most time growing the crystals for the ship's outer shell. They had to be impervious to the fluctuations of heat and cold as the star neared distant suns or sped away from them. Lara had gone over each of Jor-El's calculations. She monitored the birthing process, watched the crystals expand, examined each atom, and eliminated any with even the slightest question concerning structural integrity.

The infant fit comfortably into the star's preformed cushion, which would expand even as Kal-El himself grew.

He was an hour shy of one day when placed in the crystal star, but when it finally found its way to Earth, he would be nearly three years old.

Two

The ship had long left Krypton's solar system behind and was flawlessly navigating its way through unfamiliar space. It circled small errant asteroids as well as uncharted moons. Once free of the red star's pull, crystal spikes emerged from its shell; weapons and sensors, shielding and guiding it. Protecting the son of Jor-El and Lara was the star's prime directive.

As it soared into the seemingly endless darkness, the baby, in restful hibernation, listened as his father spoke. "Of all the Earth scientists, perhaps only Einstein understands . . ." Jor-El's and Lara's words, which would be repeated continuously throughout his journey, would not only keep him company, but teach him what he needed to know to survive on his new home.

Kal-El learned about Earth, a planet much smaller than his own. There were people there, humans much like him. He could walk among them, and they would never know how different he was, how special he would become.

Jor-El taught him Earth's history, learned over nearly a decade of observation, enlightening him with incredible stories of how the humans evolved from nearly mindless primitives to become the masters of their planet. They built great cities, not by growing and shaping crystal as they did on Krypton, but by mixing earth with water and forming dense bricks.

"Follow their history, Kal-El, for as great as these people will one day be, they still cling to their primitive ways. They have medical advances that cure most of their diseases, that extend life far beyond what their frail bodies could ever have expected, but they still fight wars that kill their young and destroy whole populations. They are a paradox of despair and hope, and they need someone to guide them."

The ship moved swiftly through space, moving in and out of spatial holes, carrying its precious cargo toward its final destination.

Jor-El's voice remained constant and loving. "Under their yellow sun, on a world whose gravity is but a fraction of our own, you will have powers that will make you appear to be a god to them. But despite those abilities, despite your powers of flesh and mind, you are, like them, only a man, with all the frailties and weaknesses of any man. Understand your place among them, Kal-El, and though they may plead for you to use your abilities to change their lives for the better, do not give in to temptation.

"Show them their possibilities, but never choose their path for them. They must advance on their own, find their own way, make their own mistakes, conquer their own fears and hatreds, and create their own history."

Months were passing, but the journey was still young.

Kal-El was nearly a year old and Kryptonian music made his sleep peaceful. His mother had programmed human art into the crystal, and through it he learned about their loves and passions. Her voice comforted him, a sweet reminder of other times, of the gentle sounds she had made once, long ago.

"My son," she said, "you can lead them only by the examples we have imparted to you. Believe in truth. Believe in justice. Believe in the hope for their greatness. And if, through your actions they yearn to be great, too, then you will have done far more for them than by making all their burdens your own. Do not fear to help where they need help, but do not impose yourself on them. Gods can become devils far too quickly. Reliance on your powers will destroy them. Belief in your values will give them strength."

The night belonged to his mother, the days to Jor-El. "Now, my little Kal-El, let us talk of Euclidean geometry and physical science . . ."

Two and a half years later his eyes opened again. The crystal wall of his ship vibrated for a moment, then became transparent, allowing him to watch as they passed a large hazy, yellow world circled with rings composed of ice and rock. The star swept past the planet's moons; there were more than thirty, he counted.

"Saturn," he said slowly, making sure he pronounced it correctly. It was his first word in English. The father crystal taught him that this was the sixth planet in the Sol system. Minutes later, he knew, they would pass another world, and this one would be much larger.

Jupiter, he remembered. He looked down at the planet, darker than Saturn, with a dull, swirling red spot in its lower hemisphere. This planet was also ringed, although faint in comparison with Saturn.

He remembered his lessons; Jupiter had nearly forty smaller bodies circling it. "Moons," he repeated.

They were moving closer to the sun. He waited. It should be coming up soon, he knew, the wide belt of asteroids that drifted between Jupiter and the final world separating him and his destination.

The asteroids rushed past, his sensors keeping the ship on course and safe. Then he saw Mars, a much smaller planet than the previous two, red in color, with only two satellites orbiting it.

Kal-El felt his ship suddenly vibrate as its crystal spikes automatically folded back into its body pod, preparing itself for descent. They passed a small dead hunk of rock. "The moon. Luna."

He knew they were close.

The star's transparent wall shimmered and became opaque again, preparing for its descent.

The ship had worked exactly as his mother and father had designed it to.

Ahead of him was the planet Earth.

His new home.

Three

They had stored the crystal star in a shallow cellar of the old barn, then placed some floorboards over it and stacked several dozen bales of hay over that just to make sure it wouldn't be seen by prying eyes, not that anyone visited them much these days.

Most of their closest friends had died, and though they were well liked and respected in town, only a few, like Ben Hubbard and the Langs, ever came over to give Jonathan a helping hand.

Jonathan Kent wished he could have dug a deeper hole—for security—but his heart had started missing a beat the year before and Doc Frye had warned him not to overly exert himself.

"Great warning, Doc," Jonathan grumbled. "I'm a farmer. How the blazes am I supposed to get my chores done without exerting something or other along the way? Conjure up a genie and wish them completed?"

Although, in many ways, that was exactly what Jonathan and Martha Kent had done.

They found him while driving across their farm. They saw the bright light, then heard the explosion that nearly rocked them off the road.

Martha cried out. "Stop!"

"What was that?" Jonathan felt his heart jump.

They scrambled out of the old red pickup and saw that whatever it was had smashed through 170 feet of corn and dirt before losing its steam and braking to a stop.

They saw him at the bottom of the crevice, standing naked and alone in the field, a brightly colored blanket at his feet.

"Martha?" Jonathan was trembling as he looked at the little boy, no older than two or three. "The first thing we've got to do when we get home is find out who that boy's proper family is."

"He hasn't got any," Martha said, staring into the still-burning crevice. "Not around here anyway."

They took him home, having no idea then how he had gotten there or where he had come from.

But a few days later, when Jonathan dug out the shining rock half-buried in the field, he saw it wasn't a meteor at all, but a large crystal orb with dozens of other smaller crystals inside it. It was some sort of spaceship, he thought, though looking nothing at all like the ones he used to see in the movies as a teenager, back when Smallville had a movie theater.

The boy, they realized, had not accidentally wandered

onto their farm; he had come with the ship. From somewhere out there, from space.

As a teen, Jonathan had read Edgar Rice Burroughs's "A Princess of Mars" and wondered if the boy was a Martian. Not one of the four-armed green guys, but the more human ones that John Carter, the book's hero, also met.

Martha didn't care. She and Jonathan had wanted a child of their own since they were married, and it had nearly torn their marriage apart when they learned she could not conceive one.

Looking at the child, so handsome and innocent, she thought they could always say he was her cousin's boy from North Dakota, newly orphaned. No one would ask any questions.

It was a good thing, too, considering they saw him lift the old truck that had accidentally fallen onto Jonathan as he tried to change its flat tire. It weighed two and a half tons, and the boy hoisted it up like it was a Tinkertoy car until Jonathan pulled himself safely away.

Maybe he was a Martian after all.

They gave him Martha's maiden name and within the week, once the legal papers were signed at the county clerk's office, he officially became Clark Kent.

Martha picked him up in her arms and kissed his full, round cheeks. They put him in the truck, stopped to buy some clothes his size at Stacy's, then drove him to his new home.

Four

Superman was dreaming of the Kents when his eyes snapped open for the first time in more than two and a half years. He could hear the soft hiss of the sleep chamber's lid reintegrate with the crystals of the ship, but he waited for it fully to retract. One of the crystals projected a holographic star chart for him to inspect. *I'm almost there,* he thought. *So very close.*

As he stretched his arms and legs, making certain they still worked, he realized that all too soon his questions might finally be answered. For a moment the thought worried him; what if they weren't the answers he was looking for?

He closed his eyes again, waiting for the ship to signal him, the comforting memories of Smallville playing once more in his mind.

His father died when he was only seventeen, but Jonathan was still alive in his dreams, working the fields just as he always did every morning starting, of course, at

5:00 A.M. on the dot. Say this for Jonathan Kent, he was a creature of habit, and those habits had served him well.

He was done with most of his light chores before Clark awoke at seven. As usual, Clark ran out to bring him a buttered seeded kaiser and Maxwell House, his favorite, with only one teaspoon of sugar and a little fresh cream. While Jonathan paused to eat and sip his coffee, Clark took over and did some of the heavier lifting.

He missed his father and those wonderful talks they had each afternoon on the way back from town. Jonathan had been a month shy of graduating Smallville High School himself when he had to take over the farm from his dad, but his education didn't stop on that last schoolday. He was a voracious reader of everything from histories to mysteries and even some science fiction, and he could talk about nearly anything, from the Medicis to the Founding Fathers, and then throw in a bit of art appreciation as well.

Every day after lunch, usually consisting of some juice, pancakes, eggs and bacon with a side of toast, or sometimes a full ham steak if a pig had just been slaughtered, he would get into his old red pickup and drive into town for supplies and a quick stop at the library. He would return yesterday's book and check out a new one, which he'd start reading while parked across from Smallville High, waiting for Clark to finish his classes.

They would always take the long way home, around the Hubbard place, which gave them more time to talk about nearly anything that came up. Some days it was about whatever was in the newspaper that morning, or about something Jonathan had read in a book, or about some problem he could tell Clark was having either in school or in life.

Thinking about it now, Superman had to laugh. Those weren't easy days. He was strong as a baby, pretty much stronger than any adult, and his powers kept growing with him. At the time, those teenage years seemed nearly impossible to get through. He had all these abilities he wanted to show off to everyone, but his dad kept insisting he had to wait. *Wait? Teenagers can't wait. Didn't he know that?*

"There's so much to learn, Clark," he'd always say. "And never any reason to rush into things without thinking them through. You're meant for something special, son, something great, and it's not hitting home runs or showing off for your friends. When the time comes for the world to know what you can do, you'll know it. But 'til then it's best to master what you are. Know yourself as a man before you have no choice but to accept your destiny."

Jonathan Kent wasn't faster than a speeding bullet, and he couldn't leap tall buildings at a single bound—the powers all those reporters in Metropolis talked about on the day Superman revealed his existence to the world—but his father was a great man anyway. He understood people and cared about them, and when he died suddenly of a heart attack, mostly everyone in Smallville came out for the funeral.

Clark missed him so very much.

He looked over the holographic star charts; they were in Kryptonian, but Jor-El's crystals had taught him the language years ago, as an infant, traveling across a universe on his way to his new home.

He felt his heartbeat quicken. The readouts reminded him he was fast approaching what was projected to be

Krypton's location, assuming it still existed. At his current speed, the crystals calculated he'd be in its orbit within the hour.

He touched one of the crystals, and the ship's opaque walls turned transparent. He stared into the blackness, searching for the star he knew had to be near.

There were so many questions: *Will I see the sun, Krypton's sun? Is it still alive, still burning? And are planets still orbiting it? If so, is Krypton among them?*

But there was a question he knew he couldn't ask, not aloud, not even to himself. *Are they alive?*

He knew, as Jor-El had explained to him, that Krypton's sun had gone supernova many years ago, and was the reason Kal-El had to be sent to Earth. But the crystals were created before Krypton's death. *What if it never happened? What if Jor-El was wrong? What if Krypton's sun still existed, then the planet could be . . .*

He turned from the window and touched the glowing white crystal his father had laid down beside his one-day-old self. "Show me the newspaper again, please," he asked.

The father crystal glowed and projected a holographic image of a nearly three-year-old *Daily Planet* headline. "Astronomers Discover Krypton Intact. Signs of Life Found." He read the article again, just as carefully as he had the more than one hundred times he read it before leaving Earth and starting this galactic quest for—?

He wasn't sure what he wanted from this trip or what he expected to find. But he knew this was something he had to do.

● ● ●

He had always felt different, especially when he was a kid in Smallville, usually when the others were playing sports, as they struggled to make it to first base or to dunk a basket from only ten feet away.

He could have done that all so easily. He could have knocked the ball to the next state. He could have dunked it into the basket from another continent. He could score a touchdown every time and nobody could ever put a hand on him. But he couldn't. *Why not?* He always questioned. *Why can't I be myself?*

He used to dream of finding someplace where he could let loose with all his incredible abilities. Where he could explode with power. He wanted to be free to be himself, not pretend to be like everyone else.

Where do I belong?

He asked himself that every night in the darkness of his room, with his eyes closed, as he slowly drifted off into his dreams of someplace better.

Smallville certainly was not the place. Perhaps Krypton.

But Krypton was dead, or so he'd been repeatedly told.

He remembered his excitement when he studied the data taken at the far end of the solar system by the Cassini-Huygens satellite, sent by NASA to Saturn to study its largest moon, Titan. The reporter who broke the story told him the satellite had taken other pictures, too, including one that appeared to be a meaningless photograph of something that looked like . . . *dust*. But once it was enlarged, it changed his world.

"You're sure of this?" he had asked the reporter.

"Everything the scientists told me says it's accurate.

You can see the planet for yourself." He handed Superman a sheaf of data. "Go ahead and check the coordinates. They match the computer calculations. You recognize it, don't you?"

He nodded. "Yes. It's Krypton."

It was exactly as the father crystal had shown him. Krypton's red sun was still alive, burning in the distance. The planet in the photograph seemed intact. More important, there appeared to be life there.

"Their theory is that only parts of Krypton were affected by the supernova. Stars have been known to go nova, expend excess energy, then return to a relatively normal condition."

Superman was trying to understand it, but he kept getting drawn to the photograph. "Theoretically, only the part of Krypton facing the red giant might have been destroyed if the planet had somehow—this is the part they had to speculate—shielded itself from the initial solar explosions."

"But there could be life there?"

"The photograph indicates that, Superman, but it's not conclusive. The trouble is, the satellite's not in the position to take any other pictures now, and it would take NASA more than five years to launch another satellite, assuming they had the financing, which they don't, and several years after that for it to reach a location from which they could take more photos. But, to be honest, with the budget cuts these days, I frankly don't see that happening. I'm sorry."

Superman kept staring at that photo. It had to be Krypton. There had to be life on it.

If Krypton lived, it meant that his father had been

wrong. Superman wondered what he thought about that. He only knew his parents from their voices. He'd seen some holographs of them, but they were cold and sterile and lifeless. He wasn't exactly sure what he was supposed to feel for these . . . *phantoms*.

He knew Jonathan and Martha Kent were his parents. They raised him. They taught him. They loved him, and he loved them.

But these *phantoms* were the people who gave birth to him, and he knew they died while saving him. He knew Lara's voice was warm and loving. He could tell that Jor-El, who diligently tried to be professorial in his teachings, felt enormous pride as he told his—as-yet-unborn— son the wonderful stories of his planet and his family. They were obviously good people, loving people. People who died long before their time.

But . . .

But if Krypton had not died, he knew he might have been walking under its bright red sun and not flying under Earth's yellow star. He would never have had his life enriched by the Kents, or laughed alongside his friends, or met the woman he'd fallen in love with so quickly, the woman he left behind two and a half years ago without explaining where he was going.

What would it have been like to have lived on Krypton? Lara made it sound so wonderful, but the holos he saw were lifeless. Where were the trees? The grass? The blue skies? He studied the pictures, but he could find no clouds drifting lazily in the sky as he had all his childhood. He remembered lying on his back, his feet propped on the trunk of the lightning-razed *halfatree,* as he called what was little more than a big stump in the middle of his parents' wheatfields, and looking up into the sky, wondering where he had come from.

He loved the beauty of the bright, freshly painted barn sitting alone in a field of green, the small blue stream snaking its way past as it made its long trek to the Milford Lake wetlands to the north. At night he'd lie there thinking about the constellations he saw and what life might have been like in those faraway places.

Still, Krypton had a—he struggled for the word—*grandeur*. The stark white mountains that covered the world were sheets of carved crystal glowing in the rich scarlet sunlight. There seemed to be no limitations there. Everything was possible.

Jor-El said they had grown their planet over the millennia, building layers upon layers, reshaping it into something unique. They didn't just live on Krypton, they made their world in their own image, eliminating all weaknesses, enhancing their greatest strengths.

Reporters on Earth had once claimed that Superman could change the course of mighty rivers, although the fact is all he could do was dam up one part of a river—something any overactive beaver could do if he set his mind to it—then dig a trench leading the water somewhere it was needed.

But on Krypton they could literally change the course of rivers—*did they have rivers? I've seen no holos of any*—grow mountains, or do pretty much anything else they wanted. They had mastered their own world. They had eliminated war and violence. They provided food for everyone. There were no awful pandemics that destroyed entire civilizations. They had turned a dark and dangerous world into a paradise.

Krypton was a world of endless possibilities that his father insisted was about to die. Of course nobody believed him. *They had built their world, for heaven's sake.*

On Earth, in his other identity, Superman was a reporter, but what would his life have been like if he had stayed on Krypton? If he had been raised by Jor-El and Lara? Superman thought he'd probably have been a scientist. He'd have been groomed for that job since birth. Jor-El's father crystal certainly taught him enough to have become one of the greats.

But science was never one of his pleasures. He knew others who relished its always fascinating intricacies, but in his mind it was a recitation and reordering of facts, needed, appreciated, but for him dry and boring. His interests were elsewhere.

"What would I have been?" he kept wondering. "Butcher, baker, or candlestick maker?"

Would he have been a soldier? He knew Krypton had an army, although it was mostly used to protect the planet from outside forces. But the crystal had told him Jor-El had sent—*what was his name?*—General Zod?—and two others into the Phantom Zone, a limbo dimension for criminals. "No. The military life was definitely out." Politician? Superman laughed. "Not likely." Educator? "Maybe." He had always thought of teaching one day.

Five

An alarm interrupted his musings. "Entering Krypton's proximity now."

Ahead of him, glittering in the endless black, was a wondrous panoply of stars and planets. But as he continued to stare at them he saw in the wall of lights a patch of . . . *nothingness,* a great circular dark spot. Something was blocking the stars behind it. *Is that it? Is it possible?*

"Over there, that dark spot. I want to check it out," he said.

The ship responded to his voice instantly. His hand brushed the crystals again, and the ship's internal lights dimmed. "Let's see how close we can get."

As the ship closed the gap, Superman continued to look at the stars, adjusting their patterns in his mind, playfully morphing them into wild constellations. The crystal star was his *halfatree,* the universe his sky.

As the ship headed toward the dark mass, Superman thought again about how he had left so abruptly, letting only his mother know why and where he was going that night when he came to say good-bye. What did his friends think happened to him?

He wished now that he had let people know what was happening. But it was so hard then. He was so afraid that he could be talked out of the trip, convinced that it wasn't worth traipsing across a galaxy just to discover where he had come from. It was so much easier to say nothing.

More cowardly, too, he thought now.

He had expected to hear his mother argue with him about leaving, or at least reminding him that Earth was his home now and that he shouldn't go gallivanting through outer space. But, just like her, she understood his need— *even if he wasn't sure he did, exactly.* All she said was she loved him and that she always would.

But why hadn't he told Lois where he was going, or Jimmy, or any of the others? But especially Lois. He felt a huge twinge of regret.

If she had looked into eyes, if she had said to him "Don't do it," he was sure he would have abandoned his quest. No matter how hard it might have been, he knew he couldn't risk that.

The crystal star activated its external lights. Superman leaned close to the transparent wall, staring as the darkness parted under their penetrating amber glow. There was a planet not far in the distance. "Where's the sun? There's got to be a sun."

The crystal star glided silently toward the planet, revealing itself as the bright lights illuminated the details of its polished surface. He saw tall, thick slices of pure crystal jutting skyward.

Crystals. This has to be Krypton.

The star descended, gliding just above the dark, lifeless crystals. Superman saw the planet's surface sweep past under him. Formerly pristine towers lay crushed in ruins, and in them Superman could see the pieces of people's lives carelessly strewn about, exposed by his harsh light; there was furniture, clothing, and even children's toys, not dissimilar to those from home—*from Earth,* he thought.

Even through the protection his ship offered, he could feel the numbing cold that hung like a dark shroud. Without a sun there was no warmth. Without a sun there could be no . . .

He refused to go there. *There has to be life. I'll find it.*

He felt tired and weak as the ship continued to soar just above the dead world. He shrugged off his fatigue; *the end of a long journey. But I can't rest. Not yet.* He saw a leveled mountain, a hole blown into its peak, one side crumbled into ruin, and his heart sank.

Is this really Krypton? he kept asking himself.

The remnants of what his father had called "a once-great civilization" were everywhere. Cities and monuments, born from the same crystal technology of his ship, lay in shattered pieces, destroyed in a single, searing moment. But where the crystal star glowed with life, this planet was dark and lifeless.

He saw a faint green glow in the distance. The star silently descended near a large mist-covered chasm. A lifetime ago Mount Argo proudly rose from these Xan mists, boasting of the teeming millions it housed. But now it was little more than a graveyard of crystal shards, snapped off the very same day Kal-El was born, and then lost in this black oblivion.

The smoldering green glow emanated from small fissures in the bottommost slabs and, barely visible, radiated outward.

Superman looked into the mists, and his face drained of all its color. "Home." He was home, where Jor-El and Lara had lived. Where he was born, then taken from only twenty hours later.

He turned away as tears filled his eyes. He felt weak and nauseous. His hands were trembling, and sweat, cold and salty, dripped from his brow. "Get me away from here. Fast." The ship rose and sped off into the distance.

Superman sighed as what had been his home disappeared behind him. "All right. I'm feeling a little better now. But keep going." He let his head fall back into the cushion, and he breathed in slowly.

The crystal star sped across the dead world. Superman gazed through its transparent walls, searching for some signs of life, but he already knew that nothing could live here. And nothing had, not in his lifetime.

The ship flew over a flat, undistinguished plain, once a thriving small city, but now dead, its homes leveled into powder and rubble. He looked, but there were no bodies anywhere. He saw none atop Mount Argo, either.

But Krypton had had a population of nearly a billion people. Where did they go, he wondered. Where are their bodies?

The ship circled over the plains, then soared upward, cresting a steep mountain, where he found the remains of what had once been a forest, but was now a charred wasteland, its tall red trees dead, smoky stumps, razed the moment after Krypton's sun died.

He began to cry, finally realizing what had happened to the people. "Why did I come here?" he said; the stark, devastated wasteland was mocking him. "This isn't home. It's Hell."

There was a large dome perched atop canyon walls rising up from a low valley not far ahead of him. He pointed to it, and the ship adjusted its course. As they approached, he could see that the dome was partially destroyed; large gaping holes pocked its once-smooth surface.

The ship slid through one of the larger gaps and found itself in a vast canyon filled with ornately designed crystal monoliths. Superman saw that the towers had been set in a wide circle and he gasped in recognition. "The Valley of the Elders."

He remembered his mother talking about this place and the spiritual effect it had on her. Unlike the world outside the dome, the great monoliths were undamaged, and their bright crystal walls gleamed in the light of his ship as they must have for ten thousand years. *They were powerful. Humbling.*

The world under the dome was like a protected snowglobe village, pristine and complete. For the first time he understood why his mother loved this place. There were more than towers and statues here, more than cold reminders of a once-better time.

The monoliths had survived planetary destruction, defiantly resisting temperatures that had annihilated seven other planets. *Look at them now,* he thought, *their pride undiminished, their resolve unquestioned.* He knew that this place, these monoliths, the great towers, somehow represented hope.

This is what Krypton must have been like.

Emotions he had never felt before flooded into him without end. His questions, his troubles, his doubts were suddenly gone; this was where he belonged.

He soared with that feeling, letting it take him wherever it wanted. After a lifetime of being different, a lifetime having to pretend to be someone he wasn't, he was home.

He had a hunger now to know everything about his people, and these towers, these magnificent monoliths, were only the beginning. He wanted to leave the strangling confines of his ship and touch them, to run his fingers across their exquisite runes, to feel in person the crystal grandeur that had been Krypton.

But he also knew without Earth's yellow sun granting him his powers, he could not survive this cold, dead, airless place.

He remained inside the crystal, safe in his own little snow globe, and as he studied the towers, he scanned the intricately carved facades and runes into the ship's memory. He knew there was no way to preserve the blissful sensations he felt seeing them for the first time, but at least he could preserve those images, those ghostly reminders of a once-better place.

The crystal star hovered in position before a tower with the crest showing Kol-Ar's open hand. It stood for "truth and justice," Jor-El had told him. It was such a simple gesture yet it held so much meaning. Intelligent species on all planets could understand it; *We are friends. We welcome you.* Appropriately, Pol-Us's sign of the open eye was on the tower next to Kol-Ar's. Superman laughed. A little paranoid perhaps, but some vigilance, he knew from harsh experience, could come in handy when you welcome in others without question.

He hovered for a long time before the third tower. Sor-El's tower. The tower built by the first of his own family. This belonged to him. This was his heritage.

He stared for longer than he probably realized at its diamond crest with the winding serpent that looked so very much like the 'S' insignia on his own chest.

His mother, his Earth mother, had seen that symbol engraved in the crystals in his ship, and somehow, instinctively, she understood its importance. Using the brightly colored threads of his baby blanket, she ever so carefully embroidered its likeness into the Superman outfit she designed for him.

"No wonder you didn't argue with me when I said I needed to go home."

From that very first moment on that wonderfully fateful morning when she and Jonathan found him naked and alone and needing their help and love, she knew he was of two worlds. She had prepared herself for the day when he'd come to her and tell her he had to leave. She would care for him until then, of course, give him all the love she had to give. She would raise and teach him to the very best of her ability, but she would never hide the truth from him, and she would not stop him from wanting to claim his true heritage when he needed to.

She knew it was as inevitable as the sunrise. On that day she would tell him how much he meant to her, wish him well, then, once he was gone, quietly pray for his safe return.

Superman felt his throat tighten and he realized how much he missed her. How much he missed his home.

He turned back to Sor-El's tower, suddenly cold and distant and impossible to touch, and in his mind he heard Jor-El's voice again. *"We were a great people once, enlightened even. We yearned to touch the impossible, and more often than not we succeeded. You will take that greatness with you, my child, and with Rao's blessing, it will comfort you and guide you."*

Perhaps Jor-El and Lara had given him life, but Jonathan and Martha Kent made it a life worth his living. All his thoughts, his attitudes, even his morality, were forged not here on Krypton, but in a small, barely recognized farming community. A dot on the Kansas map.

He had come here looking for home. Perhaps, he thought, he had found it.

He felt his throat tighten again but this time it kept getting worse, not better. Nausea quickly turned into a crippling pain, knotting his stomach and spreading throughout his body, from his kidneys to his heart. *What's happening to me?*

He felt his body collapse. He tried to catch his breath, but he was gagging, choking for air, and he couldn't make himself stop. His eyes rolled into their sockets as an unforgiving blackness overtook him.

But then a fiery green scar burned its way through the dark.

His eyes snapped open and he saw Sor-El's tower and

its serpent shield. They were also glowing green. He struggled to look closer and saw that the fire was emanating from a tapered crack that traced the contours of the winding serpent.

He recognized that green.

Kryptonite.

When Krypton died in the fires of the supernova, the molecules of its living crystals melted and transformed into a burning green radioactive mass. The mass came together for only a moment, solidifying into a single entity, then it exploded into millions of smaller fragments, all burning with that same deadly radioactivity.

The pieces cooled into small rocks as they spread across the galaxy. They crashed onto many planets, including the Earth.

They were harmless to humans, but Superman knew they were deadly to him; their singular radioactivity would, with prolonged exposure, kill Kryptonians.

They had always been yet one further reminder of how different he was from Earthpeople.

He saw his hands glowing light green, the first effects of kryptonite poisoning. Even protected by the crystal star's shielding, the radioactivity was insinuating itself into him. The green glow was emanating from the serpent shield. It had somehow fused with the crystal, disguising it, perhaps protecting it from immediate recognition.

Even before seeing the kryptonite, he'd already been feeling weak. *Why didn't I understand the symptoms?*

Why didn't I run away from here then? Another wave of nausea swept over him. His face was cold and he was sweating.

I've got to get away from here. If I stay any longer I'll die.

He struggled to speak, but his throat was constricted. "Home," was all he could choke out.

The star responded and sped toward the edge of the valley, then flew over a tall cliff, preparing to leave Krypton's space. Superman expected to see the rest of Krypton beyond it, but the world dropped away into nothingness.

Where is the rest of the world?

He thought he was delusional. The fever had taken him over: He was burning up. He suddenly needed to fly through the crystal, into the cold of space.

There were people everywhere. Their arms were raised, their fingers, white and bony, were trying to pull him to them. The crystal star began to drift backward, and he saw their faces: desiccated and fleshless, long dead. They were Krypton's ghosts, and they wanted him to come back to them.

He closed his eyes, but they wouldn't go away. He knew he was delusional; nobody was there, outside the star, calling to him. But he didn't care. He was dying.

As the star pulled away from the Valley of the Elders, he could see that what he thought had been the planet Krypton was only a broken shard of the world, a single miles-long fragment of a memory that had died a lifetime ago and was now desperately trying to reclaim its last errant son.

The fragment's underside was a shattered section of Krypton's original mantle, the kryptonite beneath was poking through, spreading its radiation farther and farther into space. Smaller crystal shards, all fused with the deadly radioactivity, had broken free and shot off into space, showering its plague in all directions.

It was so ironic. He had escaped Krypton's destruction, but the planet, perhaps realizing this was its last chance, was incapable of letting him go.

The star quickly pulled away from that skeletal mockery of what had once been a great world, but Superman was still feeling no better. Distance should have allowed him to recover, but instead he felt his heartbeat slowing. He found it harder to breathe. His kidneys were beginning to fail.

His eyes glazed over, but he could see past the star's transparent shell to the armada of asteroids that surrounded him, drawn into his ship's wake, following him like so many baby ducks to their mother.

Superman tried to talk, but his throat was constricted with phlegm. His fingers, trembling, reached for the console when he felt the crystal star shake; struck by one of the kryptonite rocks. He doubled over, gasping in pain as the ship was hit again. He struggled to remain conscious.

The star tumbled out of control, spinning across the vast pitch of space, surrounded by emerald angels of death. The star's shell fragmented and cracked with each hit, drawing in traces of the kryptonite poison, but the crystals re-formed just as quickly, filling in the vacant spaces, repairing the ship.

Another asteroid slammed into the window, and hairline cracks spiderwebbed from its point of impact. Superman struggled to his feet as more meteors slammed them.

The strikes were coming faster, and the ship's ability to repair itself was falling far behind the spreading damage.

He braced himself as another meteor struck. He could feel the ship accelerating. Space was rushing past. A new star system was within sight.

Slowly, he noticed, the strikes were becoming more intermittent; the star had outdistanced its pursuers. *Just in time.* He felt his breath slowly return as he reached to the console and punched in a series of commands.

He allowed himself one last look at the planetary shell he had left behind, whispered a quiet good-bye to the Krypton he never knew, then fell back into his seat and closed his eyes. The sleep chamber lid slid out from its crystal perch and covered him. Then he heard the now-familiar hiss as it sealed him inside, protecting him in its warm crystal cocoon.

The ship sailed toward its final destination half a galaxy away, one of many lights sparkling in the dark. He thought of his mother and father and of Smallville and Metropolis and the whole of planet Earth, and his final word as sleep overtook him was "Home."

Six

"Home, sweet, home," the man said sweetly, sitting on the large, plush bed next to the former Gertrude Vanderworth, now his dearly betrothed.

"Feeling better? Need some water? A cold drink? Perhaps some rum, my dear?"

She stared at him with dead yellow eyes that oozed with pus and God knows what else.

"That's a girl. Just rest. I'm sitting here, next to you. Promise I won't leave your side."

He saw her try to nod, but she didn't have the strength.

Outside, the storm was getting worse. The pool house door had blown in, and more than a dozen elms fell along the half-mile driveway from the gate to the main house. Lightning was creating long shadows that skipped across the bedroom, and the thunder caused the dogs to start barking wildly—*again*.

He slapped aside the two yapping beasts, noted their ridiculous diamond-studded collars—*they are so out of here*—slipped his fingers through the tangle of wires and feeding tubes and took Gertrude's sallow liver-spotted hand in his.

"I could get very used to living here, my dear. You and me. Together. Forever." Her cough sounded like the doorbell to Hell.

Her parched lips struggled into a ghastly smile, not an easy task as she dribbled over the one tube taped to her left cheek and shoved into her mouth and the two that were inserted into her nostrils, then folded back down into her throat.

He cupped a hand behind her head and propped her up just a bit as he fluffed the half dozen silk-jacketed pillows before carefully laying her back down on them. She looked at him and wondered how she had gotten so lucky.

"In spite of your past, I know you're a good man," she said, her voice so weak he had to lean an ear next to her. "And all good men deserve a second chance. Like my dear Stephen, taken before his time."

He turned to the portrait of the distinguished Stephen Vanderworth, heir to the vast Vanderworth shipping dynasty, sternly peering out from the gold-leaf frame hanging proudly over the fireplace, the sides of his powerful face obscured by the twin eighteenth-century silver rococo candleholders—his great-grandparent's—standing on the broad mantel. Vanderworth's eyes followed his as he moved.

Although he barely noticed it, she squeezed his hand. "From the moment I received your first letter, I knew you weren't like the rest." The sudden thunder caused the two dogs to leap back onto the bed, demanding attention and protection.

He glared at them, and they hopped off again, crying

and scampering back to their own beds on the other side of the ridiculously large room. He turned back to her, smiling again.

"You were saying, my dear Gertrude?"

"You came from nothing, and worked hard to get where you are, even if you made a few mistakes along the way. Not like those . . . *vultures* . . . outside who never had to work a day in their lives." The word "vulture" was spat out like vinegar, and he could hear them still pounding at the locked bedroom door, refusing to take the hint and get the hell out of here while they still could.

"Mom!" "Grandma!" "Open the door." "You bastard. What are you doing to her?" "Open the door, dammit."

"Ignore them, my love."

"Not a problem," he replied as he gave her another pill, which he helped her to take with a cup of water. She coughed into her hand, then lay back down again, looking lovingly at him, as always.

She was starting to sleep again, but he couldn't have that. Not yet, at least. It wouldn't do for her to take her final breath while peacefully nodding off.

"Gertrude!" he said sharply. Her eyes slowly opened again.

He took a sheaf of papers from the folder next to him. "Last will and testament" was typed across the top. He gently stroked her hand as he pushed the papers toward her. "We were talking, dear."

Gertrude tried to smile again, but it was the grin of rigor mortis, and it made him sick to his stomach to even look at it.

"You said if I helped you get out of prison, that you'd

take care of me. And you have. You've done so much for me. Shown me pleasures I never thought were possible."

She coughed another wad of he-didn't-want-to-know-what into her hand, then grabbed his. He almost pulled away but then thought better of it. She felt him place a pen between her fingers and guide it to the papers.

"And that's why you deserve what Stephen left for me," she sputtered again. "That's why you deserve everything."

He saw several streaks of lightning flash in the distance. *Eight. Nine. Ten. Eleven.* He heard the thunder. *Eleven seconds. The storm's moving in.*

He watched carefully, propping up the papers for her to sign. "Your name, my dear. You need to sign it here. And here. And here."

She felt tired, and her eyes were staring at the stream that used to flow by her house when she was a child, no more than five. It was just as she remembered it, and she didn't want to leave.

"Gertrude!" His shouting, sadly, brought her back. "Your autograph, honeypie." She nodded weakly.

She started to write. *Gertrude Vander*— She coughed again. The pounding on the door behind them was really beginning to get on his nerves.

"I love you, Lex Luthor," she said, then promptly died.

He quickly moved her dead hand to finish what she had started. —*worth*. Outside, the thunder was grumbling.

The dogs were barking again as he snatched up the will. He kicked them aside and saluted the portrait of her dead husband while dropping his wedding band into her false teeth glass. He watched as it sank to the bottom.

He opened the door, and her relatives shrank back when

they saw him. "Hi," he said casually. "She's gone. Better place I'm sure. By the way, she didn't like any of you very much."

He shook off the wig he'd been wearing and his slick, bald head shone under the light of the hall candelabra. He looked at the ratty hairpiece for a moment, then handed it to a little girl, Alexandra Vanderworth, age nine, fearfully clutching at her mother's skirt. "You can keep that," he said to her kindly. He looked up to the others. "The rest is mine. Now get out."

With a skip in his step he made his way down the hall, passing a beautiful maid in a very short skirt who was dusting a large display case containing a model ship. One of Stephen's, he knew. *I'll get rid of that, too.*

Lex Luthor waved the signed papers in front of her, and she grinned. "How do you like our new home?"

Kitty Kowalski threw the feather duster to the ground and slipped her arm into his, then danced with him as they descended the large, winding marble stairwell.

From the moment the stunned Vanderworth family watched Gertrude's door open, they had not said a word. Then Alexandra noticed the wig in her hand and the two lumps of something better left unmentioned stuck in it.

And she screamed.

Seven

Martha Kent was out for blood. She stared at her enemy, her eyes narrowing as she reached over the old table. "*Alien?* Is that the best you've got?"

She was a slim woman in her late sixties with bright happy eyes and a ready smile, hardly the image of someone who would get down and dirty when the kid gloves came off. She placed the tiles into position, then gave a sly laugh.

"Now this is better. *Alienation.* Five little letters but they give me seventy-four points." She marked her score on the Scrabble sheet, gave a curt smile to Ben Hubbard sitting in mock fear across from her, and laughed. "I'm cleaning your clock, Ben. Hope it doesn't hurt too much."

Ben laughed as he glanced again at his tiles. Most were vowels, and he had no place to put them. "You're not doing a very good job of letting me win." Ben was four years older than Martha, with thick silver hair and a lean, well-lined face that left little doubt he had spent many hard years working his farm as well as pitching in to help the neighbors who needed him. He was still strong and proud of it, and it took little prodding for him to pull out his old boxing trophies and Marine Corps medals from his days fighting with the First Provisional Brigade in Pusan, Korea.

Martha got up and dragged two more logs onto the fire. She glanced at the photographs on the mantel and they warmed her more than the small fire ever could.

There were at least a dozen photos of Clark, the first taken the day she and Jonathan found him in the field, and the last taken a month after Jonathan died. On the wall surrounding the fireplace she had framed Clark's first by-lined newspaper article for the *Daily Planet* and placed it next to his college diploma. She and Jonathan were always so proud of him.

She picked up her and Jonathan's wedding photo, and the memories came back strong. They were good memories of many happy years, and she cherished them with all her heart.

She noticed that Ben was looking at the furniture catalogue again. She sighed, pretending exasperation. She kissed him on his head, smelled his sweet aftershave—she had bought it for him on their last vacation upstate—then glanced down at the page he'd been looking at.

"Ben, I like my kitchen table, and I want to keep it. I'll let you win when we're playing for a new bed." She placed her wedding photo back on the fireplace mantel, poured herself another half glass of wine, and sat down again, carefully resting the glass on her napkin.

"Martha," he said, trying desperately to make his point, "I'm just thinking we'll need something new, is all."

She pulled the catalogue closer and studied the picture—not a very good one, she decided—of a small round table, smaller than the one they were sitting at. "New weathered mahogany kitchen table," she read. "Explain to me how a table can be both weathered and new."

He laughed, knowing he'd probably lose this argument, but he wasn't ready to give in yet. "There's nothing wrong with new."

Martha slid the catalogue back to him and took another sip of her wine. "Nothing wrong with old, either," she said. "And this table's already weathered."

He closed the catalogue and tossed it to the chair beside his crumpled old coat. He missed, and it fell by the dog, not quite as ancient as the coat but old enough and tired enough not to raise his head to see what had fallen to his side. The old pooch gave a little snort, then went back to sleep.

"Okay, okay," Ben said. "Whatever you want, Martha. But what's with the attachment to a table anyway?"

Martha's eyes moved to the edge of the table, and her fingers traced the letters that had been carved into it years before. "Clark."

"I just like it, Ben. It has history. Now, are you trying to distract me so I won't finish the game? You have seventy points, Ben. I have, *ahem,* four hundred and nine. Or are you ready to concede?"

"Never, woman." He laughed.

He looked at his tiles again, trying to figure out how to use two A's, one E, one I, one O, and a Q and C. "I'd like to exchange these. And yes, I know I'll miss a turn." He looked up to see her staring out the kitchen window as if there was something happening outside. "Martha?"

He felt the table move suddenly, and his Scrabble tiles gently vibrated across it. The kitchen lights blinked on and off. The cupboard doors slammed open, and the glasses, cups, and plates inside began to shake. He heard a low rumble. "Earthquake?" No. There are no fault lines anywhere near here.

"Martha, what in—?"

The rumbling deepened, growing into a deafening roar. He was frightened, but Martha was just calmly looking out the window as if she couldn't be less concerned. He thought he saw an odd smile on her face, but surely that was impossible. One didn't smile in the eye of a storm. "Martha?" he called again, but she wasn't paying him any attention. *What is with you tonight?*

He saw the night sky turn red, a dull burgundy at first, then it flared into a much brighter scarlet. It was impossible, but it appeared to him that the sky was on fire. *Is it an airplane? Or maybe the shuttle?*

Had he read that they just launched one of them, or were they going to do that soon? He couldn't remember which. *Memory. Second thing to go.*

He stood by Martha's side as the entire sky lit up like noon. Then they both saw it; a meteor was streaking just above them, right over the farm, it was round and seemed to be made of shiny glass, and it looked to Ben like it was about to crash.

There was a sudden thunderous blast. "Sonic boom." Ben knew that sound well.

Then, for a moment, everything was silent. *Is it over?* The answer came just a moment later with a deafening explosion that rattled the old farmhouse.

Ben reached for the phone and dialed. "Calling the

police," he said, but there was no dial tone. Martha's finger was on the hook.

"Martha, what are you doing?" He was concerned; She looked so strange, so different. "Should I call you a doctor?"

"I'm all right, Ben, "she said, calmly.

"But you saw that—"

"It's just a meteorite. Sometimes they burn up in the atmosphere, and sometimes they make it all the way down. No need to trouble the sheriff about it. Nothing he can do about a meteor anyway."

Something is wrong. He was about to ask her what, but Martha looked at her watch, then took his hand in hers. "Listen, it's late, Ben. I've had a nice dinner, and . . ."

Now he was really worried. "But . . ."

"It's okay. I'm fine. Really. I'll see you tomorrow night, Ben. For bingo."

"Martha . . ."

"Tomorrow. Bingo." She said firmly.

He knew that stone-faced look, it always appeared when he wanted her to do something she was dead set against. He never could move her once she set her mind. But that was okay and certainly better than someone with no mind of their own. "A meteorite, you say?"

She said nothing, but nodded while still looking out the window.

"Martha Kent, I knew you'd be trouble."

He gave her a quick kiss on the cheek, petted the tired old pooch, who still wouldn't move but acknowledged him with a snort, then hobbled out to the pickup and waved good-bye.

She watched him pull onto the main road, and Martha's smile faded. *Could it really be him?*

She pulled on a coat and got into the old truck, then hurried as fast as it could go down the dirt road toward the back fields. *It's exactly where he landed before.*

Her heart was racing. She wasn't sure she'd ever see him again. Then she shoved her happiness aside, remembering why he had left. *Did he find what he needed to find? Lord, I certainly hope so.*

The truck pulled up to the large cornfield that provided just about enough produce to pay for the farm's upkeep. She hurried as fast as she could and ran through the spaces between the cornstalks until she saw the charred trench, several hundred feet long.

Just like before.

Martha rushed alongside it, keeping off the rut, still hot and smoking. *There it is.*

There was a deep crater where there had been a large oak just minutes before. At the bottom of it the crystal ship was still glowing from the heat of reentry. Nothing had changed.

She stretched out her foot to see how hot the ground was. She felt the heat rush up into her nose, and without meaning to, she pulled back instinctively. She could feel her pulse beating. It was loud and painful, but she braced herself and started again.

But a hand, strong and firm, pulled her back. She started to scream when she heard his voice. "No. Don't. It's too hot," he said.

He was standing behind her, holding on to her. He was thinner than she remembered, and his face was drawn and pale. *What happened to you?*

"Clark. Oh, my dear, sweet Lord. Thank you."

"Mom, I—"

She saw his eyes roll up into his head and his knees begin to buckle. She braced herself as he collapsed into her arms.

For a moment she thought she could hold him, but her own legs—*damn. Everything about me is getting old as Methuselah*—wobbled and fell out from under her. They both tumbled to the ground.

"Clark, oh, no . . ."

He looked at her through half-closed eyes. His lips, dry and parched, quivered as he struggled to talk. But only one word escaped before unconsciousness claimed him. "Mom."

Martha Kent felt his weight crushing into her, but, with tears streaming down her face, she held on to him for a long, long time.

Her son was home.

Eight

The first thing he saw when he finally opened his eyes again were the familiar construction paper cutouts of dozens of small stars that he had glued to the ceiling when he was only a kid. *First grade, or was that kindergarten?* The stars were colored in crayon, and he suddenly recognized their pattern. *My God! That's the view from Krypton.* His older self had forgotten many of Jor-El's lessons, but they were still fresh in that long-ago five-year-old mind.

Clark Kent was back in his old room. He looked out the window and saw the sun just about to rise, its bright yellow rays beginning to peek through the thick clouds.

His old bookcases were lined up against the far wall and the books were in the same place he'd left them, although they were stacked neatly instead of shoved in anyplace he quickly found. There were more of his baby pictures here than he remembered, as well as photos from different birthday parties and even his high-school graduation. This room had been his life, an all-American kid's life.

He was home.

His old desk sat in the corner as it had for longer than he'd been alive. This room was once his dad's office, where he'd go for an hour or so every afternoon and write letters, make out checks, and phone suppliers and friends. His grandparents had bought the desk when Jonathan was only eleven. They certainly got their money's worth.

The door nudged open, and Shelby the old dog entered, his long droopy tail hanging between his legs. He bounded over to Clark and sniffed him. His tail began to wag as he licked his old friend. "Hey, boy," Clark said, petting him. "Still looking good for an old mongrel."

Clark saw the closet still had his clothing hanging in it, exactly as he'd left it five years before, all dry-cleaned and protected by plastic. *Sanitized for your protection!*

"They're probably out of style by now, boy, but when was I ever in style?"

He brushed his teeth and took a long shower and felt much better. The crystal star kept him antiseptic and clean, but he knew there was no way ultrasonics would ever replace a hot, lazy shower. He dried himself off and put on a pair of jeans and a white T-shirt. *Time to rejoin human-kind,* he thought.

With a slow exhale, he made his way downstairs. Shelby slowly followed.

"Mom? You here?" He made his way into the kitchen. "Mom?" There was no answer. He scanned the farm with his X-ray vision, but he couldn't find her anywhere. The old pickup wasn't there, either. He mussed up the dog's fur and headed outside. "She must've gone to town to pick up supplies. She wasn't prepared for company." The dog loyally followed.

He wandered into the cornfield and looked back at the farmhouse. It had fallen into disrepair. He could see that the tractor was rusted and the field overgrown.

He knelt and ran his fingers through the dry, crumbling soil. *Used to be the best farming land for a hundred miles. You can't harvest much in this. Guess there hasn't been much rain lately.*

The farm had changed. More than he had expected.

His memories were so clear: He was fifteen, and the cornfield just south of the house was overflowing with tall, rich stalks, planted, as his father had taught him, in a series of short rows to make it easier for the plants to pollinate during tasseling. The sweet corn had been maturing for nearly two months and was just a week or so shy of harvesting. He and his dad would get to the field early in the morning to begin their labor.

"No using your special abilities," his father would always remind him. "We pick it the old-fashioned way." He knew Clark could clear the field in less than five minutes, but Jonathan wanted to teach him patience. "Not everything has to be done fast just because you can. Sometimes it's the experience that matters, not only the results."

Clark remembered standing in the field, quiet as the proverbial church mouse, breathing in the morning air, his teenage self surveying the land. He knew then how lucky he was to be there.

The young Clark gave a wide smile and began to run. He picked up speed, sprinting through the acres of corn until he was just a blur among the stalks.

The cool wind was rushing past him, blowing his hair,

invigorating him. He let loose with a wild roar and jumped. He sailed over the stalks, ten feet straight up and fifteen feet down the row. He jumped again, higher and farther this time, thirty feet up, landing more than twenty feet from where he'd left the ground.

His powers were just blossoming, and he loved to push them to their fullest.

All right, let's see what you can really do, he thought to himself. His heart was pumping as he picked up speed. The farm was blurring around him. He kept running, faster and faster. There was a water sprinkler ahead of him. With a short laugh he closed his eyes and leapt.

When he opened them again he saw he was sailing through the air, impossibly high. He felt as if he could just hang in the air and never land if he didn't want to.

But he did. He came to rest not on the ground, but on top of the old grain bin. He was a half mile from where he started.

He looked up. The sky was a deep blue peppered with only a few errant dark smudges, leftovers from last night's rain. But farming was now the last thing on his mind. For the past year or so more of his incredible abilities were revealing themselves, and each new discovery was thrilling.

It was only last week. He was in biology class, sitting two desks behind Lana, staring at her long red hair with the perfect green bow cinching it into a ponytail that hypnotically metronomed back and forth each time she turned her head. He felt heat welling up behind his eyes, a small bonfire that was suddenly igniting into inferno intensity. He clamped his eyes tight, knowing if he didn't do something soon they would explode with fire.

What is happening to me?

He began to sweat, and he never did that. He felt his breath quicken uncontrollably. He had to release the heat fast, but he couldn't do it here; if he didn't control it, he would burn down the entire school.

He jumped out of his seat, his eyes still shut, and he ran, mumbling something like "I'm sorry. I gotta go. Must've been lunch. I feel sick."

He didn't wait for the teacher to give him a hall pass. He was already out the front door of the school, but he could hear the class still laughing; so what else was new?

They always thought he was weird, different from the rest of them. *Well yeah. Duh. I can run faster than a locomotive, you jerks. Let's see you do that.*

In less than five seconds he was back at the farm, in the north field where Mom and Dad told him they had found him. He opened his eyes and felt a massive explosion escape from them. He couldn't have waited another second. When his eyes cooled again he saw that the ground surrounding him was on fire.

Sitting atop the silo he thought about that incredible revelation. *Heat vision. I've got heat vision.* For the rest of the week he worked each afternoon after finishing his homework to learn to control that power. *Can't accidentally burn down the school, no matter how much I may want to.*

He prepared himself, then leapt off the silo. He concentrated to stay afloat this time. Not to land. In a single leap he soared over the entire field. The barn was closing in ahead of him. He tried to stop but couldn't. He tried to change direction, but didn't know how. He felt his heart thumping crazily inside his chest as he smashed through the barn roof. He was falling, and he braced himself for impact. But there was none.

He was inside the barn, hovering horizontally, just six inches above the ground. Not falling. Not rising. Just floating.

He swallowed hard and envisioned himself vertical and his body tilted upward until he was standing. Standing but still floating.

He looked down to the ground, and his eyes automatically refocused. He wasn't looking at the ground but *through* it and past layers of dirt and soil-caked floorboards, to what looked like a wooden door leading to the small cellar below it.

But it was what was in the cellar that interested him. Hidden under a tarp was a strange egg-shaped object the size of a baby's crib.

He cleared the way to it quickly, revealing a charred crystal pod under that old ratty tarp. He had never seen it before but he knew exactly what it was. *This was the ship I arrived in as a baby.*

The pod was glowing with a light radiating from the small white crystal lying inside it. *Jor-El's crystal.* As he reached in and picked it up, the light glowed brighter, bathing him in its blinding intensity.

Clark was still kneeling in the field, the dry soil sifting through his fingers. Different time then. *I was innocent and excited by everything new. It was all spelled out for me so clearly then. I had a home where I belonged. My parents knew the difference between right and wrong and did their best to teach it to me. I had school and I was ex-*

pected to achieve specific results. I had friends, and they trusted me to be truthful and honest. I knew where I stood. I knew who I was.

He patted the last of the dust off his hands, then stood up and looked at the rising sun as its bright warmth washed over him. *Yeah. Different time then.*

He felt something soft hit into his left foot. It was a tattered baseball, and it was followed a second later by Shelby, wagging his tail excitedly, trying to convince Clark to play with him.

Clark smiled at the dog's anxious face. "I was exactly like you, boy. Nothing was ever wrong." Clark tossed the ball up once or twice, the dog bracing its body, ready to run whichever way the ball flew. Clark tossed it up one more time, then threw it. Shelby began to run but then stopped suddenly. The ball was not dropping. It kept sailing through the air, disappearing from view.

The dog turned back to Clark, looking at him quizzically, as if to ask *where did it go?*

"Oops. Sorry, boy. Forgot my own strength. I'll get you a new one, I promise. But I've got something I have to do first."

He picked up a shovel from inside the barn and turned back to the field, staring at the long, still-smoldering trench receding into the smoky mist. At the very end of it, buried deep in the dirt, was the crystal star. He took the shovel and began to bury it.

After he was done, he returned to the old barn, laid the shovel once again against the wall. He saw the layer of dust and debris that covered the floor. With a whoosh of superbreath he blew the rubble away, revealing the cellar doors.

Shelby sidled up to him, wondering what he was doing. "Digging up an old, buried bone," he answered.

He pulled the doors open and saw his old childhood ship. He opened it, knowing it wouldn't be there, but he looked anyway. The father crystal was gone, as he knew it was. He'd taken it when he was seventeen. When he left Smallville and made his way . . . *north*.

Next to the crystal ship was a stack of old newspapers. Five years' worth. All the *Daily Planet* and all addressed to "Martha Kent, Smallville." His mother had saved the news for him, every day's paper for nearly five years. She never gave up hope that he was coming back. *God, I love her.*

Clark sat on the pod and picked up the most recent issue. It was filled with the typical world news: Wars. Hurricanes. Disasters. All different from the ones he dealt with, all pretty much the same. *Life goes on.*

There were no mentions of him.

He used his X-ray vision and scanned the bottommost papers.

"Meteor Shower Baffles Scientists"

He had handled that freak problem on his last day. He had hoped someone would have discovered the reason for the meteor shower by now. *Oh, well.*

He sped through the newspapers.

"Caped Wonder Stuns City"

Lois's first article on him. Superman, day one.

"I Spent the Night with Superman"

Exaggerated, he remembered. *A headline designed to sell papers, not to be factual. Still . . .*

"Superman Stops Criminal Mastermind Lex Luthor"

It took him long enough to build a solid case against that maniac.

"Lex Gets Life Thanks to Man of Steel: Swears Revenge"

Yadda yadda yadda. If I had a nickel for every threat of revenge made against me, I could give Bill Gates a run for his money.

"Astronomers Discover Krypton Intact—Signs of Life Found"

He looked away, wishing he'd never seen that one. Krypton. Not quite a lie, but it wasn't home. It would never be home.

He was near the middle of the stack.

"Superman Disappears"

"Will He Ever Return?"

Even he wasn't sure.

He scanned for more headlines, slowly getting up to date on all the news that was fit to read. War. Famine. Crime.

Each day's paper found the articles on Superman's disappearance put farther and farther into the back of the newspaper until, about a year later, just after the first anniversary of his disappearance, they finally disappeared altogether.

There was nothing about him for nearly another year, until: "Why the World Doesn't Need Superman. By Lois Lane." He pulled the paper from the stack.

I should have told her.

He began reading.

"For five long years, the world has stared into the sky, waiting, hoping, and praying for his return. We have spent our days asking where he went, debating why he left, and wondering if he's even alive.

"People have always longed for gods, messiahs, and saviors to swoop down from the sky and deliver them from their troubles. But in the end, these saviors always leave, and we are faced with the same troubles that were there from the beginning.

"So, instead of facing them ourselves, we wait for the savior to return. But the savior never does, and we realize it was better he had never come at all."

Yeah. I should have told her.

He closed the cellar doors behind him. As he walked to the house Shelby was trotting next to him, a new baseball, wet and dripping, happily ensconced in his mouth.

Was she right?

He plopped himself into the thick middle cushion of the couch and remoted his way through three hundred channels of sitcoms, dramas, documentaries, movies, food preparation shows, cartoons, and news. They flashed past him, a montage of trivia he had no interest in following.

The news shows would have once called to him.

"In yet another nighttime siege of a Chicago bank, armed robbers evaded capture by . . ."

". . . a tornado ripped through a town . . ."

". . . a family was held at gunpoint when . . ."

". . . a high-rise erupted in flames just before . . ."

Nothing.

He put down the remote, poured some cereal and, as he ate, glanced at the newspaper at his side. Lois's article was above the fold.

Was she right?

He felt the dog's nose press against his leg. Clark saw

him drop the ball, telling him to the best of his ability that he forgave Clark losing the other ball, but he still wanted to play. He petted Shelby, ruffled his fur, and scratched behind his ears. Shelby nearly purred.

Clark picked up the ball and bounced it into the kitchen. A second later the dog dropped it by his feet again, his tongue hanging over the corners of his maw, an ever-hopeful look in his dark brown eyes. Clark had to smile.

"Feeling better?" His mother was behind him. He hadn't heard her enter the room.

He got up and hugged her. She was a bit heavier than he remembered, but she seemed happier and stronger. "Getting there."

"You just needed a good night's sleep, that's all." She saw the newspaper on the couch. "I kept them for you."

"Yeah. Interesting, *umm,* reading. Thanks, Mom."

She looked out the window, concerned. Clark knew what she was looking for. "Don't worry. I buried it this morning."

But she didn't turn back to him, her eyes were fixed somewhere beyond the horizon.

"Mom?"

He could tell she was crying, but she was too proud to let him see. He put his powerful arms around her and hugged her tenderly, comforting her. She snuffled up her tears but continued staring into the nothingness of space and time.

"Five years. It was just so long. If your father was alive, he never would have let you go. And then, suddenly, you're here."

Her voice began to crack, but she couldn't stop talking. It was as if five years of worrying had to pour out of her all at once before she could go back to some sort of a normal life.

"I almost gave up. There were times I thought I'd never see you again."

He continued to hold on to her as she wiped some new tears away with the sleeve of her blouse. "Did you find what you were looking for?" she asked.

He shook his head sadly. "I thought . . . hoped . . . it might still be . . ."

"Your home?" Martha finished for him.

"Well, one thing I learned. This is my home. That place . . . was a graveyard." He paused, trying to say what he knew to be true, but the words still stuck in his throat. "I'm all that's left."

"The universe is a big place, Clark," she said softly, comforting him now, the anger gone, the mother back in place. "You never know who's out there. And even if you are the last, it doesn't mean you're alone."

She stood on her toes and pulled him to her, kissing him on the forehead. His body seemed to relax. At last she let go and stepped to the mirror hanging near the fireplace. She pulled out a pair of earrings from her pocket and fastened them.

He was smiling. *It was right to come back here. To come back home.*

"So, when are you planning on heading back to Metropolis?" she asked, checking the mirror, making sure her earrings hung right and that her necklace was in place.

Clark hesitated before answering. "Actually, I was thinking about sticking around the farm. It wouldn't take much time for me to repaint the barn or replant the field. Place could be shipshape in just a few weeks."

She pulled out lipstick from her purse and removed the top. "What about that girl you used to like. Lois Lane? The one you had me send all those postcards to? I have to admit I got pretty good at signing your name."

She noticed he didn't respond. She put down the lipstick.

"You know, since you've been gone the news hasn't been quite what it used to be. The world can always use more . . . good *reporters.*"

Clark smiled, understanding. "It's hard for me to live my life . . . keeping secrets."

He turned away. The memories of Krypton, of death and shattered crystal lying side by side with those great ancient towers of hope, rushed back to him. He grew the crystal star from Jor-El's gift and risked everything to go there, not just because he believed that Krypton was still alive and would welcome their long-lost son back to their fold, but because it would have allowed him to put aside those secrets, to forget the deceits he needed to keep up in order to live each day.

He knew for Superman to exist there needed to be a Clark Kent. But inside him, in the deepest core of his thoughts, he was Clark far more than he ever was this . . . *savior,* as Lois had called him . . . this symbol of perfection everyone thought him to be.

But Lois was wrong. They were all wrong. He might have powers, but he didn't see himself as any kind of god come to walk the Earth and show mankind where it had gone wrong. He only came to help.

He wasn't raised on Olympus, but in Smallville, given the values of two of the best people he had ever known, but he was still prone to mistakes and fits of temper and errors of judgment, just as anyone else.

He used his powers for good, but he had come to feel the weight of his destiny crushing him.

He needed relief. He needed his own hope. He needed his own Superman to guide him.

He felt his mother's hand take his. "Clark, your father and I wanted a child so much, and when you came to us, well, much the way you did last night, we knew if anyone found out about you, or the things you could do, they might take you away. Or worse."

She looked outside the window, the sun now overhead. "It was a secret your father and I gladly kept our whole lives."

For several minutes he didn't respond. He had never fully thought out the words before—they were feelings that churned inside him, never verbal and specific—and they were awkward for him to finds words to describe. He was the one who was supposed to have all the answers, not just more questions.

"I don't know if I'm that guy anymore. I don't even know if I'd be welcomed back."

Martha laughed. "That's preposterous, Clark. The notion of anyone who cares about others not wanting you back, I'm sorry, but I have to laugh. How could you ever believe that?"

Of course, she knew the answer: He never understood his own power or the power his . . . *goodness* . . . had on others. He carried with him the wisdom of a universe, but at times he was also so naïve it startled her.

"Your father used to say that you were put here for a reason. And we all know it wasn't to work a farm."

He knew she was right. She usually was, but Smallville was his home. This farm was where he belonged.

He noticed the newspaper again. Lois's article was screaming at him. "I don't know, Mom. I still think I should stay. Maybe not for the long haul, but right now."

A knock on the door interrupted him. *Good,* he thought. He was happy to drop the conversation.

He turned to see Ben Hubbard at the door. "Martha?" Ben's ready smile reminded Clark how much he had liked him.

"In here, Ben," Martha said. "Come on in. Look who's here. You remember my son, Clark."

Ben entered, a small bouquet of flowers in his hand, which he gave to Martha as he kissed her on the cheek. Clark's mouth dropped. "Mr. Hubbard," he finally said when he found his voice again.

Ben Hubbard smiled again. "My, my. The last time I saw you, you were packin' up for the big city. A lot skinnier, too. So, you flew in last night?"

"What?" Clark was startled. What did his mother tell him? He turned to Martha suddenly, his eyes panicking. *What do I say?* She nodded back to him. *It's all right.*

"Yeah," is all Clark said.

Ben grinned. "You missed the big event, Clark. Meteor struck here last night, too. Lit up the whole sky. You would've been amazed."

"Meteor." Clark breathed out. "Yeah. Sounds spectacular. Wish I'd seen it."

Ben turned to Martha, who finished applying her makeup. "You ready?"

She picked up her purse and took his hand. "Can't keep me away."

"Where are you going?" Clark asked, still unsure what exactly was going on.

Martha smiled. "It's Wednesday, Clark. Bingo night."

Clark looked at them hand in hand, both very happy. He was starting to put things together. "You two . . . you're *dating*?"

Martha glanced at Ben, who understood and headed out. "I've got to start the car. Sometimes it gets a bit cranky, you know. I'll see you in a minute. And nice seeing you again, Clark."

"Uhh, right. Good seeing you, too, Mr. Hubbard."

Martha waited for Ben to leave, then turned to Clark, her old hands gently touching his face. "Clark, dear, no one will ever replace your father. But Ben and I have found something special. Together. And, well, this might all come as a shock . . . another shock . . ."

What now? How bad is this going to get? Tell me, Mom. Level with me.

"I'm selling the farm, Clark. We're moving to Montana."

All he could do was repeat what she said. "Montana?" His mouth was still hanging open, and he was sure his eyes were as wide as one of those old, cracked googly dolls his mother had as a young girl and now kept on a dresser drawer in her sewing room.

"The lakes are great, and we love the fishing."

I'm not back on Earth. I'm in some alternate mirror dimension.

"Fishing? You . . . like . . . fishing?"

She turned his head so their eyes met. Hers were sad but firm; she knew this was coming the moment she saw the sky turn red with fire just as she knew she was not about to back down.

"Clark, you've been gone a long time. And not even you can stop the world from spinning."

Once again she pulled his head low so she could kiss him on his forehead. "We'll talk more tomorrow. Don't wait up."

Clark walked her outside and saw Ben open the car door for her to get in. "It's good to see you again, Clark. Welcome back," he said. Clark nodded and watched the car take off down the road into town.

He sat down on the couch again. Shelby dropped the baseball onto the newspaper at Clark's side, on Lois's article, then curled up next to him. With a heavy sigh Clark took the ball, spun it on his finger a few times, then threw it, gently this time, into the next room. But instead of chasing it, the dog simply yawned and rested his old head against him. Clark's hand found its way onto Shelby's head and scratched it. "Yeah, welcome home."

Nine

Outside, the air was thick with snow and sleet. But inside the sleek 271-foot yacht—*skinflint Vanderworth couldn't have sprung for the 280-foot model?*—Lex Luthor didn't care about the raging arctic storm. He knocked a few pool balls into their pockets—perfect three-cushion ricochets—looked down at the glass floor; the lights were on, revealing an array of colorful fish swimming below, settled into his cushy lounger, and was listening to *Carmen* playing over *The Gertrude*'s sound system as he pored through the last of the nearly one hundred books he had brought with him on this trip: *Crystals, The Definitive Guide; The Crystal and Mineral Guide; The Geologist's Guide; Make Your Own Crystals; Minerals' Physical Geology; The Crystal Atlas,* and *Gems and Crystals.*

He put down the books and ran his fingers through his hair as he snuck a peak at the small makeup mirror on his desk. *Only the best hair for the brightest mind,* he thought as he adjusted the wig a bit to the right.

He looked across the sprawling thousand-square-foot stateroom, past the pool table and the piano where he assumed dear old Stephen used to serenade Gertrude, then to his desk, formerly Gertrude's desk and, before her, Stephen's, and rifled through the stacks of articles and papers he had assembled over the years on Superman and the fabled planet Krypton.

He picked up a five-year-old copy of the *Daily Planet* with the brash headline, "Astronomers Discover Krypton Intact. Signs of Life Found," and he smiled. "Gotta love the classics."

He glowered toward the bar. "Kitty! Where are you, my dear." No response. He sighed and turned back to *The Geologist's Guide*. He went through its table of contents for the article he marked on molecular crystal recombination. This will do for now, he decided. He would deal with Miss Kowalski later.

On the deck of *The Gertrude* the four men went about their daily tasks. The twin 2000HP Caterpillar diesels pushed the boat to over thirteen knots, but Grant knew that wasn't nearly fast enough for the boss.

Short and squat, and looking even rounder under his five layers of cold protection, Grant sported a six-day-old stubble that itched enough to constantly scratch but not enough to remind him to shave it off in the morning. Binoculars pressed to his eyes, he stood on *The Gertrude*'s teak deck, searching for . . . *something*.

Maybe Mr. Luthor had described what they had come to this frozen hellhole for; he even drew him a picture, but Grant still wasn't sure what they expected to find here, in the middle of this frozen wasteland. "Nothing," he shouted so he could be heard over the wind. "It's always nothing."

"Well, keep looking," Brutus snapped back to him. "Mr. Luthor's getting pretty angry it's taking so long." Brutus grumbled. He hated being here, in the cold. Alone. With nobody to hurt.

"I still don't get it. Why couldn't we stay in Metropolis? Why did we hafta come here?"

Stanford looked up from *The Gertrude*'s controls. "You rob banks, because that's where the money is, right?"

"That doesn't make sense, Stanford." Brutus was scratching the hood of his parka, trying to make it all work in his mind. "There's no money here. Come to think of it, there's no banks here, either."

Stanford shook his head. "Brutus, we're not here for money. Mr. Luthor could get us money anytime he wanted. What we're after *is* here. Somewhere. Just keep looking."

Stanford glanced back at the sonar image on *The Gertrude*'s radar screen. Still nothing. But Luthor swore it was close. Suddenly, a large blip danced across the radar. Something . . . it looked to him like a *structure* of some kind was just ahead of them.

Just as suddenly, the blip disappeared, and the image of—*whatever it had been*—was gone.

Stanford nodded to Grant, who pressed the intercom. "Mr. Luthor?" There was no answer. All he could hear was some opera—*what the hell does the boss see in them anyway?*—blaring over the com. "Wait here. I'm going in."

Grant saw Riley following him. The skinny weasel had his camcorder in hand, as always, recording their every movement, including bathroom breaks. Luthor's orders.

"Document the trip. The breakfasts, lunches, dinners,

and snacks. And make sure you record every brilliant word that trips liltingly off my silver tongue. It all must be recorded for posterity. People will know that greatness began here, on this oversized canoe, initiated by the world's greatest criminal genius that is Lex Luthor."

Riley was, as always, in the way. Grant pushed him aside and headed for the stairs to the main stateroom. "Get that thing out of my face," he barked. Riley stopped and let Grant pass. Then he picked it up again and continued filming, this time from the back. *When Mr. Luthor said record everything, he meant everything!*

Kitty was breathing hard as she hurried to the bar and began pouring drinks. "Sorry, Lex. I was—"

Luthor cut her off. "It is five after three, Miss Kowalski. I don't see a drink in my hand. Do you see a drink in my hand?"

Kitty shook her head and poured one drink, then set it down to get a second glass. He liked two martinis at once. The yacht leaned to the side, and the drink slid off the bar, shattering on the wooden floor. "I'm sorry, Lex. Really sorry," she said, mopping up the mess.

Luthor held up a hand, palm out. "It is now six after three, Miss Kowalski."

She quickly poured him a drink, dropped in two olives, and carefully walked across the swaying deck to hand it to him. She said nothing while he sipped it. "Ahh, better," he finally said. "My second one," he demanded.

This time she was ready. She handed it to him and settled back, relaxing at last. "Stanford was rude to me again. Your friends give me the creeps."

Luthor held the second martini glass up to the light, squinting as he checked it out. "Prison is a creepy place, Kitty, and one needs to make creepy friends in order to survive. On the inside, even my talents were worth less than a carton of cigarettes and a sharp piece of metal in my pocket."

"Did you really have to make friends with *them*, Lex? What about . . . ?"

"Your poor former boyfriend whom you dutifully visited each Tuesday afternoon and every other Saturday? Do you think he would have worked to my benefit once he learned that you and I, well, he must have wondered why his conjugal visits were suddenly cut off."

"Andrew was small-time . . ."

"And I was Park Place and Broadway rolled into one. With a dash of Marvin Gardens for spice. Yes, yes, one can't blame you for seeing the light, but you have to admit our extracurricular dalliances limited my henchman options."

With a disgusted look Luthor put down the martini glass. "Hmmpfff."

Kitty looked curious. "What?"

"Is this the reward for the man who patiently waited by Gertrude Vanderworth's bedside, feeding her prunes, reading her Dickens, *washing her*?" He shuddered at the thought.

"What are you talking about, Lex?"

"And what did I do that all for? So we could live in the kind of opulence a girl like you only reads about in magazines." He picked up the glass again. "Is this the reward, Kitty? A martini with one withered olive?" With two fingers he gingerly picked it out of the glass and held it up as far away from him as he could, shunning it.

Kitty snatched the martini back. "My name is Katherine. And that wig makes you look old."

"So does yours . . . Kitty."

She grabbed her hair, embarrassed, and walked back to the bar, trying to keep her dignity as well as her balance. She hated boats. She hated how they moved. She hated everything about this stupid trip. "Some ocean voyage you promised me."

She grabbed the side of the bar for support, then turned back to Luthor.

"So now that we're out in the middle of nowhere, away from prying eyes, does the oldest criminal mind of our time think I'm worthy of hearing his plan?"

Luthor snorted. "Small doses for small minds. Another martini, please."

She poured another drink and let him see her fill the glass with thick, fat olives. She handed it to him. "Thank you, Kitty," he said.

"So what is it? Clubbing baby seals or selling ice to Eskimos?

Lex pinched an olive out of the glass and tossed it into his open mouth. "Do you know the story of Prometheus?" Before she could answer, he continued. "Of course you don't. Prometheus was a god who stole the power of fire from the other gods and gave control of it to the mortals. In essence, he gave us technology. He gave us power."

Kitty looked out the window, then back to Luthor. "So, we're stealing fire. In the Arctic."

He took another olive and dropped it in his mouth. "Actually, sort of. You see, whoever controls technology controls the world. The Roman Empire ruled because they built roads. The British Empire ruled the world because they built ships. America built the atom bomb . . . and so on and so forth."

He put down his glass, picked up *The Science of Crystal Technology* and opened it to a full-color double-page spread of a crystal garden complete with cutaways dealing with light dispersion and polarization, color, cleavage, piezoelectric compression, and the birefringence refraction of light. Kitty looked at it, turned the book upside down to see if it made any more sense that way, then stared confused at Lex.

"I just want the same thing Prometheus wanted," he said, matter-of-factly.

"Sounds great, Lex. But you're not a god."

He was about to reply when Grant entered, still dripping wet. "We found something."

He held up a hand as he turned back to Kitty. "God? Gods are selfish beings who fly around in little red capes and don't share their power with mankind. I don't want to be a god, Kitty. I just want to bring fire to the people . . ."

She stared at him. *I'm not buying this, Lex.*

He continued. "And I want my cut."

Satisfied, he turned back to Grant.

Lex Luthor left *The Gertrude* anchored near the icy shore as they began the harsh inland trek through the shrieking winds and endless snow. If his memory was correct—and it almost always was—he knew they would only be outside in this flesh-freezing blizzard for about an hour or so.

Even if they couldn't see it, it was close. He could feel it in his bones.

His men, he thought, were working out well, as he knew they would. Grant and Brutus, both carrying heavy totes laden with Luthor's equipment and other necessities, struggled to keep up with the others. Luthor had observed and studied them for the entire five years he was in prison. He knew that though their combined IQs were probably in the gerbil range, they were loyal and followed orders. What more could he want?

Stanford was in the lead, constantly checking the GPS for any minor course corrections. He was a real find, and Luthor knew it. What were the odds, after all, of uncovering a tech like him, an expert in crystal manipulation, behind bars, serving the first of fifteen to twenty years and more than willing to do anything if it meant getting out early?

Luthor knew Stanford wasn't a scientist or even half as smart as he, but then, who was? Still, he could take Luthor's crystal theories, execute them to perfection, and not concern himself with all those finicky moral implications.

Luthor stomped ahead, a man on a mission. He allowed himself a small smile as Kitty put her arm in his and trudged alongside him. Despite how she presented herself, he knew her IQ was considerably greater than her bust size, which in itself was quite ample. Natural, too, a rarity for the girlfriends of lowlifes and criminals who these days would throw half their first illegal haul into nip-and-tuck surgery.

He knew Kitty was always scheming and plotting, something he admired in anyone, especially a woman; but he also knew as sure as he was a certified genius with the papers to prove it, compared to him she was dog-paddling in the shallow end of the gene pool. If she ever tried anything against him, he knew he'd be prepared for it. But at least for now she'd do.

Riley followed behind, his camcorder documenting the journey as always. Like Stanford, Grant, and Brutus, Luthor had met Riley in prison. Riley had always been into movies; he shot a couple of well-received blue films, acted in one of them as well. He also shot a commercial for some Japanese cinnamon gum with a burning after-kick. As far as Lex Luthor was concerned, Riley had 20/20 vision and could hold the camcorder steady. Any other skills would probably get in his way.

Luthor stared into the endless snow and ice. As soon as they entered it, he remembered the valley as if it were yesterday. He'd flown over it the first time he had come here, and walked past it on the way back, before finding a trawler that would take him the rest of the way home.

He clearly saw the scene in his mind. The landscape was going to change, he recalled, in about twenty minutes, once they passed the glacier that was looming just ahead of them.

They circled the glacier and pushed their way through the sudden swirl of snow that tried to drive them back. "Keep going," Luthor shouted.

Kitty was screaming at his side. "But, Lex, it's freezing. Can't we turn back?"

"No, we're close. We're nearly there." He took her hand and pulled her ahead with him.

Stanford turned back, looking quizzically at Luthor. "Is this it?"

Luthor nodded. "His security system and early-warning device all rolled into one. Just keep moving. He built it to frighten us, not kill us. Stupid blue Boy Scout. Never knew how to use his powers right."

They made their way past the freakish storm and saw that the flat plains had become a landscape of tall, icy columns that stretched up into the blinding arctic sun.

"You were right," Stanford said. "There was some kind of unnatural weather pattern keeping it hidden."

"I'm always right." Lex paused then grinned. "We're here."

Kitty looked around and saw nothing but more ice and more ice towers. "Here? Where's here? We're nowhere, Lex."

He sighed. "None are so blind as those who will not see."

She ignored him as she looked at the column in front of her and touched it, then quickly drew her hand away. Puzzled, she looked at it again, then took off one of her gloves and touched it again.

"This ice is warm," she said, turning to Luthor, confused. He was smiling knowingly.

"It's not ice. It's crystal."

Stanford saw her running her fingers over the column again, then licking them. He rolled his eyes as he looked at Luthor. "Why is a guy like you with a girl like her?"

Luthor grinned. "Why do beautiful women carry around ugly dogs, Stanford? Why do people volunteer with the mentally challenged? Work in hospitals . . ."

Stanford waited for an answer, but Luthor's attention was already elsewhere. Behind him he heard Kitty's voice over the roaring wind. "I can hear you," she was shouting.

Ten

They crested the ridge, then saw it rising up over the horizon, the size of a cathedral with crystal architecture reminiscent of a world Luthor had never seen but had studied intimately. *Designed on Krypton, built on Earth.*

"Superman's Fortress of Solitude."

They made their way through the maze of towering crystal columns and watched in awe as light refracted through them, forming a million overlapping rainbows. Luthor waited impatiently, then snapped at them to follow. "People! We didn't travel more than thirty-five hundred miles for you to go flower child. We have work to do."

"You are such a spoilsport, Lex," Kitty fumed. Luthor snapped his fingers at Riley, who suddenly resumed his filming. "Sorry, boss. I got, *uhh* . . . distracted."

Grant tried to see the Fortress ceiling, but it was lost somewhere in the misty haze high above him. All he could see were refracted rainbows amidst the skyscraper crystals. "Was this his house?"

Luthor removed his goggles and stuffed them in his back pocket, then took in a deep, brisk breath of cold air. "You might think that. Most would. But, no. He lived among us."

Luthor ran his hands over the crystals. *They're beautiful, and they're mine.* He snapped his fingers, and Riley turned the camera from taking generic background pictures they could cut to, to him. This was going to be an important pronouncement, Riley knew. He moved in for a tight close-up.

Luthor waited patiently for the signal that he was in focus, then continued. "This is more of a monument to a long-dead and extremely powerful civilization. It's where he learned who he was and where he came for guidance." He slid his finger across his throat and whispered, "Cut." Then he pointed ahead and Riley focused the camera on the next room.

They continued into the central chamber, an immense almost circular hall with smaller adjoining rooms jutting off around its perimeter.

The chamber, with its sweeping vaulted ceiling rising hundreds of feet overhead, appeared to Kitty, to have been altered in some way, as if crystal chunks had been removed willy-nilly. Off to the side she saw signs that a large wedge of crystal had been removed from the wall as if something grew there, then broke off. "What's this, a garage?" she asked.

Luthor laughed. "You're not so far off, Kitty. The leading theory is that he took off from here in a futile attempt to find his home world."

Kitty heard Stanford stifle a laugh as Lex glared at him. *What are those two up to?*

Luthor ran his fingers over the edge of the broken crystal. "If so, even he would have to rely on a craft of some kind, and I'll bet Gertrude's last dollar that's exactly what used to be parked there."

Kitty looked again at Stanford, still smiling, then back at Luthor. "So, did he?"

"Did he what?"

"Take off for his home world?"

She saw Lex smile at Stanford again. "Well . . . we gave him a little push."

Lex turned away, and she saw him quietly counting to himself as he stepped under a large opening in the ceiling into the faint shaft of light that it cast there. He took one step forward, then another and another, slowly and deliberately measuring the distance of each purposeful stride.

"You act like you've been here before," said Kitty.

He rolled his eyes and held a hand to his lips to shush her. He took another step forward, and then—*VWOOM!*— he was suddenly enveloped by a bright white light that seemed to respond to his every movement.

"Here it is, just as I said. And yes, my dear, this is not my first time."

She growled at him and stepped back, along with the others. Grant leaned to Riley and whispered to him. "Whatever you do, don't stop shooting. Get it all. If the boss survives, he's going to want to watch it over and over again." Riley nodded nervously and zoomed in for another close-up.

The crystals beneath Luthor's feet appeared, to Kitty, to be growing. Then another crystal, one more columnlike in its shape, rose from the ground directly in front of him.

Luthor assumed it was nearly identical to the control column in Superman's crystal star.

It rose to just over four feet before stopping. Kitty saw Luthor breathe in deeply, lustfully leering at it as he had never leered at her. She wondered why she was feeling jealous over a piece of rock. She pouted as he ran his hands over its surface like a concert pianist. *He never touched me like that.* He was *playing* the crystal.

She saw a single large crystal set among the others on the console. This was the father crystal, the one Jor-El had placed beside his son as he sent him spaceward to find his destiny.

It pulsed gently as Luthor removed it from its pocket. There were many other openings on the console. He turned to Kitty with a smug grin—*Told you I knew what I was doing*—then turned back and fit the father crystal into the largest, highest hole.

A perfect fit.

Shafts of light filled the Fortress. Whispering echoes hummed from its every corner. The lights came together forming multiple ghostly faces, all of them of the same handsome white-haired man.

"My son." His voice was soft but compelling. While Kitty, Brutus, Grant, and even Stanford stepped back in fear, Luthor stayed his ground, his eyes riveted on this stranger from another world.

"Who is he?" Kitty asked.

Luthor ignored her as the voice continued. "You do not remember me. I am Jor-El. I am your father." Lex turned to Kitty. "And he thinks I'm his son."

"Embedded in the crystals before you is the total accumulation of all literature and scientific fact of other worlds spanning the twenty-eight known galaxies."

Jor-El's voice continued. "There are questions to be asked, and it is time for you to do so. Here, in this *Fortress of Solitude,* we shall try to find the answers together."

"Can he see us?" Kitty wondered aloud.

Luthor shook his head. "No. He's dead. Now shhhhh."

"So, speak, my son. Speak." Jor-El instructed, then went silent, waiting.

"What are you going to ask it, boss?"

"Quiet, Grant. Don't distract me. A great mind is at work here."

Luthor thought for a moment. He had the secrets of the universe in front of him. He could ask for the knowledge to cure all diseases. How famous would he be then? *My God, how the masses would worship me. But then, I've always hated their kind.*

If he wanted to, he could acquire the secrets of building great starships that could span the universe. He could ask anything he could imagine, and it would be explained to him in glorious detail.

But he knew he had only one question. The one question that had caused him to trek all this distance to this cold, arctic Fortress.

"Tell me everything, Father," he said. "Starting with the crystals."

The father crystal pulsed and hummed, and Lex smiled. He would soon, he knew, have a grand new home.

Eleven

The cab driver didn't bother looking into the backseat as he checked the meter, "That'll be thirty-four fifty, bud." He got out of the car and flipped open the old, dented-in trunk to find the two large suitcases wedged between the spare tire and the jack. As the passenger clumsily sifted through his wallet, he reached in to pull them out. The suitcases barely moved. "Whaddaya got in these things, bricks?"

He tried again and nearly dislocated his shoulder. The passenger smiled gently as he lifted out both of them at once, rested one of the suitcases on the ground, the other tucked under his arm, handed the driver two twenties, picked the suitcase up again, and headed for the plaza entrance of the Daily Planet building.

He was greeted by Edward the security guard, looking only a bit older than the last time they had seen each other.

"Hey, long time no see."

"Been traveling, you know. Here and there."

They talked for a few minutes about his extended trip, Edward's grandchildren (both were doing well), his wife Stephanie (she had broken her hip but was recovering), and Edward's upcoming retirement. The man said he'd be sure to come to the party and was happy he got back to town in time.

He then got into the elevator, and when the doors opened again on the editorial floor, he stepped out into the wild chaos that had been his home for so very long.

Nothing had changed in the five-plus years he'd been gone. Rows of reporters and rewriters, stuck in cubicles much too small for them and their desks, were still hunkered over computers, typing away furiously, forwarding their stories, articles, classifieds, or whatever to editorial, who would then process the material and send it on to layout. Assistants and copyboys were scurrying about like crazy mice, navigating through the maze of desks, rushing to make crucial deadlines.

There was a certain frantic quality here that energized him. *Yeah, this was the right thing to do.*

He passed a row of televisions, all set to different news channels. A difference at last: These TVs were LCD widescreens with a picture quality he had never experienced before. FOX was talking politics. CNN was airing an exclusive interview with the prime minister of Japan. MSNBC had one of its talking heads arguing with three guests, shouting them down over some new congressional scandal. *No. Nothing's really changed.*

He made his way through the bullpen, his suitcases clumsily knocking into one desk after another. A table boy saw him coming and jumped out of his way in time to avoid being hit by the edge of an errant suitcase. The man smiled apologetically as he passed him.

He turned an aisle and his suitcase hit into another desk. A camera, sitting precariously on the edge, shook itself off and began to fall. He dropped the suitcase, reached down—faster than the eye could follow—and caught the camera before it fell onto the marble floor.

"Careful, care . . ." a young voice cautioned him before stopping in midword.

The man gave an embarrassed smile. "Sorry, Jimmy."

Jimmy Olsen's eyes went wide.

"Mister Clark," he sputtered. Then realized what he said. "I mean Kent. Mister Kent. You're back! I don't believe it. Wow."

Clark stuck out his hand, expecting Jimmy to take it. He had been just a boy when Clark took off on his . . . *exploration.* Now Jimmy was probably in his early twenties, clean-cut and dressed in a conservatively cut shirt and bowtie perhaps one size too large for him.

Jimmy kept staring at him. "Oh, wow. Oh, my God. Welcome back! Hey, come with me. No, wait. Don't move." Jimmy stood gaping at Clark for another few seconds, then rushed off, suddenly. "Stay here," he shouted back.

Clark waited in front of Jimmy's cubicle, his six-foot-four-inch frame topping over the short walls.

He glanced around, looking for any differences in the place since he left. New people were busying themselves with work. But then newspaper offices were always filled with hopeful wannabes. Some made it. Others fled, for jobs with less pressure.

New family photos were sitting on desks or tacked to cubicle walls. There was a new coat of paint along the back walls, and, he noticed, the original asbestos ceiling had been removed and replaced with new, safer materials. The Planet office was both new and familiar. A nostalgic smile spread across his face.

"Behind you, Mister Kent," Jimmy's voice called. Clark turned to see Jimmy holding a plate covered in aluminum foil. "Here. I made it myself."

Clark peeled back the foil and saw there was a cake on a plate, but its whipped cream frosting was smeared by grubby fingers. It now read, "We om ack lark." He swept a finger across it, scooping up a small piece and dolloping it into his mouth. "Delicious."

Jimmy saw that part of the cake was already gone. "Oh. I guess the other guys got hungry," he said, disappointed. He had wanted Clark's return to be special.

Clark was about to console him when another voice boomed out. "Olsen!" Clark smiled. *I was wondering where he was.*

Perry White stormed in. He was in his midsixties with a thick mane of stark white hair, but he moved like he was still a young reporter bulling his way into major scoops. He was, as usual, growling, about to snap in anger. Clark couldn't remember when Perry White had looked any different. "Where are those photos from the Sixty-sixth Street birthday clown massacre? Compositing needs them now."

Jimmy's face lost its color. "Right away, Chief. Hey, look who it is."

Perry turned to him and stifled what Clark knew was going to be a smile. *Couldn't have that now, could he?* "Kent," he barked. *His way of saying hello.*

Clark didn't expect more. Perry was Perry, and he was

never going to give in to showing his emotions. Just as well. Clark preferred him this way.

Clark remembered that when he announced he was leaving Perry took him to lunch and spent about two hours trying to get him to change his mind. When Clark said he couldn't, Perry wished him the best, paid the check, and left without another word.

Clark put out a hand, but Perry didn't take it. "Hey, Chief. Thanks for giving me my job back . . ."

But Perry was already halfway back to his office. "Don't thank me. Thank Norm Parker for dying."

Jimmy nodded to Clark. "It was his time."

"Well, I do appreciate it, Ch—"

"And don't call me Chief," Perry said, slamming his office door behind him. *Thank God some things don't change.*

"Come on. Let's get you set up," Jimmy said as he reached for one of Clark's suitcases. He grabbed the handle and tried to pull it, but it held firm. He used both hands, and the suitcase tilted just a bit, enough for its rugged polyolefin wheels to gain traction. Jimmy dragged it slowly across the floor before he noticed Clark was walking the other way toward the cluster of reporters' desks. His old desk.

"Mister Kent. Over here, Mister Kent." Jimmy was motioning Clark toward the other end of the room. Clark looked back to Reporters' Row, then back at Jimmy, and followed him. Jimmy was, as always, exuberant.

"So, wow, you sure are lucky. Hitting the open road, hitchhiking around the world like that. I can't wait to hear all about the Peruvian llama rodeo."

Clark was confused. "Llama rodeo?"

They stopped at a small desk near the back wall, and Jimmy was relieved to let the suitcase drop with a heavy thud. "Yeah. I kept all those postcards you sent. Hey, gotta run. I'll check on you in a bit, okay?"

Clark nodded and sat at his new desk. *Llama rodeo? I'm going to have to ask Ma exactly what she wrote in the postcards.* He opened a few drawers, scooted his chair across the cubicle to test the wheels, then returned to the desk. "Oh, hey, do you know where I can find . . ."

He looked up but Jimmy was already gone. ". . . Lois?"

Clark sighed as he looked for something to do. Next to him was a massive stack of newspapers, magazines and, there was no other word for it, junk. Norm Parker's junk. The stack was so high he couldn't see over it into the next cubicle. *This all gets thrown out tonight.*

He hefted one of his suitcases onto the desk, shaking the stack of papers.

He was about to open it, then noticed the door behind him.

Not here. The janitor's closet.

He shut the door and pulled on the chain dangling in front of him. A small sixty-watt bulb warmed up the tiny space. There were buckets of cleaning solution, wash rags, mops, solvents, brushes, and squeegees cluttering the closet shelves. A janitor's uniform hung from a hook that had lost one screw and was tilting forward precariously. Anything heavier than the shirt and pants would pull it out of the wall.

He cleared a space on the table and opened the suitcase. Inside were dozens of pressed suits and shirts. He removed some books and toiletries, then picked up one final item, a framed photo of his mother and father, Jonathan and Martha. He looked at it for a long time before carefully laying it aside.

Underneath the photo was a large red "S" embroidered on a bright yellow diamond-shaped shield; his Superman uniform, cleaned and neatly folded by his mother. He gently touched the symbol, now just a reminder of the shattered crest he found on that ancient tower in the Valley of the Elders.

Without a word he closed the case again and hid it on the lower shelf of the storage cabinet in the back of the closet.

"Clark, come here." Jimmy was calling him. "Hey look. It's Lois."

Clark's eyes widened. She was here. He took a long, deep breath, composed himself, and slowly walked back into the office.

His lips were dry, and he felt a coarse tickle in his throat as he looked for her. *Come on, don't make this harder than it has to be. Where are you? Let's get this over with.*

He couldn't see her anywhere. He swept the room with his X-ray vision, but there was still no sign.

"Mr. Kent. Over here. See? Right there. In front of the guy from the *Post*."

Jimmy was standing next to Gil Truman, one of the other Planet reporters. Clark followed Jimmy's gaze up to the TV monitor on the wall. They were watching a live video feed of a press conference taking place on board a modified Boeing 777 already in mid-flight.

Bobbie-Faye, a stunning blonde with searing blue eyes, looked more like a model than the jet's public relations spokeswoman. She was standing in the front of the plane, smiling professionally to the reporters who furiously wrote down her every word. "You should already have the technical specs as well as the flight profile, so if you don't, please let me know, and I'll get them to you."

A longtime aeronautics professional who had begun working on the space shuttle program two weeks after graduating from college, Bobbie-Faye was used to dealing with the press, and she made certain that as her eyes slowly swept the crowd, they momentarily came to rest on each reporter—followed by a quick smile—to give them the feeling she was talking only to them.

"Main engine cutoff and external tank separation will commence approximately eight minutes after launch and just before orbit insertion, which varies, of course, according to each mission. By the way, did you know the 777 is the first airplane to have a rose named after it?"

She smiled again, and the reporters laughed, right on cue. She could rattle off a thousand different impressive statistics about the plane, but the rose story, and it was true, was the one that always appeared in their articles. *Give the people what they want.*

"With a takeoff weight of nearly three-quarters of a million pounds, in the past the space shuttle needed twelve million pounds of thrust, just in its initial launch phase. By piggybacking the *Explorer* on this Boeing 777 . . ." She was about to continue when a hand popped up, nearly blocking the TV screen. *There's always one who won't let me finish before having to ask their questions.*

"Yes?" She was a good actress, and there was no sense of impatience in her voice.

A tall, slender woman stood up, her hand still waving. Clark stared at the TV, transfixed. She was a little more mature than the last time he had seen her, but she was just as beautiful, and he noted, just as spunky, as ever.

"Lois Lane, *Daily Planet*. Piggybacking? Is that official terminology?"

Bobbie-Faye held in her annoyance. "Yes, Miss Lane. It is." *Go away. Sit down. Stop asking stupid questions!*

But Lois was just beginning. "You stated that this shuttle will usher in a new era of travel, enabling the average person to afford transcontinental flights via outer space—but can you tell us the exact price an 'average person' will be expected to pay?"

The cracks in Bobbie-Faye's picture-perfect makeup were beginning to show at the corners of her mouth. "I think you'll find that answer in your press packet, Miss Lane. Feel free to take your time looking for it."

Jimmy was grinning as Lois sat down. *She always asks the great questions.* He turned to Clark, who seemed confused. "What's going on there, Jimmy? What is this?"

Jimmy turned back to the monitor screen as Bobbie-Faye took a question from Laura Dane, a young reporter from the *Tribune* Jimmy had dated twice about a year ago.

"Oh, it's the first dual-craft launch of a privately funded orbital shuttle that uses onboard SRBs instead of external fuel tanks."

He noticed Clark's confused look. "SRB. Solid Rocket Boosters. They're going to launch it off the back of a jet."

Clark looked worried. "Sounds dangerous."

Gil thrust his face in front of Jimmy's. "Olsen, I can't hear her. Turn it up."

Jimmy was suddenly flustered as he grabbed the remote control and fumbled with it. The TV flickered and changed to a live baseball game.

"Sorry. Sorry."

As Jimmy tried to operate the remote, Clark made his way to Lois's desk, cluttered as always with books, files, and nicotine patches—*Still? What am I going to do with her?*

Sitting atop a folder, an engraved letter. "Lois Lane, As a Recipient of This Year's Pulitzer Prize, You Are Formally Invited to the Awards Ceremony . . ."

She won. Good. She deserved it. That's so good.

He was still beaming when he noticed the grouping of framed photos crowding the desktop. Lois with her family. Lois with her sister. Lois with a handsome young man. Lois with a little boy.

Who are they?

He looked up to see several child's crayon drawings pinned or taped to the cubicle wall. They all read, "To Mom." He turned back to the photo and studied it . . . trying to make heads or tails of the two strangers whose happy faces were beaming out at him.

"He looks a lot older now. Kids grow up so fast," Jimmy said.

Clark looked at him, a bit overwhelmed. "His mother?"

Jimmy saw his confused face. "Oh, gee. Oh, no. You've been gone. Well, Clark, you better sit down because you will not believe this. Fearless reporter Lois Lane is a mommy."

Clark felt every muscle in his body stiffen. He didn't know what to say. "Sorry," was the only thing that stumbled out of his mouth, and he wasn't even sure what that meant.

Jimmy was smiling. "I'm surprised she never told you, Clark."

Krypton was . . . it was worse than dead. My mother is involved with another man, not my father, and they were moving to oh, good God, Montana. Lois is, he could hardly even frame the thought, *a . . . mother? Is that even possible?*

He knew Jimmy had no idea that everything in his life suddenly seemed to unravel. He took control, or what little control he could, and forced a fake calm smile. "I haven't really been reachable." He let it drop when another thought struck him. "Wait. She's married?"

"Yup, well, no. Not really," Jimmy said, trying to sort it all out in his mind. "More like a prolonged engagement. But don't ask Miss Lane when they're tying the knot." He looked around and leaned closer to Clark. His voice fell to a conspiratorial whisper. "She hates that question."

Clark still wasn't sure what Jimmy had said. He glanced at the TV monitor again and heard Lois's voice drowning out the other reporters'.

"Bobbie-Faye, if this launch is as pivotal as you claim, why is it only being covered by one news network?"

Clark turned away from the camera and looked again at the photo in his hand. Lois. Her son. And him, the . . . *what was he? Her boyfriend? Lover? Fiancé?*

"You all right?" Jimmy asked. "You look like you could use a drink."

Clark stared ahead. Everything was a blur that he knew not even his telescopic vision could sharpen. "It's almost noon, Jimmy."

Jimmy nodded, grinning. "You're right. Almost lunch hour. We better hurry."

Twelve

They entered the Ace O' Clubs, and Jimmy pointed Clark to a seat in the back. "Hey, Bo," Jimmy said to the tall white-haired man working out the crossword puzzle on the cartoon page of the *Daily Planet,* "we'll sit back there, okay?"

Bo shrugged. "Whatever." He went back to figuring out a nine-letter word meaning to connect or divide.

Save for one unconscious Japanese businessman slumped over on his bar seat, the bar was empty, but Clark still felt out of place. "Shouldn't we get something to eat first?"

Jimmy laughed. "Bo serves up a great plate of pretzels and peanuts. So what do you want?"

Clark sat down and squinted at the wall of bottles shelved behind Bo. "Just water, please. Flat."

Bo raised his head from the puzzle and gave him a strange look. Clark turned to see Jimmy giving him the same look.

"You sure?" Bo asked.

Clark noticed the TV above the bar was set on the shuttle launch. The camera swept across the Boeing 777's cabin, and for a moment Clark saw Lois, seat-belted in place, trying furiously to get Bobbie-Faye's attention, but the PR woman kept talking. ". . . now, when we hit forty thousand feet, the shuttle will detach, ascend, and fire the first of the two propellant systems: the liquid fuel boosters."

She pointed to a monitor screen and the four astronauts strapped into their seats. Steve Yeager, the shuttle commander, waved at them. "Our heroes," Bobbie-Faye said. "But they're busy now, so why don't we let them get on with their work while we show you exactly how separation will occur."

The monitor screen changed into a picture of an animated version of the jet. As Bobbie-Faye continued to talk over the picture, the cartoon pictured the shuttle separation procedure in bright colors and loud music. "Then, when the shuttle reaches the stratosphere," she said, "the insertion boosters will fire, sending the craft into orbit."

Clark heard Lois's voice calling faintly from the back of the plane. "I'm sorry. Did you just say 'insertion boosters'?"

Bobbie-Faye held back her temper. *It won't be much longer. Just a few more minutes.* "Yes, Miss Lane. I did."

Clark heard Lois pipe up again. "Right. Of course."

Clark called back to Bo. "Actually, make that a beer, please." Bo nodded, unimpressed.

"Anything else?"

Clark looked at the TV again. "Yeah. Isn't there a game on?"

Bo nodded, grabbed a remote, and the baseball game appeared. The Ravens were playing the Fins. It was the third inning, and the Fins were ahead two to one. "Thanks," Clark said.

"No problem," Bo said. He turned to Jimmy. "The usual?" Clark saw Jimmy eagerly nod. A second later a beer was sitting in front of him, and a shot of whiskey was placed before Jimmy. *What's going on here?*

Clark noticed the clock, and it was suddenly 1:15 P.M. He looked at his bottle and saw it was empty, and Bo was dropping his previous bottle into the recycling bin, along with seven others. He turned to see Jimmy, his head on the tabletop. His eyes were open, but just barely.

"Another?" Bo asked Clark. Clark stared at the empty bottle in front of him and shrugged. *Why not? I'm not driving. Flying maybe, but not driving.*

Jimmy smiled a sloppy grin. "You know, Bo, ever since Superman took off into—where did Superman take off to, anyway?—anyway, since he went bye-bye and all our worlds went a little weird . . ." Jimmy tapped his empty whiskey glass against the counter. Bo filled it again. "Well, since then, Clark took off, too. Y'see, he's been doing a little soul-searching for a few years. He saw llamas."

Bo looked at Clark sipping his latest beer. "Oh, yeah? Coming back must be tough."

Clark was confused. "Coming back? What do you mean?"

"You know," Bo said. "To work. To start up all over again."

Clark nodded. He saw Johnnie Davis knock out a triple, bringing a man home. It was three to two now. "Yeah, well, you know. Things change. I mean, of course things change, but sometimes things that you never thought *could* change. Look at Lois. A woman like her . . . I thought she'd never settle down."

Jimmy was swirling the grains of salt that had fallen from the pretzels onto the table into a little whirlpool design. His head rotated with the movement of his finger. He looked up to the TV, not realizing the channel had been changed. "If you ask me, 'cause she'll never say it, but I think she's still in love with you-know-who."

Jimmy reached for his glass and chugged it while Clark stared at him, intrigued.

Gertrude Vanderworth's dog was quietly chewing on a bone in the corner of the hallway. A common fabric collar had replaced her diamond-studded showstopper, but the dog didn't seem to care. The dog—was it Tala or L.D.?—Luthor could never tell the difference—perked up, her ears rotating to a distant sound. She discarded the bone into a small pile of matted fur and scampered over the tile floor and down the stairs to the front door, where the alarm panel was beeping. The dog stood back and watched the door swing open.

Kitty Kowalski stepped inside and made a face. "Ack. This place is so tacky. Lex, why are we back here?"

Luthor grumbled as he pushed past her. "Kitty, while you were doing your nails, I was unlocking the secrets of one of the most advanced civilizations in the universe."

The dog watched Luthor march past, barely acknowledging Kitty's presence. Kitty paused to scratch the dog behind her ears. "Hey, weren't there two of these?" Luthor continued walking, ignoring her, then was joined by Brutus, Stanford, Grant, and Riley, his camcorder in hand, recording everything. She hurried to catch up.

"You see," Lex continued uninterrupted, "unlike our clunky earthbound methods of construction, the technology of Krypton, that's Superman's home world by the way, was based on manipulating the growth of crystals."

Kitty wasn't impressed. "Sounds like hocus-pocus to me."

Lex paused and growled as he glanced back at her, taking her chin in his hand. "Of course. To a primitive mind, any sufficiently advanced technology is indistinguishable from magic."

Luthor opened the basement door and headed down the staircase. "Cities. Vehicles. Weapons. Entire continents. All grown."

They reached the bottom of the stairs. The room before them was dark, but the echoes reverberating through it indicated an impressive size.

"Crystals. To think one could create a new world with such a simple little object." He removed the white crystal he took from the Fortress and held it in front of him for them to see. "It's like a seed. All it needs is water."

"Like Sea Monkeys," Kitty said dryly.

Luthor continued to stare at it. "Exactly, Kitty. Like Sea Monkeys."

Luthor turned the lights on revealing a huge, sprawling room and an immense model train set sitting on a table. Tiny people, miniature vehicles, and even a small, quaint town filled in the spaces around the tracks. In the center of the set was a small lake, filled with real water. Toy planes and jets circled over the town, suspended on nearly invisible wires.

"Wow," Kitty exclaimed. She walked around the train set, staring at the hundreds of tiny figures going about their lives. There were policemen, bus drivers and cab drivers, utility workers—one was perched atop a utility pole—and passersby.

In front of the grocery store a heavyset man in an apron was holding a bag of fruit. A small woman with a boy in tow was in front of the store, posed as if she was about to enter it. There was a line of people in front of the post office and about a dozen children making their way past a crossing guard as they headed to school. One of the child models was lying on its side. Grant cackled, assuming a car had struck him.

Kitty noticed the little church and the small wedding party on its front steps. A bride and groom were standing in front of a minister. She picked up the groom. "I, Lex Luthor, give you Katherine Kowalski, everything," she whispered.

She giggled and put the groom down again. *Lex can have whatever he wants. But I'll get everything else.* She laughed. She saw Stanford, tools in hand, hunched over a small workbench, staring through a microscope, across the room from her.

"Careful, careful," Lex cautioned him.

Stanford was using a miniature diamond saw to shave off a thin veneer from the edge of the white crystal. A small flake fell to the side. Using calipers, he picked up the tiny sliver and walked toward Lex, proudly showing him the slice.

"But it's so small," Kitty said.

Lex stared at it. "It's not the size that matters. It's how you use it."

Kitty rolled her eyes. "Still using that line?"

Lex glared at her for a second—"Funny"—before turning to Riley. "Are you getting this?"

Riley turned the camera to Luthor and gave a thumbs-up sign. "Not me, you idiot. Him." Riley quickly turned the camera back to follow Stanford, ever so carefully holding the crystal sliver as he slowly made his way to the small lake in the middle of the train set. "Careful," Luthor said. "You know what to do."

Stanford leaned forward as his foot snagged a train set cable that snaked across the floor to the 220 outlet on the other side of the room. He lost his balance as the calipers and crystal flew out of his hands and dropped into the center of the lake. He fell to the ground, waiting for the explosion.

Nothing.

He stood up again and saw that everyone else had nervously moved to the other side of the room. He glanced back to the lake and saw his calipers leaning up from it, its closed jaws submerged. He scurried across the room and joined the others. "Sorry, boss," he said to Luthor.

Kitty chuckled. "Wow. That's really something, Lex."

But Luthor was still smiling. "Wait for it."

He held his breath. *C'mon. What the hell are you waiting for? Do it!*

Nothing. He turned from the set, disappointed. "All right Riley, shut off the camera."

Riley was zooming in on the calipers. "But I'm getting it."

Lex shook his head. "I said shut off the damn camera."

Riley turned off the camcorder and started to put it down when the train set lights suddenly flickered and died. He looked up to see the basement lights go black. "Did I do something wrong, boss?"

Luthor turned back to the train model. He felt his heartbeat quicken. "No. That wasn't you. Turn it on again. Turn it on."

The model lake was beginning to bubble. Through a thin layer of fog he could see that the crystal was glowing.

The hallway lights died. The living-room lights died. The first-floor lights, then the second-floor and the attic-area lights all died, too.

Even in the darkness, Luthor was staring at the glowing crystal and the bubbling water.

Beginning in its middle and radiating outward from there, the house began to shut down. Outside, in the great gardens, the sprinkler system suddenly stopped, and the garden lights exploded.

The blackout continued spreading from there.

Thirteen

Clark Kent downed his eighth beer when the lights went out at the Ace O' Clubs. He didn't care. Bo picked up the phone to call the power company, but the familiar dial tone wasn't waiting for him. He looked at the receiver as if he could intimidate it into working, but the phone wasn't afraid of him. "That's weird. Must be a blackout."

Clark glanced up and lowered his glasses. His eyes focused, and the back wall to the bar disappeared, revealing the street beyond. Streetlights blinked off. Store-window lights went dark. Cars slowed to a stop, bumping into each other as their frantic drivers tried ineffectively to turn their steering wheels.

Bo hung up the phone, shrugged, and turned back to Clark. It didn't matter what was going on outside. In here, he controlled the world. "Want another?"

Clark blinked as his eyes refocused. He turned back to Jimmy and saw his head still resting on the table, his snoring growing louder. Clark shrugged, looked up at the TV, its screen thankfully dark. "Sure," he said. *Why not?*

Inside the Daily Planet the lights suddenly went out without explanation. As one, a hundred reporters, secretaries, and assistants hit the SAVE keys, but their computers were already down. They all tried to remember when they saved last and how much they would have to retype when the power returned.

Perry White looked out his office window and onto a city that had come to a dead stop. Cars weren't moving. Horns weren't blaring. The eerie silence was frightening. High above, on the roof, the Daily Planet globe stopped rotating. Perry turned back to his office not realizing he was humming *It's the end of the world as we know it.*

The blackout continued on its outbound journey, not yet nearly sated.

John Williamson sat back in Mission Control and stared at the display screens. *So far so good.* The shuttle commander's voice was coming in loud and clear over the radio. "Mission Control, booster ignition is at T-minus one minute, and we are prepping to disengage couplings, and—

The power died abruptly, and the screens flickered off. Williamson shunted to emergency power, but it didn't respond.

He fell back into his chair; contact with the Boeing shuttle was lost.

• • •

In the *Explorer* shuttle, the four astronauts were strapped into their seats when the blackout hit. The lights on Shuttle Commander Yeager's console shut off in sequence. He hit the con, but neither the familiar beep nor static greeted him. "Mission Control? Come in, over." It was dead. *What the hell is going on?*

Inside the jet cabin, the lights suddenly flickered and went out. Bobbie-Faye's animated cartoon moaned its way to a stop. Lois looked outside the window and saw the ground. It seemed to be closer than before.

In the cockpit, Captain Hamilton heard the engines die as his stomach felt the plane suddenly drop. He remained calm as he tried to regain power and contact with Air Control.

Then, just as suddenly, the power was back. Hamilton put the plane into a light dive, then brought her out again. Inside the main cabin, Bobbie-Faye's animated cartoon groaned its way back to its story, but nobody was paying any attention.

Inside the shuttle, Commander Yeager and his men allowed themselves a sigh of relief.

The jet leveled off, back on course. All was well again.

The TV turned itself back on in the Ace O' Clubs as Jimmy pulled himself back to a sitting position and nursed his unfinished drink through a straw. Clark was looking at him hopefully.

"When you said Lois was still in love with you-know-who . . . who did you mean?"

Jimmy turned to Clark, his eyes half-closed and his smile wide as if he knew great secrets better left unspoken. He hiccuped, and that wise, knowing look disappeared again. He turned again to his shot glass and held it up to the light, a diamond inspected. "Did you know I haven't had a picture published in two months?"

He let that hang. Clark tried to get Jimmy's attention, but his eyes were focused somewhere else. "No, I didn't. But Jimmy, when you said that, did you mean that Lois is still in love with Superman?"

Jimmy turned back to Clark, bleary-eyed and confused. His words were slow as he tried to control the pronunciation of every last syllable. "I don't remember saying that. You must be drunk, Clark."

Clark's voice softened. "Actually, I've always had a pretty high tolerance. But about what you said . . ." He saw Jimmy staring mindlessly at his drink, then watched helplessly as the boy's eyes closed peacefully and his face sank, almost in slow motion, to the tabletop, where he started snoring again.

Bo placed another beer on the table in front of him. Clark stared at it as if it were about to perform some kind of trick.

He thought about everything that had happened since he came home.

Home! That was a laugh.

He thought about growing up in Smallville, remembering the time just before his powers began to really blossom. He had few expectations back then. It was the ride that mattered, not the goal.

Lana. Pete. All the others. All his friends. They were important to him. But after the change, after *his* change, he knew that as much as he might have wanted it, it could no longer be that way. He had a mission. Jor-El himself had told him that.

It changed after Smallville. After his father died. *My real father,* he thought. *Jonathan Kent—the man who raised me. The man who loved me. Not the man who gave me a mission and then walked out of my life.*

It changed so much after he took Jor-El's crystal from the barn, asked Ben Hubbard to help his mother look after the farm, and made that long trek north. Everything changed after he threw the crystal into the frozen arctic waters, and it bubbled and frothed and then grew into his Fortress of Solitude.

Fortress of Solitude!

He hated that word.

Solitude.

His father promised him he would never be alone again, but then why build a place for solitude?

Maybe that was supposed to be my home, because right now nothing much else feels like it is.

He lived with that solitude for years, his only company Jor-El's quiet voice reminding him that he had a destiny, then training him how to fulfill it.

What if I don't want to have a destiny? What if I don't want to be special? You said I wasn't a god, but you turned me into one anyway. Lois called me a savior. But she said the world shouldn't have saviors because people would come to expect us to solve all their problems for them.

If I'm not a god, then what am I? If I shouldn't be a savior, then what should I be?

Clark stared at the beer sitting on the counter in front of him. He wasn't drunk, he was sure of that, but he certainly felt a little buzzed. He looked out the bar window again. Krypton wasn't home. Smallville wasn't home. Metropolis wasn't turning out to be all green lawn and white picket fences either.

Where was this mythical home he was looking for? Where did he belong?

He turned back to the beer and reached for it . . .

. . . then pushed it away.

Riley turned on his camera again and aimed it at Luthor. Kitty was thinking, *What the hell just happened?* Stanford was counting his fingers, making sure he was intact, while Brutus and Grant were just happy to be alive. But Lex was still staring into the lake, waiting.

"That's it?" Kitty asked, indignantly. "All that jazz for some itty-bitty poof?"

Luthor didn't turn to her. "Nope. Are you getting this, Riley?"

Riley nodded and moved closer. With shaky hands he aimed the camera at the small lake in the middle of the model railroad set.

The table began to shake as the rumbling began again, at first slowly, like some high-speed train rattling its way just outside their window, then it grew louder and louder like roller-coaster screams. Kitty saw the train set vibrate. The tiny church steeple slipped off its base, crushing the hopeful wedding party. She watched the trains crash as cracks tore through the model landscape like a ravaging earthquake. *Everyone has a fault. Mine used to be in California,* Luthor thought. *Now it's here.*

Buildings shattered and overhead, in the real world, the basement lights exploded and the water pipes split, spraying boiling water everywhere.

Kitty fell back as the mansion's walls and floor cracked exactly as the model city had moments before.

Luthor watched and smiled. It was all so much better than he had expected.

John Williamson was hunched over the Mission Control con as data spooled across the bottom of his computer screen. "*Explorer,* not sure what just happened, but it looks like we're going to have to scrub the launch. Copy?"

Yeager's voice came over the radio. "Roger that. Aborting booster ignition."

Lee Aaron, his copilot, flipped open the control panel and entered the abort sequence. He waited for the green light to turn to red, but it didn't happen. He reentered the sequence a second time. Still no change. "Sir, boosters are not responding. We are still counting down for ignition." He was looking to Yeager for a suggestion.

"Can we release the couplings?"

Aaron entered a new sequence and heard the shuttle couplings fire. He checked the monitor. They had not disengaged. "Negative."

Yeager checked the panel again. There was only a handful of seconds remaining before the boosters, still attached to the jet, fired. The commander took a moment to calm himself as he reached for the radio. "Mission Control, we have a malfunction. Can you do a remote override?"

He knew if they couldn't, the booster ignition would destroy the jet as well as their shuttle.

Williamson saw Curtis enter the codes. "Negative."

The worst was happening. Astronauts knew in advance of any mission that there was always a possibility they could die. Drawn by both the need for adrenaline as well as the thrill of exploration, pilots have, since the dawn of manned flight, put themselves at risk to push new technologies to their limits. Risk was a necessary evil that they lived with every time they shot themselves into the sky riding in what was little more than a thin metal box.

He and Yeager had grown up together in the space program, Williamson and Yeager, pushing each other, always trying to outdo the other. If they hadn't discovered thirteen years ago that Williamson's lungs were operating at less than full capacity, he might have been in the shuttle now instead of his best friend.

Williamson swore he wasn't going to give up. Death was going to have to do double duty if it wanted to take his friends.

"Negative, *Explorer*," he said calmly, although feeling anything but. "Override is not responding."

Yeager sat back in his chair. The other astronauts had heard Williamson quietly pronounce their death sentence. "Override is not responding."

Maybe, but they still had work to do. Through his seat cushion he felt the boosters rumble and shake. Outside, he knew, they would just be starting to smoke.

Although she had no idea what had happened, Bobbie-Faye was keenly aware that something had gone wrong.

Her job required her to keep smiling no matter what, to keep on her talking points, present that happy face to the press, all the while minimizing potential problems. Every time she felt the engines groan her smile widened just a bit more.

If the reporters weren't asking themselves why the shuttle hadn't disengaged when they felt the shudder rumble its way through the jet, they might have realized the look in her eyes didn't quite match the happy face she was presenting to the world.

"Now," she said, keeping her voice light as if the engine groans were either anticipated or natural, "if you look out to the right side, when it is time you'll be able to see the shuttle climb into the stratosphere. And if you're lucky, you may hear the faint pop of the sonic boom."

Everyone jumped as they heard the boom, then they settled back, applauded, and laughed. Obviously everything was under control.

"See what I mean?" Bobbie-Faye was laughing with them, but she was the only one in the passenger compartment who knew that boom was not the one she had been talking about. "Okay, everyone settle in for a while. I'll fill you in on what's going on"—she looked at her watch—"in just a few minutes, give or take."

Lois Lane pressed back into her seat, worried. She wasn't laughing. She'd flown with Superman. She knew what sonic booms sounded like, and that, sister, whatever the hell it was, was no sonic boom.

The primary boosters had fired, and the blast had already begun to melt the jet's tail. The jet began to shake as it and its shuttle cargo rocketed up into the sky.

"Everyone, please make sure your seat belts are fastened." The captain's voice was coming over the intercom. "We are experiencing separation problems with the shuttle. I'll get back to you as soon as I have any information." The com clicked off abruptly, and the reporters went wild.

Lois felt the jet rattle and lurch forward, then she saw Bobbie-Faye thrown back and tumble to the floor. She was grabbing the seat legs to stop her slide to the back of the jet. Everyone was screaming as they found themselves plastered to their seats, flattened by the pounding g forces. The roar of the boosters and the screech of the buckling metal hull were suddenly deafening.

Commander Yeager noticed the airspeed indicator lean into the red zone. He turned back to the radio. "Mayday, Mayday. Boosters have fired, and we are not disengaged. I repeat, we are not disengaged."

He knew there was mayhem in Mission Control as the brass and the techs ran one emergency scenario after another, hoping against hope that there was something they had overlooked, while never allowing themselves to acknowledge that even if they found it, there was probably still no way to save the jet and the shuttle in time.

They were scientists, not miracle makers. But they weren't about to give up.

The reporters covering the launch on the ground reluctantly pulled themselves away from the Mission Control monitors and called in their stories. This was the part of the job they prayed they never had to report. Most of the reporters knew Williamson and Yeager personally from working with them closely over the years. They had gone out to lunch and dinner with them and one or two had become close friends. They knew how close those two were and what must have been going through Williamson's mind as he tried to find a way to save his friend as well as everyone else on board. The flyboys were about fun and hard living and the reporters, despite the scoop this provided, never wanted to write their obituaries.

When Daily Planet reporter Curtis Wayne was just a kid, no more than thirteen, he used to get up at midnight to listen to the news of the latest rocket launch or space mission taking off from Cape Kennedy. Later, he would spend hours listening over and over again to the homemade tapes he made of Walter Cronkite announcing to the world that man had landed on the moon.

He had volunteered to cover the shuttle launch story, but Lois Lane got the assignment instead. She always got the assignment. Curtis could have resented her, and sometimes he actually did, except that he knew deep down that as good as he was, she was, for all her seeming dizziness, the better reporter and the better writer.

He looked across Mission Control and saw Williamson calmly speaking with one of the techs. Curtis knew he and Yeager came up in the astronaut program together and were best men at each other's weddings. *He may look calm, but man, what's got to be going on under the surface.* He spoke a silent prayer for everyone, then he, too, called in the story, slowly enunciating every word so it could be copied correctly. "Four veteran astronauts, a Boeing 777 jet pilot and his crew of twelve, along with nearly fifty reporters, including the *Daily Planet*'s own Pulitzer Prize-winning Lois Lane, are currently in the most dire situation of their lives . . ."

• • •

Within two minutes, television stations switched over from their regular broadcasting to the news division. "This just in . . ." "The inaugural flight of the shuttle *Explorer* appears to be experiencing extremely serious technical difficulties . . ."

The newscasters were professional, coolly reading the brand-new copy off the TelePrompTers as if the words had been rehearsed.

Perry White had been told about Curtis's phone call and had the TV on in his office. He put down his cigar and helplessly watched the news. *Dammit.*

Fourteen

In the Ace O' Clubs, the Fins were winning six to five in the first game of a doubleheader that would take most of the night. The Ravens were up with two men on base, no outs, and the top of their lineup hungry for action. Clark was praying for a strike. Nothing against the Ravens, but come on, these were the Fins. The champs. They *had* to win. The game suddenly disappeared and was replaced by the WGBS-TV logo. "We interrupt our regularly scheduled program for this special report."

The image changed again to Mary Watkins, the GBS anchor.

Watkins was grim, and Clark knew that whatever was wrong had to be serious. Clark nudged Jimmy, but he was already awake and listening.

"We have an ongoing tragedy to report out of Cape Canaveral, Florida. For that we go to Flora Johnson live at the scene."

Flora Johnson, an attractive brunette in her early thirties, stared grimly into the camera as she read the news scrolling up the TelePrompTer. "We're coming to you live from the Kennedy Space Center, where it seems there is a problem with the inaugural flight of the new orbital shuttle, *Explorer.* Reports are just coming in, but it appears the shuttle's boosters have fired before detaching from the Boeing 777 jet, veering both craft dramatically off course and out of control. It is feared that when the secondary boosters ignite, both craft will be endangered."

"Lois is on that flight," Jimmy said, suddenly sober and alert. He turned to Clark, but all he saw was a wad of money rolled up on the table. Jimmy grabbed his camera and took off.

Clark rushed past the crowd clustered several layers deep in front of the window of the discount electronics store, staring at the TVs, all tuned to the same channel, all blaring news of the tragedy. He'd been following the story from the moment he left the bar, his superhearing picking up one broadcast after another as he rushed toward the alleyway across the street from the Ace O' Clubs. He had almost shrugged himself out of his shirt when he noticed he was wearing a white T-shirt beneath it and not the familiar red, yellow, and blue shirt he had expected to find.

Right! Oops.

Clark rushed into the Planet building, cursing himself for leaving behind his suitcase, leaving behind his costume. *If they're hurt because of* . . . He dropped the thought. *Just get the job done.*

There was no time to take the elevator. He hurried through the door leading to the stairs and blurred his way up the dozen floors to the editorial offices. He saw everyone engrossed watching the story unfold on the TV. He zipped past them and entered the janitor's closet, quietly closing its door behind him.

He found his suitcase and took out the neatly folded suit he'd come for. He stared at it for a moment, hesitating. *If I do this, if I release the genie, he can't ever be put back into his bottle again.*

But he knew he had no choice. Jor-El and Lara were right; he had a *destiny.* Jonathan and Martha Kent were also right; he *was* put here on Earth for a reason.

The suit felt comfortable and somehow reassuring. He took a long breath, stepped outside, and made his way to the nearest window. Everyone was still watching those horrifying images flickering across the television. He caught his reflection in the glass; he was still wearing Clark's glasses. *It has been a long time.* He slipped them into his cape pocket, then stepped out into the cold air.

He found the wind against his face bracing as he soared over Centennial Park. It had been more than five years since his last flight, and though he felt a pang of guilt for thinking it, especially now, considering, flying felt . . . *natural.* It felt good. Somehow empowering. He realized how much he had missed it.

He flew over a bronze statue of himself in the middle of the park, near the lake and the carousel, standing tall and proud, holding a meteor over his head—one of the actual meteors he had caught on his last day on Earth. People were sitting on the benches circling it, having lunch, talking and laughing, happily living their days, temporarily unaware of the problems plaguing the rest of the world.

His telescopic vision let him read the engraved plaque partially buried in the ground in front of the statue. FOR SUPERMAN, OUR SAVIOR. He winced.

He never wanted to be a savior, or even to be thought of that way. Yes, he knew he wasn't just a policeman who came with something *extra*. He acknowledged his powers separated himself from nearly everyone else, but he didn't think of himself as special. *Why did they have to?*

He glanced up and concentrated, focusing his eyes until he located a long trail of smoke climbing into the upper atmosphere, halfway across the United States. He trained his telescopic vision to find the head of the comet and saw the shuttle, its boosters still firing, dragging along with it the helpless Boeing 777.

He switched to X-ray vision and checked inside the jet. He saw a blond woman, Bobbie-Faye, crawling across the floor, struggling her way into a seat. Oxygen masks were descending from the overhead compartments, and passengers were securing them in place as instructed by the preflight movie.

He searched aisle after aisle until he found Lois. *Thank goodness.* She had grabbed her mask but was failing to put it on properly. A reporter next to her helped fit it into place and begin the flow of oxygen.

The smoky trail was now directly ahead of him, so he banished his doubts and streaked toward it. Within seconds he saw the 777 with the piggybacked shuttle climbing higher into the atmosphere, two fighter jets attempting to follow but unable to keep up.

His X-ray vision allowed him to see the astronauts,

calmly flipping the switches on the panel that should have detached them from the jet. The system had short-circuited, somehow taking its backup with it, and nothing was working now. He could clearly hear Commander Yeager speaking with Mission Control. "Entering mesosphere in sixteen seconds. Secondary booster ignition in twenty seconds. It doesn't look good, John."

He heard Mission Control respond, their voices calm, despite the obvious stress. "*Explorer*, Houston, UHF comm.— check. Do you read?"

Perhaps, he realized, that one of the reasons he hated that term *savior* applied to him was that he believed he wasn't taking real risks doing what he did. Most of his actions, he felt, weren't life-threatening. He was invulnerable; almost nothing except for kryptonite could harm him. But policemen, firemen, people like these astronauts, they put their lives on the line every time they tried to help mankind take yet another small step forward. They were the real heroes, and he wished they received the acclaim they deserved.

Hank Josephs, the navigations officer, glanced at the radar screen and saw a small blip rushing toward them. "Sir," he called out, "picking up something on radar."

In Mission Control, John Williamson looked at his own screen and saw the same blip closing in on the jet. *Bird? Missile? What the hell—?*

"We see it, too. Can you get visual contact, *Explorer*?" Josephs looked out the cockpit window, but the shuttle was surrounded by clouds. "Can't tell, Mission Control. Not yet."

Williamson's voice sounded resigned. "Keep looking, *Explorer.*"

Peering inside the jet, Superman saw Bobbie-Faye struggling to stand. The plane jerked suddenly to the side, and she fell again. He saw Lois unbuckle her own seat belt. She reached out to grab Bobbie-Faye as the jet banked to the right. Lois held on to her seat with one hand and grabbed Bobbie-Faye by the wrist with the other. She pulled her into a seat.

The fighter jets leveled off as they reached maximum velocity. On their radar they saw what appeared to be a *third* jet screaming toward them.

No. Not a jet. What is it?

The lead jet banked. "Sir, we're seeing something passing us. Can't make it out yet. Oh, my God, sir."

Superman was closer now. He could make out the 777 and shuttle less than a mile away.

Josephs checked the console. "Secondary booster ignition in five. Four. Three . . ."

Superman was within a hundred feet of the jet when the secondary boosters ignited and blew off the 777's tail. The blast rocketed both craft forward while blasting Superman back.

He tumbled until he was able to regain balance, then, with just a pause, he rocketed ahead again. He saw Lois's face, framed by the jet's window, staring at the vast curvature of the Earth far below. She looked up and saw that the shuttle was climbing toward outer space, dragging the helpless jet with it.

Her eyes widened in surprise as he passed her at superspeed. She looked again, wondering if what she saw was real or just wish fulfillment.

Superman scanned the 777 and saw that the couplings were still secure. He strained to pick up speed. The jet was less than a hundred feet away now.

I can do this. I have to do this.

For just a moment he felt calm, almost serene. He closed his eyes and let the cool wind rush past him. He was a runner hitting his stride. He was there. He was ready. *In the zone,* he remembered it was called. His muscles relaxed. His face, taut with worry, gave way to relief.

The jet was directly below him.

He grabbed its cold, metal skin and pulled himself slowly across its belly. He held on, fighting both the wind and gravity, which were conspiring to toss him off as quickly as they could. *Forget it. I'm here, and I'm not leaving 'til I get what I came for.*

Hand over hand he pulled himself across the body of the jet, fighting the relentless pressures pushing against him. His muscles tightened as he strained to gain every inch, every foot.

Gods could do this without any problems he thought. They could wish the jet to safety. They could make everything right again just by snapping their fingers.

But his fingers ached as he pulled himself across the jet's body, the wind slamming at him, trying to fling him back into space. It had been five long years since he had exerted himself in this way. Five years sleeping in stasis, living in his dreams, and his movements now felt awkward, and his balance was precarious; the jet's slick metal body was not designed to be climbed over like some playground monkey bars.

The jet metal bunched as his fingers dug into it. Then, as he continued, each handhold became a foothold, something for him to push against, making the next several feet seem possible to advance. Despite the awkwardness and pain, he had not considered giving up. This had to be done, and even if it tore him apart, he was going to save the jet.

He reached the couplings and pushed at them. The wind was doing its best to tear him away, but he held on, pushing harder and harder until they finally snapped. He could feel the two craft detaching.

He backed off, hovering for an instant, regaining just a fraction of his strength, but he knew it would have to be enough. He pushed again, forcing the shuttle skyward, into space, safely away from the jet.

Mission Control's voice crackled over the radio. "*Explorer*, UHF comm. Check. Do you read? Over."

There was silence. The kind that cut directly through Williamson's heart. But then, "Ground control, we have . . . liftoff? I mean, we're in orbit. Don't ask me how, but everything is okay."

Superman checked inside the jet again and saw the passengers experience a brief feeling of calm as their pens, glasses, magazines, and other loose items started to float; they were in zero gravity. Superman heard his own heart thumping; he knew what was going to happen next.

The jet, having reached its apex, began to plummet.

He glanced up, saw that the shuttle was safely moving

into orbit—*one less worry*—then dove for the jet free-falling like a bomb toward the ground, smoke trailing behind it, marking its doomed descent.

He knew what he had to do: *Grab its wing. Pull on it. Slow down the jet.*

But the 777 was spinning too fast and hard. The wing strained, then bent, and finally broke. Superman tumbled off, hovering for a brief moment, then he reoriented himself as the jet arced downward in a continuing nosedive.

A moment later the wind and pressure shattered its left wing, cannoning it into Superman. He flew through it without pause or thought. *They're panicking inside. Screaming. I see the fear in Lois's eyes, but she's forcing herself to be calm by talking into her tape recorder, reporting on the fall. Nothing fazes her.*

Superman saw the horizon spinning below him. He pulled himself across the hull, shooting past the windows toward the jet's nose. Astonished passengers gawked at him from inside.

Fifteen hundred feet. Twelve hundred feet.

He made it to the nose. He grabbed it, then pushed against it, trying again to slow it down and control its descent. His feet floundered; there was nothing to push against but his own indefatigable will.

A thousand feet. Nine hundred feet.

He heard their cries, and though he wanted to give them their privacy, he was unable to shut them out. There were reporters from fifteen countries, and they prayed in a dozen different languages.

His mind triggered another memory of another time.

Strange how life works, symmetry. My first appearances then and now, both connected with falling airships. Both with Lois Lane.

It was the Daily Planet helicopter. Its landing skids had snagged a loose cable on the Planet's roof helipad and the copter was unable to take off. It was yanked back and fell against the side of the building. Pedestrians on the street below saw it hanging precariously from the roof. The police and fire department moved in. Reporters suddenly appeared, from nowhere, their camera crews recording every moment.

Everyone was watching. Waiting. She was dangling from the copter, holding on to a fraying seat belt. Then it snapped, and she fell.

He only had an instant to make a decision then, like now. One decision that would change his entire life. And like now, he had no choice.

He flew, readying himself to grab her as she fell. As he did he lowered himself just a bit, breaking her fall gently.

She stared at him as if she couldn't accept that she was safe in this person's, this stranger's arms. She was about to scream when he gave her a slight smile and spoke to her softly and reassuringly. "Easy, miss. I've got you."

She kept looking at him as if she were having a dream, then she looked down to the ground, no longer rushing up to her, then back up at him, still disoriented, perhaps even more than she'd been a moment before. "You've got me? Who's got you?"

Before he could answer they both heard the helicopter's skids snap. The copter was falling directly at them.

He held onto her with one hand and grabbed the copter with his other. She looked at him again. *What are you?* He continued smiling as he flew his precious cargo back to its rooftop pad.

As he let her down, she began to wobble a bit, unsteady on her feet. "I certainly hope this little incident hasn't put you off flying, miss," he said lightly, trying to diffuse her nervousness. "Statistically speaking, of course, it's still the safest way to travel."

She nodded, still quiet, still unsure if she was dreaming. Or dead. Or something else. He started to leave when she finally called to him. "Wait. Who *are* you?"

He turned and smiled again. "A friend." He then quietly climbed into the night sky and disappeared into the distance.

He remembered she stood there for a while, quiet and numb, trying to make sense of the impossible. It was the only time in all the years he'd known her, before or after that day, that she had ever been speechless.

Fifteen

Seven hundred feet.

Lois was falling. Again. But this time it wasn't from a helicopter. From something light enough that he could catch and hold steady with only one hand. This time it was a speeding deadweight that was not about to cooperate with him or anyone else. From head to tail the jet was 195 feet, 9 inches long. It weighed more than four hundred thousand pounds. Without the passengers. That was not its plummeting weight.

If he could move worlds like they used to have him do in those comic books they made about him, then this would be no problem. Then he would be the next closest thing to a god, as Lois had said.

But, despite his gifts, as miraculous as they were, he was just a man. He had no three wishes he could utter to make this go away. *Peter Pan was just a story,* he had once told Lois.

But this was no fantasy. This was reality.

He looked down again and saw the large Florida city, its wide avenues congested with rush-hour traffic. There were more than fifty thousand people filling nearly every block, walking its streets, shopping their way across town, driving their cars, living and working in the city's proud office buildings and high-rises, many built back in the '30s when art deco was king, and the others, constructed more recently, designed to fit into the cityscape, a retro view of what the future should be.

The passengers' screams interrupted his reverie. But along with the screams he heard moments of cheering. *Why? Who?*

He scanned the area and looked to the north, just across the bridge to a large park, which occupied nearly two hundred prime acres of land. The lights of the stadium were announcing to all within fifty miles that the Fins were playing. *Come on down and join the fun.*

The Ravens had come from behind to win the first game eleven to seven. They were now in the bottom of the fourth of their doubleheader. Alvin Wayne of the Fins had just hit a home run with three men on, a grand slam that put the Fins ahead six to nothing. They weren't going to let the Ravens have their way with them again.

Jerry Harlan hit a fly ball that shot straight up in the air. Forty thousand fans craned to see it, but their attention was drawn to something other than that high-flying ball.

Most of them hadn't seen him for more than five years. Some of the younger fans thought he was just some figment from myth or history, from way back, you know, before World War I or Vietnam or some time long ago. But they all knew his costume, they all knew that red cape.

His name quickly spread through the stadium. *He was back. Superman was back!*

He was in front of a jet *heading directly for them,* and they saw his face contorted with pain as he pushed against its nose with every iota of strength he could summon.

Some of them began to run, but others, the older ones mostly, the ones who remembered seeing him fly through the city on his way to save . . . *someone* . . . didn't bother to leave their seats. *He's back.*

They picked up their binoculars, brought to the park to watch Christopher George or Mort Schwartz steal third or slide into home.

Through their binoculars they could see him straining as he pushed against the falling jet, as he was pushed down by it.

You can do it, Superman. You can do anything.

They were falling, but it appeared to those watching that their descent was occurring in slow motion. The fall was being controlled. He was lowering the jet toward the field. *He was holding a half-million-pound jet, for cryin' out loud!*

As Superman and the jet drew closer, the players ran to the edge of the field to give him room. Maybe the people in the stands had come here to see the so-called superstars play a game, but both teams knew better; he was the real superstar. He was the pro.

The stadium lights flickered and exploded as the remains of the jet's wings tore through them.

Inside it, while some passengers prayed and others screamed, Lois remained calm, her eyes closed, her breathing normal. *Superman is back. Superman is here.*

They were directly over the diamond, but still falling

fast. *Too fast,* Superman thought. He braced himself again and gave the jet one last, massive push.

The hull groaned as a wave of kinetic energy rippled through the steel, traveling the length of the jet until it finally slowed to a stop, only a few feet above the ground.

Lois felt the cabin jolt. Most of the people around her screamed again, not sure what had just happened. She gripped her seat arms tighter. *He's back. He's here.*

He hovered over home plate, about a dozen feet above ground, holding the jet straight up. The muscles in his arms were bunched and strained, and he felt like they were going to burst. He wanted to toss the plane aside, to get rid of the massive weight he was trying to hold steady, but, despite the pain, he forced himself to lower it slowly to the ground. His feet touched the plate.

He held firm for what seemed to him to be hours, then he carefully tilted the jet and lowered it until its wheels hit the ground, kicking up clouds of dirt and dust.

He stepped back and took a long, deep breath, then jumped to the passenger door and pulled it free. He stepped inside the jet and looked around.

"Is everyone all right?"

They nodded, unsure what had just happened.

He scanned them quickly; no broken bones.

He smiled, and their anxieties seemed to disappear. "I suggest you all stay in your seats until medical attention arrives."

They nodded again, without saying a single word.

He noticed Lois peeking out from behind a seat. She looked frazzled, but beautiful. *She was always beautiful.* He made his way down the aisle to her. The reporters let him pass, the questions they were waiting to ask evaporating as he stepped past them.

She undid her seat belt and stood, still shaking, but looking only at him. The jet could have been on fire. People could have been burning and screaming, but all she would have seen was him walking closer and closer, those deep blue eyes staring into her soul.

"Are you okay?" he asked.

She opened her mouth, but all that came out was a small squeak. He smiled again, gently brushed away some of her hair, and let his hand fall, just for a moment, on her cheek.

Superman realized the others were looking at them. He gathered himself, winked at Lois, then turned to them.

"Well," he said, "I hope this little incident hasn't put any of you off flying. Statistically speaking, it's *still* the safest way to travel."

He remembered. Lois let herself laugh as Superman turned from her and walked back up the aisle. He stepped into the doorway and saw the stadium crowd staring at him, the TV cameras, taping the doubleheader, trained on him, a close-up of his face dominating the stadium's Jumbotron screen.

They had all been quiet, as if silence had somehow been ordered by some higher authority, but as soon as they saw him step into the doorway, their inhibitions disappeared. They began to cheer and applaud more than they ever had at any game. More than they had when the Fins had won the World Series.

$\bullet \bullet \bullet$

In the Daily Planet offices, the staff screamed when they saw him. Perry White, sitting alone in his office, watching the small TV on his desk, took two aspirin as he gave his silent thanks.

Superman's image was on every monitor screen in Mission Control. The normally reserved scientists were shouting, dancing out of control, like five-year-olds, and not caring who was watching.

Superman looked at the crowd, feeling a bit intimidated. It had been so long. They were hooting and waving their Fins' giant flipper-on-a-stick signs, and yelling out his name, hoping he'd hear them and look their way. Their cheers kept growing louder and louder. He was almost ashamed to admit it, but it felt good. He nodded at them, waved good-bye, then rose into the sky and flew off, happy he was home again.

It was a good first day.

Sixteen

The town had been completely destroyed. The post office was still on fire as was the police station, the row of office buildings next to it, the block of small homes that dotted the landscape and, in an ironic twist, the firehouse. The fast-food restaurant had sunk into the massive hole in the town center, which had also swallowed at least nineteen of the town's cars. The ground was filled with holes and cracks, and there were bodies everywhere, many of them crushed beyond recognition. The lake had been emptied of all its water.

Lex picked himself up from behind the model train set table and looked at the former Vanderworth basement, charred, in shambles, and filled with several inches of water that had spilled out of the cracked pipes. Debris floated on its surface along with several other disturbing piles of unrecognizable things Luthor chose not to identify.

He looked ahead, and his eyes widened, then he turned

to Riley with hopeful anticipation. "Did you get that? Are you still getting it?"

Riley, holding the video camera in his trembling hands was nodding repeatedly. "Yeah. I got the whole . . . scary . . . thing."

Luthor turned back to the huge crystal structure that had grown up through the train set, towering over the destroyed cityscape. The crystal formation started where the lake had been and looked nearly identical to Superman's Fortress of Solitude, as well as the ruins of Krypton, only in miniature scale; the train-set version, only real, he thought.

Kitty looked under the table that held the demolished model and saw that the crystal structure had grown through the bottom as well, with crystal tendrils piercing the basement's concrete floor, then moving down into the ground below. She shook her head, not believing what she was seeing. "Lex, your little crystal broke everything."

Lex was grinning as he checked out the devastation. "So it did."

Perry White circled the conference room, glaring at the reporters sitting around the table, their slim notepads in front of them, pens in their hands, taking down every word he said. "I want to know it all! Everything!" he shouted.

He waited for the fear to fill their eyes. Fear was good. Fear would get their hearts pumping. Fear would get them working harder and faster. Fear would make tomorrow morning's edition of the *Daily Planet* sell twice as many copies as their closest competitor.

As he walked around the table, he clipped Jimmy Olsen's chair, startling the young photographer, who was trying to decide if he should ask Donna in the secretarial pool if she wanted to go to a movie with him on Friday. "Olsen, I wanna see photos of him bathed in stadium lights!"

"Uhh, Chief, he flew off. How am I—"

Perry had already moved on to his next victim. "Sports: How will this event change baseball? How will they get the plane out of there?" He turned to Alice Travers and his eyes bored into hers. "Travel: Where has he been? Was he on vacation? If so, where?"

He circled the room again. They were tense, waiting for the music to stop and for him to steal their chairs, if not their souls. "Fashion: Is that a new suit? Health: What's he been eating? Has he gained weight? Business: How will this affect the market? Short term? Long term?"

He paused, and they waited for his next tirade, but none came. Had he extinguished the flame burning in his belly, or was he waiting to catch his breath and begin all over again. Still nothing. He was staring at them, and that made half of them reach for their stomach acid pills and the other half for their Valium.

"Well, what are you standing around for?" he shouted. "GO!"

They ran out of the conference room, back into the bullpen, where they grabbed their coats and took off before he had a chance to scream at them about something else.

He walked back into the bullpen and saw the last of them cramming into the elevators.

Fear good. Fear very good.

Lois Lane was sitting at her desk, hunched over her

computer screen. She turned to Gil, working in the cubicle next to hers. "Gil, how many F's are there in catastrophic?"

Before Gil could respond, Perry interrupted. "None. And what's the usage?"

Lois glanced at him, then back to the screen. "This mysterious electromagnetic pulse knocked out portable devices and entire power grids, causing a catastrophic event during the highly touted—"

Perry didn't let her finish. "Lois?"

"Yes?"

"In my office." Then he paused and looked up to the few reporters still lingering in the bullpen. "This goes for everybody. The story isn't the blackout. It's Superman."

Lois followed Perry, and once they were inside his office, he shut the door behind them.

In the back corner of the Planet's editorial floor, Clark looked up from his current obituary column. "Agnes Dreyfuss, born 1927, died—" he left that blank.

Through the glass walls, he noticed Lois standing in Perry's office, arguing with him. He concentrated, focusing his superhearing. He was suddenly listening in on every conversation taking place on the editorial floor. He worked to filter out the other voices.

"I'm telling you, you're dead wrong here." Lois was complaining. *So what else is new?* "The story is the EMP, Chief. Every electronic device on the East Coast goes dark—"

"Lois," Perry interrupted, "there are three things that sell papers in this world: tragedies, sex, and Superman. I'm tired of tragedies, and you can't write worth a damn about sex, so that leaves one thing." He pointed to the TV, once again showing Superman's rescue of the Boeing 777. It was the seventy-eighth time the network played it that morning. "Him."

"Fine. He's a story, I agree. 'Superman Returns,' *blah-blahblah*. Front page. Maybe a few more pages inside. We'll only be a day behind every TV station in the country, using the same photographs they used, only ours won't be moving. But Chief, he's not the only story. Maybe not even the most important one."

"Lois?" The voice was younger than Perry's but had the same intonation. She allowed herself a huge smile and turned to see her fiancé, Richard White, entering. "Richard? What are you doing here?"

He gave her a big hug and shot a glance at his uncle. "I'm interrupting something, aren't I?" Lois and Perry both turned to him. "Yeah," they said simultaneously.

"So that's her fiancé," Clark noted. Richard White was a tall, broad-shouldered man with a lean face topped with dark brown hair. He looked like he worked out two or three days a week and applied himself to the task. *Yeah, let's see you lift up giant jumbo jets, pal.* He had a ready smile to which Clark took an immediate dislike.

"'Scuse me," a voice said, interrupting him. Clark looked down to see a frail-looking five-year-old boy standing next to his desk.

"Hi," he said. The boy took a hit off the inhaler he had pulled out of his pants pocket. Clark looked toward Lois's desk again in the editorial wing. His X-ray vision picked out the picture of her with a young boy. *This is Jason. This is her son.*

"Who are you?" Jason asked.

Clark leaned in closer, smiling. The boy was working hard to control his breathing. "I'm Clark Kent. An old friend of your mom's. From before you were born."

"Really?" Jason said. "She's never mentioned you."

"Never?"

Jason shook his head as he heard his name being called. "Jason."

He turned to see his mother determinedly making her way through the jungle of desks. She wrapped her arms around him and hunkered low to look him directly in his eyes.

"I told you to stay in Daddy's office."

The boy made a face. "Daddy's office is boring." Clark stared at him. Maybe he was a little small and frail, but it was obvious there was a fire burning in that little body. He definitely had Lois's steadfast determination.

Lois finally noticed Clark, and with a wide smile she kissed him quickly on the cheek. For a moment he became light-headed. "Lois."

"Clark, welcome back." As he stood, she hugged him. "I see you've already met the munchkin."

Jason was looking bored as well as annoyed. "Yeah, we were just talking. He seems like a great kid, Lois." But Lois had already turned back to Jason.

"Did you take your vitamins? Eye drops? Preventil? Poly-Vi-Flor?" Jason nodded after each item on his mother's check list. Clark could tell they'd done this routine before.

"Yes, Mom," he said, still bored, with no sign of relief ahead.

Lois turned back to Clark, shaking her head in despair. "He's a little fragile, but he'll grow up to be big and strong like his dad, won't you?" Clark saw Jason reflexively nod again. He wasn't paying attention.

She noticed her watch and was suddenly concerned. "Richard?" She seemed impatient, but Clark couldn't tell why.

She had changed since he last saw her, five years ago, when Clark told Perry he was going to leave on a world trip to "Sort things out, you know. Everything's changing so fast these days." She was at her desk, working, oblivious to what was going on across the hall. And after he told her he was leaving, she smiled at him, half-hearing what he said, and muttered a noncommittal "Bye. See you later, Clark."

She was focused on her article detailing how Superman saved the city . . . *again* . . . this time from a meteor shower that without him, she wrote, would have completely destroyed Metropolis. He wasn't sure the city would have been "completely destroyed," but there would have been extensive damage.

Clark watched as she called Richard's name again, exhaled impatiently, and blew away a wisp of hair that had been resting on her cheek, harming nobody.

He was struck by how beautiful she still was. Blessed with perfect bone structure, she would never change, but it still made him stare at her, even after all this time. He thought about the Lois he used to know. That woman's focus used to be solely on her work. *I'm on a story. Get the hell out of my way.* As for kids, that was something other people had and best to avoid.

He was amused as he watched her dote over the tiny five-year-old. Who'd have ever suspected she had maternal instincts? *Miracles will happen.* She was straightening out Jason's shirt, rebuckling his belt, and rifling through his pockets to make sure he had all his pills, sprays, and other medical aids. Clark watched her hug and kiss him on his cheek. He was feeling strangely odd. He was thrilled that Lois had a son she loved so openly, but . . .

He wasn't sure what was wrong. Was he surprised that after leaving her for five years without a word of explanation that she had done the adult thing and moved on? Maybe he was jealous that Jason wasn't his? Was he annoyed the man she was with was actually a good man? Someone to admire? Someone who made her happy? *If he was a creep, I could . . .*

No. Don't think about it!

Still, his stomach knotted. He felt strangely . . . *queasy.* He was bothered by the way he felt and knew he had to get past it quickly.

Clark called to her. "Lois, I saw you on TV, in that, you know, the jet. Are you okay? I mean, wow. It must have been such an ordeal."

She reached past him and grabbed a stapler off his desk. "Oh, yeah. It was nothing. Hey, can I borrow your stapler?"

She had already taken it. "Sure. Oh, and congratulations on the Pulitzer. That's incredible. Really."

She cuffed Jason's pants—from their frayed edges he'd obviously been tripping over them a lot. "Yeah. Can you believe it. Richard!" she yelled again.

She stood up and admired her son, then leaned over and kissed him on the top of his head. "Practically perfect in every way." Jason giggled as she looked back at Clark. "He just loves watching *Mary Poppins*," she said, explaining. "I think he actually just loves those penguins. So, I wanna hear all about your trip. Where'd you go? What'd you see? Meet anyone special?"

"Well, there's just so much," Clark began. She saw a smudge on Jason's shirt and wet her handkerchief with her tongue to rub it out.

"*Umm*, so where to begin," Clark continued. "Well, I was in South America. I, *uhh*, think I sent you a postcard from that, *uhhh*, Peruvian llama rodeo? Does that strike a bell?"

"You screamed for me?" Richard White said as he entered. Clark was floundering for something to say and didn't mind the interruption.

"Hi, Daddy," Jason shrieked. White picked up Jason and gave him a squeeze.

"Are you getting into trouble again?" Lois was checking herself out in her compact mirror. "What's he done this time? Destroy the presses? Erase your story again?" He turned back to Jason. "Is that what you did, you little monster? Destroy all of Mommy's hard work?" The boy giggled and threw his arms around his father.

Lois was already going ninety in a fifty-mile-per-hour zone. "I've got to run out. Can you book his flu shot? I forgot with everything going on."

Richard nuzzled his son's cheek. "Already done. Next?"

"Great. And work some family magic to get your uncle to stop giving me a hard time about my article, please."

"Again?"

Lois was finally satisfied with how she looked. "Again. Gotta go," she said, kissing Richard. It lasted longer than Clark thought appropriate.

Clark shifted uncomfortably and cleared his throat. Lois saw him, did a double take, then remembered he had been standing there. "Oh, right. This is Clark. Richard, Clark. Clark, Richard."

Clark extended his hand. Richard set Jason down and took it quickly. "Clark Kent. Nice to meet you."

"Hi. Richard White."

Lois was checking out her handbag as she continued. "Richard's an assistant editor here who's basically saved our international section. He's also a pilot and likes horror movies." She closed her bag, continuing. "Clark is, well, Clark."

Richard was warm and friendly. "Great to finally meet you. I've heard so much."

Clark eyed Lois. "You have?"

"Yeah. Jimmy just won't shut up about you."

Lois kissed Richard again. "Gotta run," she said as she kissed Jason. "Love you, honey."

"Love you, too, Mom."

"Love you more." She mouthed his cheek until he started laughing. He had a good, happy laugh.

He's had a good life, Clark understood. But he didn't know what to think of that.

"Where are you going? Richard asked.

Lois made a face. "You heard Perry. Superman's back,

and he thinks I'm the only one equipped to . . ." She paused, suddenly deciding not to continue. "*Never mind.*"

"To what?"

"It's nothing." Clark could tell that Lois was trying not to answer. Obviously Superman was a sore point between them. He smiled, then immediately regretted it.

"I don't know what the problem is, hon," he said, still playing with Jason. "I mean, it is Superman."

Clark turned away. He didn't need to know how much he was hated by the man Lois obviously loved.

"He was a hero. He was the best there's ever been. And if you were close to him, well, that was then. It's okay. He's back and that's great, too, and if you can get the exclusive on him, that's even better. But if you're afraid in any way it would bother me, it won't. What can I say? He's Superman. Go for it, honey."

Clark turned to him, his eyes narrow. *He's a fan? He's a good man. He loves Lois. And he's a fan? Could it get any worse?*

"Maybe you could introduce me to him. I'd love that."
Why is my mother moving from Smallville?

"Richard, you don't get it," Lois said, fuming. "It's me. I don't want to be on the story. That part of my life's over, and I don't want to go back. I don't want to speak to him."
It's Lois.

Richard stood in front of her, gently cradling her face. "Honey, I love you. You know that. And if it's going to hurt you in any way to do this, then don't. You know whatever it is I'm on your side."

"But Perry's insisting . . ."

"So don't listen to him. He has the rest of us on that story. I don't think he'd even know you were elsewhere."

"I'm not planning to. I'm going to the power plant to look into the blackout. Seeya." She gave him another kiss, this time on the cheek, then took off quickly.

Richard shouted after her. "When will you be home?" But she was already out the door. He stared as it closed behind her and turned away only after he saw her get into the elevator.

"Wow, she hasn't slowed down for a second," Clark said. "Still the same old Lois. You can't keep her in one place for long."

Richard nodded. "Tell me. No matter how close we are, that woman will always be a mystery to me. But I love her anyway, and have since the day I first met her." He turned to Clark and lowered his voice so Jason wouldn't hear him. "But frankly, she's a little pissed. I was out flying when she was . . . in trouble. I think she was disappointed I didn't somehow swoop in and save her like Superman. Not that I could."

He picked up Jason and held him in the crook of his arm. "Well, I'm sure I'll be seeing you around the office. If you ever need me, I'm right over there."

He gestured toward the large office next to Perry's. "Nice office," Clark said.

Richard laughed. "Yeah. I'm not sure if I got it because I'm the assistant editor and deserve it, or because I'm the editor's nephew. But you know, the view's the same." He turned to leave but noticed Clark's computer. "What's that you're working on?"

Clark checked the screen. "Obituaries."

Richard read the piece. "Nice writing, but those people aren't dead yet."

Clark sat down at his desk and flipped through a thick

file folder filled with papers. "Yeah, but you know your uncle—*um*—Mr. White and that Eagle Scout banner he's got over his desk.

Richard laughed again.

"Always be prepared." He and Clark echoed the same words.

"Right." He glanced at his son in his arms. "C'mon, monster. Say good-bye to Clark."

"Bye, Clark."

"Bye, Jason," Clark answered with a smile.

He sat back down as Richard walked off, Jason in tow. He saw Richard bounce a bit, then heard Jason laugh again. *Good laugh. Honest laugh.*

He watched Richard leave, waving to one of the reporters who was asking him a question. Richard smiled as he answered something about Singapore and its legal system, and Clark was struck by something he hadn't noticed before.

Richard looked very much like *him*. Or actually, like him without the glasses and the timid attitude.

More like Superman.

Wow.

Seventeen

Lex Luthor was not a happy man. He had picked up a copy of the *Daily Planet* from behind the rosebushes near the front porch stoop where the paperboy had tossed it, and stared at the headline for the third time. "The Man of Steel Is Back." Under the headline, which he thought filled the entire page, they fit in a full color shot of that super*creep*— the photo captured from the cameras covering the game. He was holding up a damned jet by its nose. *By its nose!*

"This is impossible. Do you have any idea how many laws of physics this defies? *All* of them."

Luthor was girding for an extended rant. "It's doctored, that's what it is. Look at it. It's been expertly changed using that cheapjack computer photo-retouching software they're selling these days. Probably done by some ten-year-old brat with a drawing tablet and an hour of free time between playing video games."

Kitty peered over his shoulder and looked at the picture of Superman, standing in the jet's doorway, his smile radiating more wattage than Luthor's little crystal shard was capable of dimming. "Hell-oh," she said, admiringly. "It says here he saved everyone as the jet was falling to its doom, and after they landed he personally checked to see if the passengers were all right. What a man."

Luthor pulled the paper away from her. "Man? Man? He's not a man. He's an alien. Probably hides his bug eyes and tentacles under that cape. And furthermore, this has to be a lie. He can't be back. Not now. Not ever."

Gertrude's dog was barking at him. The damned dog was always barking at him. He took the paper and raised it to slap the mangy mutt. The dog yipped and took off before it could be hit. "And stay out," Lex shouted.

He took another look at the newspaper and angrily stuffed it in his back pocket. "Follow me. I've got plans."

They had started back into the mansion when they heard the minivan pull into the entranceway. It screeched to a stop in front of them. Inside, Grant, Riley, Stanford, and Brutus were sweating profusely; their faces were bruised black-and-blue.

Luthor ran his fingers across the side of the minivan. There were at least a dozen bullet holes dotting its side. He stuck his finger into one of them. "Run into trouble?"

Grant put on his macho look. "You should see the other guys."

Brutus opened the rear hold, revealing a long crate inside. He grabbed it and slid it out. "Hey, I can use some help here."

Luthor glared at Grant, who rushed to catch the back end of the crate before it tumbled out of the trunk, "Sorry, I was still breathin' hard. Gettin' shot at isn't as easy as it looks."

Brutus and Grant carried it around the back of the mansion, to the docks, where *The Gertrude* was moored. Luthor followed, still grumbling over the newspaper. "Careful with that. It's worth more than either of you."

They made their way onto *The Gertrude* and set the crate in the main cabin, where Luthor had prepared a place for it. Luthor followed, and Stanford rushed behind to catch up.

"So, what are we going to do?" Stanford asked, trying to catch his breath.

"You're going to modify it according to the plans and attach it to the stern. I don't care if the instructions are in Russian."

Stanford shook his head. "You know what I mean, Lex. He's not stupid. How long do you think it's going to take him to trace all that stuff back to me and you?"

He waited for a reaction from Luthor, but the boss was already poring through the books spread across his desk. *Crystals, the Definitive Guide* was sitting on top of a half dozen others about crystals, gems, and minerals. "He was supposed to die up there, Lex."

"I know what he was supposed to do. But do you? What have I told you about annoying me while I'm working? What am I doing?"

"Reading?"

"And these books, why am I reading them?"

"Work?"

"Connect the dots."

Luthor felt his leg being clawed and saw Gertrude's dog pawing him and sniffing the floor. Infuriated, Lex hurled the newspaper at the animal but missed. The dog sniffed it, then squatted and peed on the paper.

Luthor was about to throw a heavy book at the whimpering dog when his eyes went to a small headline on the urine-soaked paper. The dog finished its business, and Luthor picked up the paper and handed it to Stanford. "Stanford, you worry too much."

Stanford looked at the stained article. "World's Largest Collection of Meteorites on Exhibit at Metropolis Museum of Natural History."

"How fortuitous." Luthor walked past Stanford as he continued to read the article. He paused and turned back. "And find that dog a nice home."

Superman's photograph was everywhere. It was shown continuously on all the news stations as well as on the front page of every newspaper in the city. The *Daily Planet* published three extra editions, each one with a larger photo of Superman on the front page than in the previous edition. If the *Tribune* sized their cover photo at 60 picas, the next *Planet* edition had theirs at 110.

"The larger the photo, the better the sell-through," promised Perry. Although Clark was doubtful, it had worked. Sales of the *Planet* were up a whopping fifty-one percent.

Clark was crammed into the left corner of the Planet elevator as it made its way to the lobby floor. More than a dozen Superman head shots and headlines separated him from Lois, crushed on the other side of the car. Lois glared at the photographs and tried to turn away from them, but wherever she looked, he was there, smiling at her with his perfect teeth and those penetrating blue eyes that glittered like starlight. She shut her own eyes and waited for the elevator to ding. The door slid open, and she pushed her way out.

She was hurrying out of the building. "Uh, Lois," Clark called to her, trying to catch up.

Lois noticed him and smiled, but continued on her way. Clark had to rush to keep up.

"Hey, Clark. I haven't seen much of you. Been really busy, as usual. So, how's your first week back at work?"

"It's okay. Kind of like riding a bike, I guess."

"A bike?" Lois didn't understand, but then she rarely understood anything he said.

"Yeah, you know, you never forget how. Like an elephant." He realized she wasn't following him. "Never mind."

They made their way outside into a street crowded with people rushing home after work. "Superman Returns" was on the glowing light banner that circled the Planet building. "Man of Steel Saves Shuttle."

"Everyone knows that already," Lois complained. "God, you can't walk anywhere without someone sticking some photo of him in your face and gushing that he's back, he's back. Well, where the hell was he? That's what I want to know. And why the hell didn't he stay wherever the hell he was? Now that's a question that needs answering. And if I cared enough, I'd suggest it to Perry for an in-depth article. But I'm too busy. It's yours, Clark, if you want it."

Clark struggled to keep up with her. "Gosh, thanks, Lois. But I was thinking since I've gotten back we haven't really had a chance to catch up. Would you want to—?"

Lois interrupted before he could finish. "Hey, can I ask you something?"

"Sure."

She looked at him for a long time. "Have you ever been in love?"

Clark started to answer, but then Lois interrupted again.

Maybe, he was beginning to think, she didn't really want to hear his answer.

"Or at least, have you ever met someone and it's almost like you were from totally different worlds, but you share such a strong connection that you knew you were destined to be with each other? But then he takes off without explaining why, or without even saying goodbye?"

He was staring at her, and she laughed. "Sounds cheesy, I know."

"Taxi!" she shouted as she stepped into the street and raised a hand to catch a cab. A half dozen sped past. Two had actual passengers in them.

Clark's voice was soft, as if he was having trouble talking. "Well, maybe saying good-bye was so hard because he didn't know whether it would be good-bye for a little while or good-bye forever."

Lois was looking down the street, getting more and more annoyed as taxis flashed past.

"And maybe he had to go and he wanted to say good-bye, but he couldn't find the guts to do it, because if he saw you, even one last time, well, maybe he was afraid that if he even looked at you just once, he would never be able to leave."

He paused, took in another gulp of air, then finally said, "Maybe it was too difficult for him."

She whirled to face him. By the look on her face it was obvious that he had accidentally hit a very raw nerve. "Difficult? Difficult? What's so difficult about it? Good-bye! See? It's easy. What's so hard about saying good-bye?"

Her intensity was overwhelming him. Clark backed up a few steps, then found his voice again. "Who are we talking about?"

Lois stepped into the street and began whistling and waving for the cab. "Nobody. Forget I said anything," she said. Then she screamed, "Taxi!"

Clark looked around awkwardly, and his voice rose a full octave. He continued to stammer and stutter. "So, do you want to grab a quick bite? My treat."

Lois turned to him and let her anger fade. He was a friend. Sort of. Why was she going Attila the Hun on him? He's not the problem. Clark Kent is never the problem.

"Oh, I'd love to, but Daddy took the car, and it's my turn to cook the family dinner, which means I've got just enough time to get back to the suburbs and order Chinese food."

"Suburbs?"

She was smiling and never looked more beautiful. "Yeah, we have a really nice place on the river. You should drop in sometime."

Clark felt his heart racing. "I'd love to." Another cab rushed past, ignoring them. Clark stuck his two fingers in his mouth and whistled. The shrill sound was loud and piercing, and even as a small dog a block away whimpered weakly in response, a cab suddenly screeched to a halt and backed up to them.

"Uhh, sorry 'bout that. You call a cab?"

"Wow, thanks," Lois said, impressed, as she climbed into the backseat. "Three-twelve Riverside Drive." She turned back to Clark and opened the cab window. "G'night, Clark."

He stood to the side of the street as a dozen cars blared their horns for him to move. But he was watching her cab make its way down the block and turn the corner.

"Good-bye, Lois."

Eighteen

Long before they saw him coming they heard the familiar whoosh of wind. Old-timers knew he was heading toward them, soaring through Metropolis at superspeed. *Able to leap tall buildings at a single bound,* as they used to say. When they saw him, however, he wasn't flying over the skyscrapers; he was no more than twenty-five feet off the ground, corkscrewing his way through the city streets and alleys, in and around the buildings. They could tell he seemed . . . *distracted.*

They called his name but he didn't appear to hear them. Perhaps, they thought, he was on his way to some emergency and had no time to acknowledge their presence. They waved and jumped while shouting at him, trying to catch his eye, but he continued meandering through the city, heading east down Broadway, then hopping over the Metropolis River, flying parallel to the City Bridge, then west to the suburbs.

He studied the rows of luxury housing built along the

shore, back in the sixties when the suburbs were just beginning to boom. This was before shopping malls equalized opportunities and before transportation made it just as fast to get to the city center from the heights of Wedgemore as it was from the upper west side.

Single men and women lived in the city's high-rises, taking in its nightly events, clubbing their way downtown or just luxuriating in a city that never seemed to sleep. But married couples, overflowing their tiny apartments with burgeoning families and two oversized cars, moved farther away, searching for a less harried lifestyle and affordable two- or three-bedroom homes with fenced-in lawns where their kids could play safe and protected.

Superman hovered over the homes. He looked up and down the streets until he saw a seaplane floating next to a small dock that led to a large yard and a fancy all-wood swing set. The lights inside the two-story house were on and he could see its owners rushing about inside, preparing for dinner.

This was it. He quietly lowered himself behind the trees, hovering just outside the dining-room window, unseen.

He could hear "Heart and Soul" being played over and over again inside. He focused his eyes, and the outside wall seemed to disappear. He could see a child's bedroom on the second floor. The parents' bedroom was across the way. Both were messy.

The boy's room had a small bed tucked to the side of a long wall. In front of it was an old toy chest, filled beyond capacity, its top unable to lie flat against it. A desk, just about large enough for a kid, was pressed against the wall under the open window. He saw toy airplanes hanging on fishing line from the ceiling, and toy trucks sitting atop a small dresser drawer. *Typical boy's room,* he thought. *One that shows there's a lot of love here.*

Superman wanted to leave—he knew he shouldn't have come in the first place—but for reasons that escaped him he continued to linger. He turned to the kitchen. It was a large room with a center island. He saw Lois emptying boxes of Chinese takeout onto serving plates while Richard was fumbling with chopsticks, fitting them between his fingers as the instructions on their paper holder told him to, trying to make them work together in synch.

Jason was playing "Heart and Soul" on a small electronic keyboard. Every time he struck an incorrect note, he stubbornly started again from the beginning.

"You can keep playing, son. You don't have to start over," Richard said.

"But I want to, Dad. I want to do it right."

He was just like Lois.

She brought in the first platter. "Kung pao shrimp," she announced.

Jason hurried to the table, excited. "Mine."

Lois laughed as she shook her head. "Nice try, kiddo. No peanuts, no seafood, and definitely no wontons." She opened a separate box for him. "Just rice and snow peas for you."

Jason sneered, then went back to his keyboard and started "Heart and Soul" from the beginning again.

Richard looked at the kung pao. "Why do we get Chinese food if he's allergic?"

"Because he loves the peas," Lois said, ladling out the chicken. "And I think we all prefer egg rolls over macrobiotic shakes."

Jason was nodding. "Macrobiot-ICK!"

"Good point," agreed Richard.

Richard watched as Lois scooped out food for everyone but, as always, she gave herself a smaller portion. He then noticed the lines creasing her forehead and the downward turn to her mouth. He wanted to say something that was on his mind, but wasn't sure how. Or even if he should.

She wasn't talking as she ate, and Lois always talked, whether or not there was anything to talk about. He swallowed hard and headed for the deep water:

"I've noticed you've been acting a little different lately."

Lois didn't look up. "Have I?"

He hesitated, but then continued. "And I promised myself I'd never ask you about this, but now that he's back . . ." He paused then continued. "Your article . . ."

"'Why the World Doesn't Need Superman'? What about it?"

Richard shook his head. "No, no. The other one. From years ago. Before we met."

Lois was baffled. "Which article? I wrote dozens about him. I was practically his press agent."

He didn't want to go there, but he continued anyway. "That first one. 'I Spent the Night with Superman.'" From the look on her face he knew it was a mistake to ask, but there was no way to retract it now.

She gave him a look, then laughed. "Richard, come on. That was just a title for an interview. Plus, it was your uncle Perry's idea. Nothing happened then. I swear."

He felt a cold sweat forming around his ears. "I was just . . ."

She turned his face so he would have to look at her. He

was so sweet and so loving. She hadn't been thinking about it before, but of course he'd be worried about *him.*

"Richard"—her voice was quiet and loving—"that was a long time ago." She tried to be reassuring, but she was afraid the trepidation in her voice would tell him it was not long enough.

He laughed. "No, no, no. I mean. You. Him. God, any woman would want him. Plenty of guys, too. And yeah, I know it was a long time ago. Trust me. I'm fine with that.

"But I just wanted to know . . ." He kept his eyes low, still trying to avoid hers. *Don't go there. Don't ask.* "Were you in love with him?"

She answered him quickly. It wouldn't do to linger on this. "He's Superman. Everyone was in love with him."

"But were you?" he was now looking into her eyes. There was a pause, brief, but it held there longer than she would have wanted.

"No," she said, firmly.

Superman quietly rose into the sky. The moon was full, and he cursed its light.

Lois looked at Richard, who was staring at her curiously, then she glanced down again to her plate. *Just eat. Don't say anything. Just eat.* She picked up her chopsticks and used them expertly to lift some of the kung pao. She felt a breeze, but when she checked, she saw the windows were closed.

"Lois, are you okay?" Richard asked.

She shook her head and snapped out of her unexplained reverie. She laughed without reason and swallowed her food. *It was good. Really good.* She looked at one of the paper cartons, opening it to see its contents. "Yeah. Sorry. I'm fine. Hey, didn't I have four wontons?"

Jason was stuffing a wonton into his mouth, trying to eat it before they noticed. "Jason!" she screamed, as both she and Richard dived at him, snatching it from his mouth before it was too late.

Superman floated in the silence of the stratosphere, staring at the blackness above him, and the lights of Metropolis shining below. The Daily Planet building was more than twenty miles away, but even without his telescopic vision he could clearly see its famous revolving globe, and its LCD rings brightly displaying the latest news.

He rose higher and looked beyond the Planet building, to the whole of Metropolis, so vast and sprawling it seemed to burst out of every map ever drawn. He felt very small in comparison.

"Was I wrong to come back?" he said, knowing there was nobody to hear him. "I thought this was right. I thought Metropolis was my home. Have I done something so horribly wrong that I can't have a home anymore? *What. Is. Wrong. With. Me?*"

The clouds moved in quickly, surrounding him. They rumbled—was a storm coming in, he wondered, or was this somehow the answer to his question. They seemed to speak to him in a voice he had heard so many times before.

It was as if he were in that crystal ship again, an infant

alone, adrift in an endless nothingness, only the voice, *that voice,* to keep him company.

He was back in the Fortress of Solitude after that long journey north from Smallville to the Arctic. Seventeen years old, afraid and yet determined, living for so long in that cold, sterile world he grew to love. That voice, that soft-spoken voice, brought him back to before he had questions, to before he had doubts, to before he lost his place, his way.

"Father?" he said.

Jor-El's voice surrounded him, comforted him. "Even though you were raised as a human being, you are not one of them."

The voice reverberated in the folds of the clouds. For a moment he thought he could see his father's face talking to him from someplace else. His eyes were filled with warmth and compassion and love for the child he had to send away, like Moses, in a small basket drifting across a long, seemingly endless sea to another place, another world. Another life.

"Why am I here, Father?" he asked.

"You have a destiny, my little Kal-El, and on Earth you shall see it fulfilled."

He knew Jor-El's wise words were uttered long ago, on a planet that no longer existed. The answer was general, picked by the crystal computer as a match for Superman's question, but not even Jor-El could speak to him directly from the grave.

Superman thought about the Valley of the Elders, dead, but still standing a galaxy away, still proud and defiant against the death that had claimed everything else around it. He thought that Jor-El was like those great crystal monoliths; gone but still alive, if only in his heart.

But that was good enough for now.

"They can be a great people, Kal-El. They wish to be."

"I've seen that greatness, Father. I've walked with them, and I know they yearn for the truth. I've seen it in their eyes. They hope. They wish. They try so hard.

"I'm not sure they need me anymore. Honestly, I'm not sure they ever did. I worry my presence made them depend too much on me, but I can't turn my back on them. I can't let them suffer when I can alleviate so much pain. I don't know what to do, Father. And I don't know where to turn."

Jor-El's words echoed in his head. "They only lack the light to show them the way. For this reason, above all, their capacity for good, I have sent them you, my only son."

Alone in the darkness of space, he hovered, still and silent, his eyes closed, thinking, meditating. He heard the city's sounds, soft at first, innocuous and innocent, but then growing into an angry violent cacophony.

He heard layers of noises: At first there were the car horns and the rattling of railroads and subways. Beneath them he could hear the electronic distractions of radios and televisions. Beneath them there was endless chattering, voices laughing or complaining, arguing or screaming.

He could hear distant thunderstorms.

There were so many noises. He focused to filter out the more chaotic sounds.

He heard an earthquake rattle its way toward a lonely Pacific island while a sudden volcanic eruption sent fire streaming toward a crowded Asian city. He heard gunfire and sirens.

He heard the noises of Metropolis coming from far below him. He heard its cries for help.

He opened his eyes again.

He was home again, and Metropolis needed him.

At least he was certain someone did.

PART TWO

TRIALS

Nineteen

"I'm bored," Kitty said again, yawning. They were watching Siegfried pledge eternal love to Brünhilde by giving her Fafner's ring. She placed it on her finger as he held up her shield and mounted her horse, then rode off into the woods.

"I can only file my nails for so long, you know. Besides, what's this 'Rope of Destiny' thing all about, anyway? And who cares if it broke or whatever it did?"

"Who cares? Who cares?" Luthor snarled but never took his eyes off the performance. "This is the pinnacle of opera, Kitty. Wagner's *Götterdämmerung*, the final act of *The Ring of the Nibelung*. All the big boys are here, the twilight of the gods, end-of-the-world stuff. And this is the first time since the seventies that the full *Ring cycle* has played in Metropolis."

"So?"

"So? Is that all you can say? 'So?' So this is like research. It has everything to do with everything we're doing. That idiot Siegfried is our so-called hero, and later, at the end, he dies. You heard it right. The hero dies. Can it get any better than that? He loves Brünhilde. You just saw him give a ring to her to prove that love. Only he gets drugged and turned into a tool of Gunther, lord of the Gibichungs . . ."

"'Gibichungs'? You're making that up."

"My talents are many, but sadly they do not include composing opera . . . I fear I have to remain only an ardent admirer. It's my single fault, you might say."

"I might. But I won't."

He snorted. "Moving along, Gunther and his half brother Hagen force Siegfried to help get Brünhilde—the woman he loves, remember—to marry Gunther instead of him, and then, at the end of the story, Siegfried is betrayed and killed. Have I told you how much I love watching heroes die? Especially when it's accompanied by the end of the gods and the world, in that order."

"You're sick, you know that?"

"Absolutely, and it's one of my most endearing traits."

She shook her head. "So what does this have to do with us?"

He rolled his eyes. "The woman needs the *Reader's Digest* version of one of the greatest operas ever written. All right, let me spell it out for you. The hero is in love with this woman."

"You already said that. I'm not dumb, no matter what you may think."

"I have never thought you were dumb, my dear. Manipulative, beautiful, crafty, sexy, untrustworthy, even criminal, all traits, by the way, that I admire and look for in a woman. And as I use you for all your obvious charms, don't believe for a moment I'm not aware that you think you're using me. Which, by the way, you can do three or four times a day at least, dear Kitty . . ."

"Katherine. Kitty sounds . . . so cheap."

"You are many things, but based on how much I have to spend keeping you in stolen jewels and pilfered perfume, cheap is not among them . . . *Katherine*. And you're also not dumb. But you are naïve."

"So?" she said, growing impatient. "What are you trying to say, huh?"

"All right. What we are watching has everything to do with our current situation, events that are already in motion, and plans that will soon rain greatness down on us."

Kitty seemed unimpressed. "You're not convincing me."

Luthor snarled, but continued anyway. "I promised you castles in the sky? You'll get that and more. You want big? You want earthshaking spectacular? Gods are going to die here, Katherine. Worlds, too, nothing's ever going to be the same, as they say, and if everything works out according to plan, cross your heart and hope to die, which you will, by the way, if anything gets screwed up, we'll be living in our new hundred-room Palace of the Gods in less than"—he checked his watch—"twenty-four hours, give or take."

Kitty had seen him sitting across and several seats down the row from her, nearly once a week for more than a year, whenever she visited Andrew in that glass-partitioned prison greeting room. She knew who the bald man was— everyone knew Lex Luthor—and she'd see him arguing with his lawyer or with one girlfriend or another, or he would be huddled in the corner writing letters to Gertrude Vanderworth, poisoning her against her own family, although she didn't know that then.

Even in prison he was powerful. The guards brought him supplies, beyond those allotted by the state. Who else was allowed to rip and burn then market illegal DVDs from his jail cell? Only Lex Luthor. He was even allowed to use the warden's private pool without anyone else present to cause him trouble.

One Tuesday, after going home, she Googled Lex Luthor, revealing more than 746,000 pages of information, most detailing his numerous crimes. A few were fan sites, which even included some fan fiction, usually romantic escapades between Luthor and the writer as together they took over countries and robbed banks.

As she read through the more factual pages, it seemed as if nothing was beneath him. He was guilty of robbery and murder, industrial espionage and several attempts at terrorism, but tucked in between trying to blow up the San Andreas Fault and assassinating the president, he also owed an emperor's fortune in traffic tickets and late library books. It was obvious to Kitty that he'd steal the money out of the church hat, if he ever went to church.

So why exactly was she drawn to him? He certainly wasn't a nice man. Not like Superman. He could be cruel, callous, and unthinking. Especially when he liked you. And his looks were certainly nothing to write home about, either. Again, not like Superman. But there was still something about that bald head and those smoldering eyes. Week by week, sitting across the aisle from him, watching him through the glass, she found he was becoming more and more interesting by the visit.

"Girls like the bad boys," her mom had once told her as a way of explaining her own seventh marriage, this one to a rich corporate raider who, less than two months later, was sent to San Quentin, the result of an embezzlement scheme that didn't quite work out right. If Mom was right, and the badder they were the more you fell for them, then she knew she was hopelessly in love.

Of course, besides the bald head and those eyes, he was rich, which was important. Long before she was done with him she knew she'd find a way to wheedle away some of that fortune. Her mother had long ago taught her the art of the "long con."

But it was more than money that had kept her with him. Six months after he first saw her looking at him, he had a guard pass her a note, suggesting a more private get-together, perhaps in a half hour, in the warden's office, on the large pool table.

She knew why she accepted.

If his confidence was electric, the power she saw burning in those incredible eyes was nuclear. When you were drawn into his circle you believed he could make anything happen.

So on Tuesday afternoons and every other weekend, she'd sit across the glass, talking sweet nothings with Andrew for almost twenty minutes, planning their future together for when he was finally released, then she would spend the next two hours with Luthor.

He revealed to her his dreams, and as sick as they may have sounded at first, they fit him. Where most people saw smiley faces in the moon, he saw worlds ripe for conquest. It was sort of thrilling.

"One day Metropolis will look up to me, Kitty," he'd say, his arms around her naked body as they luxuriated in the warden's hot tub. "I'll be sitting in my estate, high above the city, looking down on the hoi polloi, knowing all the time that they had to look up at me. There wouldn't be a moment they weren't aware that I was a force to be reckoned with."

She realized that while Andrew's dreams were of working for Blockbuster and renting a two-bedroom apartment somewhere in Suicide Slum, her dreams were of white picket fences and satellite dishes and never hallways filled with rat droppings.

Luthor's hallways would all be spotless, and the picket fences were coming, she was sure of that. As for the satellite dish, she already had more TV stations than she knew what to do with.

His booming voice pushed through her thoughts. ". . . and as the waters overflow its bank, the Rhinemaidens, carrying the ring, swim off in triumph. The curtain falls as the flames engulf Valhalla, hiding it from sight forever. The end. So, you get it now?"

"Sure. Siegfried dies along with a bunch of gods. And there's fat women on big horses. So what? Big deal. I'm still bored."

She smiled at him sweetly, thinking maybe rat droppings and Suicide Slum weren't looking all that bad after all.

Twenty

Not everyone paid attention to the news. Scott W. Mitchell for one, and for two to four, his best friends since junior high school: Steve Sava, Dave Bingham, and Len Cuden. They had spent the last two days in their fourth floor walk-up, a rotting husk of a building the town council would have condemned years ago had they bothered to go to *that* section of town.

They ordered in pizza every day for lunch from Original Pete's down the block, and never tipped the scrawny kid who had to walk up those four flights to collect his fifteen bucks for Pete's two-for-one special. Today, the kid paused on the third floor, spat on the pizza, resealed the box, then handed it to Sava, whose turn it was to pay. The kid collected his money, then made his way to his next delivery, but this time he was smiling.

The bank robbery was scheduled for later that afternoon, and Scott and the others were going over the plans one more time. They were ex-cons and had failed at their halfhearted attempt to go straight in the real world. They preferred the security prison offered them, so for the past three months they had been trying to come up with the best way of landing behind minimum security bars again, but they could not agree upon a solution.

Then, one day, they received detailed robbery plans in the mail as well as the parts for a weapon that, the letter insisted, would assure their success. The only proviso was that the robbery had to be done in a very specific town in Ohio, on a certain day and time. They would follow the preplanned escape route, and assuming they didn't botch it up, there would even be a rented copter waiting for them to make their escape. The donor neither asked for a cut of the proceeds nor told them who he was. The letter was simply signed, "A friend."

To Scott and the others, moving to Aruba with a couple hundred thou each sounded a hell of a lot better than another six-to-ten-year stretch at Mansfield Correctional. They took a vote, and four to zero they decided to give it a try.

They followed the plans to the letter, and the robbery went off without a hitch. Mitchell, Sava, and Bingham ran across the street, ducked into the alley, climbed over the fence—they had earlier placed a ladder there to make the climb even easier—sneaked into the basement of the Groiler Building on Sixth and Main, and took the elevator up to the roof, where Cuden was waiting for them with the copter.

They tossed the bags of money inside it while Cuden finished assembling the weapon, a large tripod-mounted Gatling gun. He swung it around toward the edge of the roof and aimed it at the street. Specifically at six police cars that had suddenly positioned themselves in front of the bank after the teller tripped the silent alarm.

They had been warned this would happen. Cuden glanced at his watch. He was supposed to start firing in exactly one minute. He didn't know why they just didn't take off in the copter and make their escape, but the plan had worked perfectly so far, so he decided not to ask questions. He checked his watch again and began the countdown.

The cops hunkered behind their cars and aimed their own weapons up toward the roof. Chris Dille, the department negotiator, arrived and would soon begin the long procedure to end this latest problem peacefully, he hoped. Before he could dig the wireless mike out of his case, however, a hail of gunfire began raining down from the roof. Glowing tracer bullets sprayed the police cars, tearing them apart in a matter of moments.

Cuden laughed. This weapon was the stuff that dreams were made of, at least the dreams of a psychopath who had always been too cowardly to go *all the way* until now. He kept firing even after the cop cars were reduced to slag. Then he whirled and began blasting apart a bus that had accidentally turned the corner and wandered into the crime scene. Just for grins.

"Lenny, c'mon, man. Let's get the hell outta here." Mitchell and the others wanted to leave. Why press their luck?

Cuden wasn't hearing any of it. "No way, not yet. The letter said we hadda keep firing for two minutes. I got thirty seconds left." He was laughing, spraying more tracer bullets across Fifth Avenue. "'Sides, I'm having way too much fun, man."

Two of the bank's security guards, Ed Miller and Larry Skir, had followed the four thieves from the bank to the Groiler Building and quietly made their way up the back stairwell to the roof. Both were wheezing by the time they reached the eighth floor.

They heard the gunfire through the roof door. "Remind me again, why are we doing this? The cops got it covered."

Skir shook his head. "And that's why. They're distracting them, so we're gonna march in and get the credit. After last month you wanna get another black mark?" Miller shook his head. "It's settled. You ready?"

"Yeah," Miller agreed, reluctantly.

They both raised their weapons and burst through the door, firing. They knew they hit Cuden, but he didn't fall. Their bullets weren't penetrating his flak vest.

Cuden spun around and fired, the tracer dot was targeted to Miller's forehead. He squeezed the trigger and then fired again, this time at Skir. The two guards had no time to look at each other and say their good-byes. They barely had time to realize they were about to die.

Time. Was. Slowing. Down.

Suddenly, a blurry streak of red and yellow moved past the bullets as if they were standing still. The streak stopped and came into focus. It was a yellow shield with a large red "S" emblazoned on it.

Superman's shield.

It should have happened too fast for them to see what happened, but Miller and Skir swore they saw it all. Superman, standing between them and the bullets, had just suddenly appeared, his hands casually resting on his hips, his lips curled into a bemused smile.

The bullets bounced off his chest. *Bounced!* He wasn't wearing bulletproof armor. They just bounced. The impact didn't push him back. He stood there, still smiling.

The thieves scattered, ducking to avoid the ricocheting bullets. Cuden, hiding behind an air conditioner vent, tried to fire again, but his weapon was out of ammo. He grabbed his pistol and fired, this time at Superman's head.

Superman didn't move. The bullets bounced off just as they had his chest.

At the same time, the police streamed onto the roof, weapons ready. Captain Paul Nee's jaw dropped as he saw the bank guards smiling at him. "What took you guys so long?" Skir asked.

Nee wasn't listening. He was still staring at the getaway helicopter. Its propeller was spinning lazily like a baby's mobile toy, each of the four would-be robbers tied to a different blade.

The green PT Cruiser tore down Broadway, weaving from side to side, teetering out of control. It swiped a garbage can on the corner of Nineteenth and scattered its contents across the street. Two cabs veered into each other to avoid being hit by its treasure of newspapers, candy wrappers, and half-eaten pizza slices. Pedestrians dived for cover.

The Cruiser's driver was screaming as loud as she could as she slammed the brakes and spun the wheel. The car refused to respond. "Somebody stop this thing!" she shouted. She was afraid she was going to die.

She spun the wheel again and managed to avoid hitting

a businessman, but it brought the Cruiser onto the sidewalk. Ahead of her was a crowded city square. She shrieked again.

The car slammed into an empty bench. The startled pigeons roosting on it flapped their way to safety. She continued screaming as she saw the people ahead of her trying to run away. She pumped the brakes again, but they were still refusing to cooperate. She closed her eyes and began praying.

She felt a bump and let out a low scream. *Oh, God, did I just kill someone?*

But it didn't feel like she had hit something. It felt . . . she wasn't quite sure what it was like. She no longer felt her tires treading the street, and at the same time she sensed she was slowing down but still moving, too.

She opened her eyes and no longer saw the city square in front of her. There was the park fountain, but it was below her. She was rising into the air. Then she stopped. She looked down and saw the park just beneath her. *Am I floating? Did I die and am I now rising to Heaven?*

The Cruiser was hoisted on Superman's shoulders, held just above his head. She felt the car shake just a bit as he slowly and gently lowered it back to the ground.

She saw him standing by the driver's door, his eyes even bluer than the photographs on every newspaper and TV news show had hinted. He was muscular, but not bulky in that way she never liked. More like a swimmer's body, she observed. He opened the door and reached a hand inside for her to take. "Are you all right, miss?"

She wobbled her way out of the car and noticed in the driver's rearview mirror that her makeup had smeared and that her hair was frazzled, victim of her Cuisinart ride. She grabbed her chest and gasped.

"My heart," Kitty Kowalski shouted. "I think I'm dying."

Just as she had been instructed by Lex Luthor, she fell back, knowing he would be there to catch her. She was wearing a tight, low-cut dress that accentuated every curve and left little to the imagination. She was shaking, but when she saw the crowd forming around her she suddenly pulled herself together.

A teenage boy took out his cell phone and snapped her photo. She smiled for the camera, then fell back into Superman's arms, shimmying her body again as if convulsing.

Superman was puzzled. "I'm sorry?"

She was still clutching her chest when she looked up at him. "I'm pretty sure they're heart palpitations. Here. Give me your hand," she said weakly, coughing out her words for dramatic effect. She pouted as he pulled it away, nervously. "I have heart palpitations . . . and a murmur." She coughed again. "And my back. I think I ruptured a . . . a cylinder."

Superman scanned her with his X-ray vision, then shook his head. "I don't see anything wrong."

She reached up and grabbed him, her hand lingered over his chest. *Wow!* "Please," she said, gasping for breath. "Take me to a hospital." She passed out, falling limp in Superman's arms.

He saw the crowd staring at them, waiting to see what he would do next. He shifted her to one arm and rose into the sky. "Will someone please call and have her car towed?

Thanks." Two dozen people simultaneously dialed their cell phones.

The red bus pulled to a stop in front of the Metropolis Museum of Natural History. Five passengers disembarked and made their way up the marble stairs to the museum entrance. Directly in front of them was a plastic donation box filled with cash. Attached to the front of it was a small sign, SUGGESTED DONATION: TEN DOLLARS. A hand reached into a pocket, then dropped in a nickel.

The museum guard looked at the men. "I'm sorry, sir, but we're closing in ten minutes."

"We only need five," Lex Luthor answered, checking his watch as he pushed past the guard. Stanford, a camera case dangling from around his neck, Brutus, Grant, and Riley followed him inside. "Hurry. You know what to do?"

Brutus and Grant nodded. "We went over it ten times today."

"And that's supposed to give me a feeling of confidence? Tell me again what the plan is."

Grant recounted what he and Brutus were supposed to do as they walked past the exhibits filling the Grand Hall, barely paying attention to the giant *Tyrannosaurus rex* whose massive head lowered stiffly and growled at them as they passed under it. Its head returned to its upright position and waited for the next tourist to trigger its sensors.

Brutus and Grant paused in front of a closed door marked AUTHORIZED PERSONNEL ONLY. "This is it."

"All right," Luthor said, "But if you screw this up, word of advice, don't meet up with us later." Brutus and Grant made their way down the flight of stairs to the basement hallway and continued down a narrow corridor until they found the breaker panel screwed to a far wall. Inside it were dozens of switches.

While Grant studied the hand-drawn chart the boss had given him in order to identify the different switches, Luthor and Stanford made their way to the Crystals and Gemstones exhibit. Riley lingered for a moment, lovingly staring at a large diamond sitting on a circular black felt pad. He could retire for life on what that stone could be fenced for. He looked up and noticed Lex was already on the other side of the large hall. Making sure the camcorder was focused on Luthor, he hurried to catch up.

They entered the space exhibit, a spectacular show of hundreds of different meteorites ranging in size, shape and color, with the largest of them illuminated by spotlight in the center of the room. Luthor admired it but turned his attention to a back wall filled with smaller, less impressive rocks.

He turned to Stanford. "They're going to screw it up. I know they're going to screw it up."

"I don't think so, Mr. Luthor," Stanford said. "You put the fear of God in them."

"It's me they should be fearing, not that celestial busybody. God's got nothing on me."

He waited as the last of the tourists left, hurrying to the gift shop before the museum closed to buy some cheap souvenir they'd toss into a closet and never look at again, then checked his watch again. "The goggles."

Stanford opened the camera case and removed a pair of hi-tech goggles with dials that tuned its sensitivity for minute fluctuations of radiation, heat, and light. "Right here, sir. Just making some last-minute adjustments."

In the downstairs maintenance room, Brutus checked his watch again. "Almost time." Grant nodded as he found the main switch in the breaker panel.

"Ready when you are."

In the meteorite exhibit, Stanford turned on the goggles, then tuned one of the dials. Satisfied, he handed them to Luthor. "They're ready, Lex."

Luthor snorted as he put them on. "They had better be."

He scanned the wall of small meteorites, but nothing showed up in the goggles. *Not a problem.* He checked his watch again and began to count down to himself.

Riley, checking his watch, nodded to Grant, who flipped the breaker switch. The lights throughout the museum suddenly went out.

The meteorite room was in near darkness. Looking through the goggles, he saw that the meteorites appeared in deep shades of blue. Luthor adjusted a dial on its side, setting them for a specific level of radiation.

He looked again at the back wall. A single meteorite was glowing green. Luthor grinned.

There was the sound of shattering glass, followed a moment later by a piercing alarm.

A moment later the lights returned; relays had switched the power to the emergency generators. If the guards who streamed into the room hadn't been so rattled, they would have realized that the two people who had been in the room on their last check were now gone, and that behind a shattered glass window against the far wall, one of the meteorites was now missing. The placard where it once sat had fallen over as Luthor reached in to snatch the rock. It had read, ADIS ABABA, 1978.

• • •

Kitty Kowalski was still unconscious, or at least as unconscious as she needed to be while Superman flew her across the city to Metropolis General. Superman saw the EMTs near an ambulance staring at him as he made a slow descent. As they landed, Kitty peeked a look at her wristwatch. It was time.

"All right, miss, we're here," Superman said. Kitty suddenly shimmied in his arms and bolted upright. She looked amazed as she checked herself out, patting herself down as if to make certain she was still in one piece. "It's a miracle," she exclaimed happily. "My back, my heart palpitations—healed." She was still holding on to him and pressed herself in closer. "You're a miracle worker. What did you do?"

Superman tried to step back but she held on. "Nothing. I just—"

She pressed in closer, squeezing him as tightly as she could. Her lips moved inches from his ears. "Call me Katherine."

He was trying to remove himself from her viselike grip, but she wasn't letting go. "Katherine. I really should be going."

She let her arms slide down his back and copped a quick feel. A shiver raced up her spine. She smiled sweetly as she eased back. "Of course. Places to go. People to save." She stared into his eyes, those incredible eyes, and she knew she had to grab the chance when she could. "I know this is tacky, but do you want to maybe grab coffee sometime?"

The look in his eyes gave her his answer. She smiled

again, then backed away some more, giving him space to breathe. "I'm sorry. Forget I ever said that. Thanks for your help. Bye." She gave him a quick kiss on the cheek, then scampered off.

Superman watched as she left, puzzled, embarrassed, and flattered. He saw the ambulance drivers staring at him, then he launched himself into the air, and headed up into the distance.

Josef Muller's wife had had a premonition that morning. "Something bad is going to happen," she warned her husband, as he showered and got ready for work. He kissed her on the forehead as she prepared his oatmeal, set out the bowl of brown sugar, and got his coffee ready. Eva loved him, and he had no doubts about that, but she had premonitions at least three times a week, either about danger, floods, disease, or famine, and to date none of them had ever panned out. When he'd ask her about them later, "I misread the charts," is all she'd say as a way of explaining. "But I won't do that again. I promise."

He took the brown bag she prepared that contained a sausage sandwich, apple with dried tomato, his favorite, and a banana, and waited for Hans to beep his horn and drive him to work near the center of Munich. Once there, they climbed onto the scaffold and were taken to the top floor of the fifty-six-story Shulz Building where they cleaned the south- and west-facing windows before the end of the day.

Josef and Hans talked about the soccer game that was on the television the previous night. Lukas Adalgiso had definitely been robbed. Odell Verner was overrated and overpaid, and if they had been in charge, they would have canned Yohann Stein's ass two seasons ago.

As they passed the thirty-ninth floor, Josef thought he heard a faint cracking sound. Just as suddenly, the scaffold listed to the left. They grabbed the rope just as the platform split in half, lengthwise. Josef's only thoughts as he dangled four hundred feet off the ground were, "What do you know? Eva was right."

German television, which was taping a game show two blocks away, hurried into position and trained their cameras to catch the fall, if it should happen, or the rescue, if that was even possible. Suddenly, the two men disappeared, only to show up seconds later halfway across town.

Later that afternoon, engineers had to slow down the tape in order to see the red-and-blue blur whiz past, grab them, then fly them to safety.

Gil was staring at the television monitors. "Man, it's all the same no matter where you look." He was using the remote to surf the channels.

GBS News was going through their Superman watchlist. In Shanghai, he had stopped a petty thief from robbing a small hardware store. The thief had had a gun aimed at the frightened owner, then, a second later, he found himself tied up in an electrical cord. They showed a securitycam shot of Superman shaking hands with the thief's former victim.

In Melbourne, he stopped a flood. In Cairo, he prevented a sandstorm from burying a small village.

Gil clicked to another channel where a blank-faced

anchor sat in front of a world map marking Superman's overnight feats with small "S"-shaped shields.

"Reports are flooding in from Metropolis, Houston, and as far away as Cairo and Shanghai. This is just the latest in a series of overnight appearances by the Man of Steel."

"Making up for lost time, I guess." Gil changed the channel again, to a home video taken of the Eiffel Tower. The camera suddenly whipped up in time to catch Superman streaking across the sky, disappearing over the horizon. Over the tape you could hear tourists shouting at him, trying to get his attention. An hour later, they learned, he had stopped what could have been a disastrous flood in Venice.

Clark entered the office and sat on the desktop beside Gil. He yawned as he looked up at the TV. "What's going on?"

Gil didn't bother turning. "Superman. He's been having a busy day."

Clark chuckled. "Show-off, if you ask me. Say, did you want to hear about this really neat llama race I saw?" Gil didn't seem to care.

The local news channel had a crew posted outside a small deli several blocks south of the Planet offices.

Two men in handcuffs were being led away by the police. The reporter was interviewing the anxious Jacob, the deli owner.

"Sir, after he captured the men robbing your deli, did he do or say anything?"

Jacob scratched his head, trying to remember. Suddenly, he was beaming. "He tried the hummus. He said he liked it." Jacob looked directly into the camera, becoming serious. "And Superman never lies. Jacob's Deli, corner of Fifty-third and Sixth. And if you say you saw this, I'll give you 10 percent off. What a deal."

Clark hid a small smile as he waved good-bye to Gil. Gil had changed the channel again and didn't notice he had left. He headed for Perry's office, passing another TV. This channel was replaying the scene of Superman saving Kitty, the green Cruiser held over his head.

Lois was looking at the same picture, printed in the *Planet*. She flipped the page to another photo; this one was of Superman carrying the car's beautiful driver in his arms, her head thrown back, her long legs exposed in a dress slit up to the waist. Its plunging neckline met it at the beltline. Lois then tossed the paper down, disgusted. "Eh," is all she said.

Perry picked up the paper and smiled at the photo. "'Eh?' 'Eh?' That's iconic. And they were taken by a twelve-year-old with a camera phone."

Jimmy Olsen was sitting at his desk, gazing off into space. "Olsen, what've you got?"

Jimmy looked at a photo of the skyline of Metropolis. He pointed to a small blur half-hidden by the clouds.

"He's right there, Chief. Look in the sky."

"It's a bird," Lois said, bored.

"It's a plane." Perry had picked up the photo and examined it closely.

Jimmy pointed at it again. "No, look. It's—"

"You wanted to see me?" Clark said, peeking into Perry's office, carrying his pad and pencil, ready to take notes.

"Sit down, Kent. Let's talk some halftime strategy."

Clark noticed Lois looking uncomfortable. She obviously knew where this was going.

"Not long ago, Superman and the *Daily Planet* went together like bacon and eggs. Death and taxes. Siegfried and Roy." Perry paused for effect but noticed only Clark was paying attention. "Now I want that bond back."

He turned to Lois, stabbing her forearm with his finger. "Lois, I know you've been sneaking around working on that blackout story—"

"It wasn't just a blackout, Chief," she snapped back defensively. "It was cell phones, pagers, automobiles, airplanes; it was everything."

Perry wasn't listening, "—but every other paper in town has their best-looking female reporters on rooftops waiting to interview Superman, and none of them have the history you two do."

Lois jumped up angrily. "What? No! Chief." She was furious, her face reddening with anger. "Listen to me. I've done Superman. *Covered* him. I've covered Superman. You know what I mean."

"Exactly," Perry interrupted. "That makes you the expert, so you're going to do him again."

Clark tried to interject, but he was drowned out by the shouting match in session.

"But there are a dozen other stories out there."

"Name one," Perry challenged her.

She remembered one and grinned. "Well, there was a museum robbery last night. Even Superman missed that one. He was too busy . . ." She picked up the newspaper and tossed it down in front of Perry. Kitty Kowalski's photo was staring at him. Clark peeked at it and smiled timidly. " . . . saving this stripper."

I did? he thought.

"And what'd they steal?"

Lois flipped through the article. "A meteorite."

Perry pushed the paper aside. "Boring. Gil can handle it."

Jimmy focused the lens on his camera and took an imaginary photo of Lois and Perry fighting. They fought over nearly every story. "Why don't you guys track down Lex Luthor?" Jimmy interrupted.

He was surprised when they all turned to him. Clark feigned noninterest, but was paying attention. The spotlight on him, Jimmy happily took center stage. "I mean, no one's seen him since he won his fifth appeal, and he's got more bad history with Superman than anyone. Maybe he's got something to say."

Perry shook his head, dismissing the idea. "Luthor's yesterday's news."

Lois disagreed. "No, I like that idea, Perry. Lex Luthor is a career criminal who nearly killed him, for Pete's sake. Just because Lex doesn't fly—"

Clark leaned closer, whispering conspiratorially. "Jimmy, how did Lex Luthor get out of prison?"

Jimmy shrugged. "The appeals court called Superman as a witness. He wasn't around. How much do you think that pisses off Superman now?"

"A lot," Clark said, matter-of-factly.

Lois was still arguing with Perry. "What is this anyway? A newspaper or a tabloid? We have plenty of gossip columnists equipped to cover Superman. Give it to someone else."

As she tried to think of someone to pawn the story off

on, Clark noticed her nose wrinkle. He loved that look. "Polly," she said, finally. "Give him to Polly."

They turned to see Polly glaring at them from her cubicle.

Perry stood up and glared at Lois. "Lois? Super. Man."

"What about the blackout?" she tried one more time.

Perry turned to Clark. "Kent. Blackout."

Lois fumed and stalked out. "Great. Thanks, Chief." A moment later, Clark rushed after her.

Jimmy started to follow, but Perry called him back. "Olsen, you're a copyboy again if you don't bring me one decent picture of him by the end of this week."

Jimmy's heart fell. "But Ch—"

Perry's finger was suddenly waving in front of him. "I wasn't gonna say it."

Perry sat down, turning to the computer. Jimmy stood there for another second, as if waiting for some last blistering comment or withering look, then darted out of the office. He growled at his camera as the elevator doors closed behind him. "Stay in focus next time."

Lois was already at her desk when Clark entered the cubicle. "Lois, I'm sorry. I didn't know . . ."

She spun her chair around and handed him a thick stack of files. "Here."

Clark looked uncomfortable as she forced them into his hands. "Take it. You wanted a way out of the obits? Here you go."

"No. Not this way. Not if it's going to bother you."

"Bother me? Of course not. Why in the world would it bother me that you're getting my story, the one only I've been working on, the one I've been championing."

Clark flipped through the files. "Oh, good. Because I'd hate it if this damaged our relationship."

Lois looked up to him quizzically. "Relationship?"

On the TV screen behind Clark she saw the image of Superman, in Zermatt, Switzerland, holding up a chain of twelve mountain climbers. He had saved them when the cable cars broke, stranding them on top of the Matterhorn. She rolled her eyes, then turned back to work.

She tried to come up with the best way for Superman to find her. The sooner she got past this idiotic story, the happier she'd be. *Why him? Why is it always him? I'm done with him.*

She started to type, "Fall out the window," but deleted it. *What if he's back in Zermatt, wherever the hell that is?* As she struggled for a second possibility, she heard a small voice calling to her. "Mommy."

She smiled as Jason ran into her arms. She tousled his hair and kissed him. "What is my little troublemaker doing here?"

Richard's voice piped in a second before she saw him enter, Jason's report card in his hands. "He got an A in science, but a D in gym, so we're doing something right."

Lois kissed him warmly. "At least one of us is."

Richard noticed Clark standing in the doorway, holding Lois's research. He looked back at Lois, the question obvious in his eyes.

"It's Perry," she snapped. "He just shoved Superman back into my life."

Richard shot a glance toward Perry's office; his uncle was on the phone, no doubt chewing out some paper supplier.

He turned back to Lois. "Well, I'm sure you can find a

way to interview Superman without bringing him back into your life."

On the TV behind Clark, a reporter was surrounded by people, all with binoculars and telescopes waiting for Superman to pass overhead.

"There's really no way around it, folks," he said. "Superman is back in all of our lives."

Richard sighed and looked at Clark, still standing in the way, holding the files. "How about this? We'll stay late, get dinner. I'll help you with Superman, and you and Clark can work on the blackout story together."

Lois heard Jason using his inhaler. It wheezed, nearly empty. "Here you go, kid." Lois pulled out a new one from her purse and handed it to him.

Richard turned to Clark. "So, is that good for you, Clark?"

He nodded. "Sounds swell."

Lois and Richard both looked at him. *Did he just say "swell"?*

Jason was beaming as he pulled up his sleeve and showed Lois the Band-Aid on his upper arm. "Look, Mom. I got my flu shot."

"Did it hurt?" Lois asked, cleaning a smudge on his face.

"Not a bit." He grinned.

She leaned in and kissed him again. "That's my boy."

Twenty-One

Lex Luthor settled into *The Gertrude*'s leather easy chair, put his feet up on the large desk and closed his eyes for a few minutes as Haydn played in the background. As his thoughts took off on a moment of fantasy, he pretended he was conducting the orchestra, bringing up the wind section, lowering the strings, deepening the percussion. Soon, he thought, he wouldn't have to pretend. He'd have his own orchestra and they'd play whatever he chose exactly as he desired it.

The concert over, he looked up at the framed nautical map screwed to the wall, then to a second map, this one rolled up in his hands. He started to unroll it when he heard the clackety-clack of Kitty's high heels descending the stairs, heading toward him.

"Ah, I was wondering what was taking you so long, Kitty."

He turned and smiled as she slapped him hard across the face. He grabbed his cheek and looked hurt. "Something wrong, my dear?"

She leaned in close, and snarled, "I was gonna pretend my brakes were out. Like we talked about. *Pretend!*" Her voice was shrill and rising, nearly out of control. "You didn't have to actually cut them."

He leaned back into the chair, closing his eyes once more. "Of course I did. A man can always tell when a woman is pretending. Especially Superman."

She tried slapping him again, but he caught her wrist and held it firm. She tried to pull it away, but he wouldn't let go until he felt her back down.

"Did you at least get your dumb rock?" she said weakly.

He nodded, smiling, as he pulled her closer to him. *She was a hundred kinds of trouble, but she came wrapped in an irresistible package.* "I did. Now ask me about the map."

She looked at the map on the wall. It was just an ordinary map with all those lines that went up and down and from side to side that meant nothing to her. "That map?" she asked.

He laughed. "No. This one," he said, holding up the rolled map in his hands. "This map is the future."

He pulled her closer, their lips almost touching.

"Mr. Luthor," Grant's voice boomed over the intercom, ruining the moment, "they're about to start, sir." He let her go, and she scurried back a few feet.

"Thank you, Grant," he said, annoyed but anxious to get to work. He glanced back to Kitty. "Well, duty calls, Ms. Kowalski. We'll talk more about this later."

She was quiet as he put the tube away and looked down at the newspaper on his desk. "Nice picture," he commented as he brushed past her.

As he slammed the stateroom door behind him, Kitty saw the copy of the *Daily Planet.* There was a full-color photo of Superman holding her in his arms. *Those powerful arms.* She smiled at the picture. *And those blueeeee eyes.*

She glanced at Lex's computer and saw some meaningless diagrams on the monitor. Although she didn't know what they meant, they were models of Kryptonian crystal technology as well as crystalline vehicles and large tracts of land. Even had she recognized what she was looking at, she could never have understood their importance.

Instead, she stared a few more minutes at the picture of her looking giddy in Superman's arms, then went back to her cabin to dream wonderful dreams.

Luthor stepped onto the bridge as Stanford was carefully removing the explosives from a missile, then setting them aside in a drawer. He measured the missile compartment, then turned to the small, rocky meteorite they had stolen from the museum while they kept Superman busy elsewhere, fighting evil, injustice, and bad brakes.

Stanford chipped off pieces of the meteorite's outer shell as Luthor gazed over his shoulder, staring at its inner core. It was glowing green.

Stanford chipped away some more rock and exposed more of the kryptonite beneath it. A long, sharp sliver of kryptonite broke off onto the counter. It was about six inches long and tapered to a point. Luthor slipped it into his pocket.

As Stanford carefully placed the remaining chunk of the kryptonite into a metal vise, just under the drill, he waited for Lex's go-ahead signal. Luthor finally nodded, and Stanford started the drill. He then lowered it slowly until its tip started drilling into the glowing green stone.

Twenty-Two

"Crap."

Jimmy Olsen was one step away from jumping out the Planet window, with no expectations that Superman might be around to save him. His stomach was knotted as he sat hunched over his keyboard, popping another stomach acid candy while staring at his computer. A calamitous slide show of his latest photos flickered past, one after the other, all disappointing: Photo 1 was a patch of blue sky. He could see a single puffy cloud floating in it, but no image of Superman. *What was I thinking?* The cloud dissolved into photo 2, which was an out-of-focus shot of the side of a building. He remembered thinking he saw Superman streaking past. If Superman had ever been there, by the time the shutter recorded the image, he would have been halfway to Toronto. Photo 3 was no better, a blurry image of what could have been a man, or possibly a tree. Or a shadow.

The sidewalk pavement was looking good. The only thing that did these days. He watched as a few more horrendous images stuttered past. "Crap," he said again.

Clark looked up from the watercooler, worried. Jimmy had always been so upbeat. *What happened to him?*

Jimmy stared at a picture of another useless streak of blue sky. "The guy just moves too fast. I haven't gotten one decent shot. Perry's going to fire me. I just know it. God, my stomach." He swallowed another two candies and washed them down with some soda.

Clark felt bad for him. "Keep at it. He's got to slow down eventually." Clark rested a friendly hand on Jimmy's shoulder and watched more of the slide show. He had to admit the photos were pretty bad. "You've got to be patient. And you want to know another secret?"

Jimmy cocked an eyebrow. "What?"

"Perry won't respect you until you talk back to him. He and Lois fight all the time, but you know how he feels about her. You've got to stand up for yourself, Jim. But when you do, you've also got to know you're right. That's what he respects above everything else."

"Yeah. But what if I'm not right?"

"Then don't say anything until you're sure you are."

Jimmy had begun at the *Planet* about the same time Clark had, and was one of the first people Clark met the day he interviewed for the job. He started in editorial as a table boy, shuffling papers from one office to the other, fetching coffee if he was asked to or carrying stacks of art or edited columns up to syndication on the twenty-ninth floor. When the Planet installed its internal e-mail system, most of those jobs went away. But as long as there was a need for coffee, and as long as Jimmy's part-time pay was low and didn't include medical, he was relatively safe.

He had wanted to be a photographer from the time he was twelve. For his sixth-grade graduation, his father had bought him a pawned old Hasselblad, and Jimmy spent the summer bicycling around the Clearview section of Metropolis, taking photographs of everything he thought looked interesting. In September, he showed his seventh-grade teacher the best of the photos, and with her encouragement, he organized them into a show for the school's art gallery.

The photos were seen by one of his classmates' parents, who worked at the *Clearview Shopper,* a local free paper that published a few articles, but made its money selling advertising to local merchants as well as the big movie chains trying to lure the suburban homebodies downtown for the weekends. The *Shopper* paid him $25.00 for three of his "Back Alleys of Clearview" photos and published them on its front page, the beginning of Jimmy's dream.

Several years later he joined his high-school newspaper and had nearly a hundred photos printed during his time there. He used those photos in his portfolio and because of them got a job interning at the *Daily Planet.*

Jimmy held no delusions that he was going to be a star right off the bat. He assumed when he was hired that he'd start by working with their staff photographers, loading film, developing negatives, in short, learning the ropes, then, after proving how good he was, he thought he'd quickly graduate to junior photographer. After five years he envisioned himself as a senior photographer, assigned, perhaps, to the crime beat. He clearly saw a series of his crime photographs printed in hand-tooled leather-bound editions, perhaps being used to teach photography at Metropolis U. But after three years as table boy, then another as copyboy, and later under the generic title of "Assistant," he had not been allowed to pick up a camera, let alone load or use one.

"I am so out of here," Jimmy whined. "Perry's already fed up with me, and these"—he looked at a series of photos of the attractive blonde he saw walking across Binder Boulevard, none with Superman anywhere in them—"are not going to help me in any way. I used to be so much better."

CLANG! Jimmy and Clark heard a ruckus behind them and saw Jason, wearing a trash can on his head, rampaging around the office like a giant monster. He roared wildly, "GROWLLLLLLLLLL" as he slammed into walls, but kept going.

"Jimmy, is he . . . okay?" Clark whispered to Jimmy.

Jimmy nodded. "Yeah, he's fine. A few weird allergies, asthma, but the kid's come a long way since he was born."

"What do you mean?"

"Well," Jimmy began, then lowered his voice, "Miss Lane doesn't like to talk about it, but Jason was born a little premature. They weren't sure if he was even going to make it."

Clark kept watching Jason running through the office, growling like Godzilla.

He saw Jason run across the floor to his mother sitting at her desk, checking over city maps.

Jason began hopping around Lois, then finally ran out of steam and sat down next to her. Richard plopped down beside him and put an arm around his son. He kissed Jason on the forehead, and they sat there while Lois worked.

Lois pulled out a map of the East Coast and placed it over the others. She used a compass to draw a series of concentric circles, based on the time and location of each blackout. They began to show a pattern that would get her closer to its point of origin.

Lois turned to Richard and noticed that Jason was asleep. She kept her voice low. "Weird. If these times are right, it looks like the blackout spread from a specific point."

"Where?" Richard wondered.

She checked the map again and shook her head. "I'm not sure yet."

Jason rolled off Richard and went to sleep on the floor. Richard flipped through piles of old articles and research papers dealing with Superman that were crowding her desk. "He's certainly a lot taller than I thought."

Across the room, Clark suddenly perked up, listening in on their private conversation.

"Six-four," she said.

"I love that he can see through anything. I'd have fun with that."

"Anything but lead," she smirked.

"And what's that other thing he does with his eyes? Laser blasts, or, what were they?"

"Heat vision. But he doesn't use it much. He also has telescopic vision. That lets him see long-distance. If he combines X-ray vision with telescopic vision, there's probably nothing on Earth that can hide from him."

"Unless it's covered by lead," Richard added.

"Yeah. Unless it's covered by lead."

Richard picked up a photograph taken on that first day Superman had let Lois interview him. "I bet he's . . ." He didn't have to continue.

"Two hundred and twenty-five pounds, faster than a speeding bullet, invulnerable to anything but kryptonite, and he never lies."

"Kryptonite?"

Lois glanced up from her work. "Radioactive pieces of his home world. It's deadly. To him. Why?"

"Just asking. Wow. Sounds like the perfect guy."

He turned to see Clark standing near Jimmy. They were obviously engaged in some serious discussion. "Hey, how tall would you say Clark is?" he whispered.

Lois shrugged. "I don't know. Maybe six-three, six-four?"

"Around two hundred pounds," Richard added.

Lois paused and looked up again. "Sure, why?"

She followed his gaze as he turned to see Clark. He looked up and smiled nervously as if he realized he was being watched. He coughed into his hand, then waved at them. They both began to laugh to themselves. "No reason. Never mind."

He saw Jason waking up. "Hey, Jason, Jimmy, let's go get these intrepid reporters something to keep them going, okay?"

Jason was already on his feet. "Burrrrrritos! Roarrrrr!"

Lois watched them take off, smiled at Clark, and went back to work. The silence was uncomfortable. He kept sneaking looks at her, trying to find a way to start a conversation. Any conversation. He decided he was going to ask her about the blackouts. Before he could, Lois started talking.

"So. Have you found a place to live yet?"

He shook his head. "No. I'm still looking."

"Where have you been spending your nights, then?"

Clark shrugged. "Oh, here and there."

He looked back at the janitor's closet, then turned back

to her. "You know. Umm, Lois, I wanted to ask you about that article . . ."

She stood up, cutting him off before he could begin. "Hey, I'm gonna run downstairs for some fresh air. Let's talk when I get back. Okay?"

"Sure. Later then."

She grabbed her purse by one handle, spilling its contents over the floor. There was a small makeup kit, a tape recorder, and a pack of cigarettes. She shoved them back into her purse and gave Clark an embarrassed smile. He was about to say something when she darted to the elevator.

As the door slid shut he raised his glasses, focused his eyes, and saw her inside, grabbing for her pack of cigarettes. She pressed the button for the top floor of the Planet building and headed for the roof.

The air was brisk and clean, and she drew in a long breath as the wind rushed past her. The Daily Planet globe was revolving just above her. She sat down on the ledge and looked around her suspiciously. There was nobody here. *Perfect.* She took out a cigarette and stared at it, then flicked her lighter and it ignited. But as soon as she touched the flame to the tip, it went out.

She tried again. The lighter lit for a moment, then extinguished itself again. She tried again, flicking it harder this time, but it accidentally dropped from her hand. Kneeling, she groped under a rooftop vent searching for it.

"You know, you really shouldn't be smoking, Miss Lane."

OhmyGod! She knew that voice. Knew it as well as Jason's, knew it perhaps better than anyone else's.

Twenty-Three

She yelped as she saw him land on the ledge.

"I'm sorry. I didn't mean to—"

Close up he was just the way she remembered. She drew in another breath. *Ready now!*

She straightened up, composing herself. "I'm fine. Really. I just wasn't expecting you."

He stepped closer, and she stepped back in response. "So where—?" She started to say, even as he spoke.

"I'm . . ."

It was an awkward silence.

Lois knew she had to take control. If she didn't, this could turn out so wrong. "You first. I can wait."

She could see him straighten up, composing himself. It was as awkward for him as it was for her. *Good! He deserves it!* She was angry, and although she wasn't sure she wanted it, she was getting the chance for some kind of closure.

"I'm sorry," he began. "For leaving like that. And . . .

with all the press on the plane, I wasn't sure if it was the best time for us to talk."

Press? Lois was confused. She struggled to make sense of him, then suddenly remembered. "Oh, right. The jet. Well, there's no press around now. Except me." She let the "me" hang, demanding his explanation. She could tell he was struggling for an answer. *Yeah. Do it. Struggle.*

"I know people are, uh, asking a lot of questions now that I'm back, and I, uh, think it's only fair that I answer . . . those people."

Those people? "So, you're here for an interview?"

He nodded, not certain what else to say. He realized that coming here, coming to her, was a mistake. Her life was settled. She had a kid. She was happy. *Why am I trying to upset the applecart? Why did I come here?*

"Okay then." The anger was thick in her voice. "An interview it is.

She reached for her purse, to get out the tape recorder. She fumbled for it amidst all the stuff she had tossed in without planning. "Where did I put that thing . . . ?"

"The right pocket, Lois," Superman said.

"Huh?"

"The tape recorder. It's in your right pocket."

"Okay. Fine. An interview. Sounds just about . . . *right.*" She turned the tape recorder on. *He wants an interview? He's gonna get one he won't ever forget.*

"Let's start with the big question. Where did you go?"

"To Krypton," he answered, without pausing.

Lois was confused. "But you told me it was destroyed. Ages ago."

He didn't answer her quickly, and she could see the pain behind his eyes. When he finally spoke, his voice had quieted a bit. It felt sad. "I did. It was. But when astronomers thought they found it . . . I had to see for myself."

What happened out there? What did he see? She heard his voice weaken, and she realized how much his answer affected her as well. *Dammit! Why couldn't you just tell me you moved in with some bimbo or something?* She paused to get her bearings.

"Well, you're back, and everyone seems to be happy about it."

He shook his head. "Not everyone," he said quietly. "I read the article, Lois. 'Why the World Doesn't Need Superman.'"

She'd been waiting for that. "So did a lot of people. Tomorrow night they're giving me the Pulitzer for it."

He looked at her, trying to read her thoughts. It was the one power, right now, he was thankful he didn't have. "Why did you write it?"

Lois clicked off the tape recorder and turned away. She walked to the other side of the roof and stared into the night sky. She felt her cheek moisten as she wiped her eyes with the back of her hand.

"How could you leave me like that?"

He stopped, caught off guard.

"I'm sorry if I hurt you."

She felt the knot in her stomach. She had lived with that pain for five years. *Where are you? Why did you go? Are you ever coming back? Did I do something—?*

It was only in the few last months that she had been able to put even a small part of it aside.

"No. The time to say sorry was five years ago." She kept staring into space, trying to regain some modicum of control. *I am not going to cry. I am not going to cry.*

Her words were deliberate, spoken slowly as if trying to twist them into something calmer, less potent, than she felt, but her anger still shook him. "I moved on. I had to. And so did the rest of us. That's why I wrote it. The world doesn't need a savior."

"I never wanted to be a savior. I never tried to be one. I just wanted to help the best I could."

"You sure screwed that up, didn't you?"

They stood quiet, neither having anything left to say. He watched her for several minutes, knowing she was right, of course. He should have told her before . . . He should have explained it all to her, but he didn't. He couldn't.

"Lois, will you come with me?" He wasn't sure why he was asking her or what he'd hoped would happen if she said yes. All he knew was he couldn't let her go like this. Not now, after all this time.

"Why?"

He didn't really have an answer. "There's something I want to show to you." She continued staring at the sky-line, ripe with the colors of an early dusk. "Please," he said finally.

She was hesitating, wanting to go but knowing she shouldn't. "I can't be gone long," she said, then cursed herself for opening that door again. *Nothing good can come from this.*

He smiled sweetly at her. "You won't be."

She stepped closer to him, regretting it already, but also knowing she couldn't refuse him. She never could. She kicked off her heels, then placed her feet on his. Finally, she looked up into his eyes.

"Clark says the reason you left without saying good-bye is because it was too unbearable for you. Personally, I think that's a load of crap."

Superman smiled in that way that melted her heart. "Maybe Clark's right."

She tried to turn away again but couldn't. "You know, my, *umm*, Richard, is a pilot. He takes me up all the time."

"Not like this."

She looked down and gasped. They were already fifty feet above the rooftop and moving over the edge. She was shivering, and her foot slipped off his. Gravity tugged at her, and she held on to him tighter. They began to rise again.

She kept staring as his warm blue eyes reached into hers.

She knew they had done this all before. That magical night. When she held on to his hand as they floated past the city and over the water, alone, looking at each other as if no one else existed, that night when she fell in love with him knowing there could never be anyone else.

But there was someone else now.

They were both silent as he finally stopped, hovering high above the city. They floated there for what seemed like forever.

It was all the same, yet so different.

"What do you hear?" he finally asked her.

Lois shook her head. "Nothing. It's quiet."

He smiled at her. "Do you know what I hear? I hear everything." His smile faded.

"You wrote that the world doesn't need a savior. But every day I hear people crying for one."

She felt her heart sink. *This isn't the same. It is different.*

He was still looking at her.

"I'll take you back now," he said.

• • •

The stars were twinkling in the darkness when he reached out to them. They magically rippled at his touch. Lois saw herself as they flew just inches above the river, his finger running through the water, fragmenting their reflection.

They flew past rows of shore homes. She saw a glimpse of her own house as they headed for the Metropolis Bridge, then dived under the structure.

They glided past a section of scaffolding where sparks from blowtorches rained down around them like fireworks. Construction workers turned and gawked as they continued on to the city.

Metropolis's majestic towers were bathed in golden light as they soared over and between them. He pulled to the right and carried her toward a tall building. It didn't look like he was planning to stop. Lois braced herself, but he rose suddenly, and they began to turn and spin, wrapped in each other's arms, like some slow dance in the middle of the sky.

They continued rising higher, until the Daily Planet globe appeared. He hovered there for another moment, then gently lowered her to the roof. She looked into his eyes again, their faces inches apart. *It would be so easy.* She moved closer to him, then suddenly pulled back, dazed.

"Richard's a good man," she finally said after a long moment. She could barely catch her breath. "And you've been gone a long time."

"I know," Superman said.

She was standing on the roof again. He let her go and she gently reached down and picked up her shoes. She walked unsteadily to the rooftop door, then turned back to him. "So, will I see you? Around?"

He smiled again and nodded. "I'm always around. Good night, Lois."

He looked up into the sky and was suddenly flying through it. Lois watched until he was gone.

After a few minutes, she quietly made her way down the stairs to the editorial floor. Her thoughts were frazzled, and that bothered her. She liked the life she had made and didn't want anything—*not even him*—upsetting it.

She entered the conference room and saw Richard, Jason, Clark, and Jimmy eating takeout. Her smile returned as her son ran to her. "Mommy, we've been having fun."

She kissed both of Jason's cheeks, then gave Richard a kiss on the lips. "Love you."

"Back atcha," Richard said as he moved a few of the containers closer to her. "We've got beef, honey. Do you want the veggie or tofu wrap?"

"Honey beef," she said.

"What?"

She shook herself out of her reverie. "Sorry. Veggie. I'll have the veggie wrap."

Richard watched her staring out the window, into the distance, as if looking for . . . *something*. Her hair was windblown. "Lois, where have you been?"

She noticed Clark watching as she answered him. "I was just on the roof, getting some air."

She smiled at him, but the look in his eyes said he was suspicious. "Tell me the truth, Lois."

She was trembling. Nervous.

"Have you been smoking?" he asked her.

She grinned sheepishly. "Caught."

Twenty-Four

She plopped down onto the living-room couch, the laptop resting on her lap. From where she was sitting she could see the fireplace mantel and the cluster of pictures of her and Richard and Jason that covered it.

He was such a good man, and she loved him. She didn't have to look to know there was a picture of them, taken at the Metropolis County Fair, on their very first date, sitting on the mantel's left side.

She realized how strange it was. He began working at the *Planet* a few weeks after Superman . . . *vanished.* Clark had taken off, too—and sometime after Superman disappeared he sent a postcard saying he needed to find himself, or something like that. *Fine. Whatever.*

She'd met Richard before, although only once. She thought he was good-looking, but they hadn't talked, and she didn't think much else about him. Besides, he was working on the *Planet*'s international side, based out of London, so the odds of seeing him again were slim at best.

But at Perry's urging he'd come back to Metropolis, to head up the *Planet*'s International Bureau from the main office. On his third Friday working in Metropolis he complained to her that he didn't know anyone in town, then asked if she would accompany him to the county fair. He said he really wanted to see it but didn't think he could go alone. A macho thing.

A harmless enough get-together, she thought, hardly a date, with them and thirty thousand others crowding the narrow Fairplex streets. She wasn't looking to meet anyone. She hadn't yet accepted the idea that Superman was gone. But the fair sounded fun, dumb fun, a not-altogether-terrible way to spend a free Saturday.

"A Little Bit of Country in a Whole Lot of City," was the slogan that year. As they entered, a young girl who couldn't have been more than seventeen, dressed in country-girl gingham, snapped their photo, gave them a coupon, and said it would be ready, if they wanted to purchase it, when they left the park that night.

Lois had no intention of doing so, but nine hours later, sated or perhaps wired by ice cream, veggie corn dogs on a stick, lemonade sold to them by teenagers wearing striped clothing and hats, BBQ corn, deep-fried Twinkies and laden down with a half dozen giant stuffed animals he'd won for her at the sideshow, well, the picture had come out looking really good, and, besides, it no longer seemed like a totally dorky idea.

She was glad now he insisted on buying the picture for her. It was a memory of the first day she stopped crying and started to laugh again.

She told him up front she wasn't interested in a relationship. He said he had no problem with that.

"Trust me. I'm not looking to settle down, either," he said more than once. "For all I know any day now Uncle Perry's going to ship me back to London. But it'll be fun while it lasts."

Fun. Fun would be okay. Fun would actually be different.

He was nice. Funny. Handsome. Exciting. Smart as hell. They had great times together, but she still wasn't looking for anyone. For a long time she didn't even want to admit there *was* a relationship brewing, but slowly, and so imperceptibly neither of them noticed it, over a long time, it seemed to her now, it became one nevertheless.

And when Perry finally did talk to him about returning to London, Richard turned him down. "Nope. Not really interested. Besides, I can do the job just as well from here," he guaranteed. When he told her what he had done, she shrieked with joy.

She wasn't quite sure when she had fallen in love with him, but she knew he was not only there for her when she needed him, she knew she wanted to be there for him, too. To help him when he needed her. That was different for her. That hadn't happened in any of her previous one-way relationships. Especially not with *him.*

He didn't need help. He certainly didn't need hers.

She knew she was a handful. Hell, it had taken a Superman to deal with her, but Richard knew how to challenge her. Keep her off guard a little. He wasn't someone you could steamroller. But he was someone she wanted to share a life with.

Lois enjoyed their nights together, curled up on the couch, reading books, watching DVDs, playing with Jason. Richard was a really good cook, an incredible father, and an even better lover. There was a comfort there, of course, but it was more than just that.

One day she woke up at three in the morning, rolled over in bed, looked at him sleeping beside her, and realized how much she adored him.

She glanced at the laptop again and shivered, suddenly feeling cold. She bundled the afghan that Richard had bought for her on one of their weekend trips to the Pennsylvanian Dutch country around her, and she wrote into the night. At nine the next morning, she handed the interview to Perry.

"Is this real?" he asked. She didn't bother replying. "How'd you find him?"

"He found me."

"Great. I can't wait to read it." He turned to the first page, but she was still standing in front of his desk, waiting. "What!"

Somewhere from deep inside her Lois found a way to be sweet. Or at least to talk sweetly. She gave him the most demure smile she was capable of making. "So, Mr. White, about that blackout . . .?"

Perry put down the interview and gave her a confused look. "Lois, this is the biggest night of your life, and all you care about is that story? Have you picked out a dress? Something snazzy, I hope?"

"It just feels a little weird winning for that article," she said, showing more regret than she had intended. "It doesn't seem right anymore."

"What doesn't seem right?"

Even as she wrote about *his* return she spent most of the night awake, trying to put words to her mixed feelings. "Getting an award for an article called, 'Why the

World Doesn't Need Superman.'" She held up a copy of that morning's *Planet*. "When, according to this paper, it does."

Perry shook his head as he got up from behind the desk. He put his arm around her shoulder and began to walk her outside. "Lois, Pulitzer Prizes are like Academy Awards. Nobody remembers what you got one for. Just that you got one."

Lois was about to question him. "But—" she started to say.

"This night's for you, Lois. Just enjoy it. I'm sure Kent's on the blackout."

She started to protest when the door to his office closed in front of her. He had led her into the bullpen without her even realizing it. She looked back through the glass partition and saw he was already sitting at his desk, going over her interview, a red pen in his right hand. She growled at him, and though he didn't look up to see her, he waved his left hand good-bye then turned to page two.

Twenty-Five

The northern lights were shimmering in the dark gray sky as Superman flew past the Queen Elizabeth Islands and the Alpha Ridge to just north of the Fletcher Abyssal Plains. As far as he could see there were vast miles of unspoiled whiteness punctuated only by small pools of crystal blue water. Seals dotted the area, hopping in and out of the holes, searching for enough food to sustain them during the oncoming long winter. Normally, he would have paused to watch them playing, perhaps even diving into the water beside them to help them dig out food that was buried too deep to find easily, but today was different. Today he didn't much care about anything.

He was angry, then felt angrier for feeling so angry. *I went away. Was the world supposed to stop spinning until I got back?* But he knew reality didn't matter. He couldn't get rid of the painful hole he felt burning in his stomach.

He flew through a thick, misty bank and emerged about

a mile away from his Fortress. It stood, crystal shafts gleaming in the bright arctic sunlight.

He came because he needed someone to talk to and here, unlike in Smallville—or was his mother already in Montana?—he could say whatever was in his heart. He knew Martha would tell him he had to forget Lois and move on even as she had. Lois had her man and her son, and it wouldn't be proper for him to come between them. By speaking what he already knew was the truth, Martha would break his heart, and he didn't want that, as right as she would be.

He needed anything *but* that now.

All he wanted now were for the ghosts to listen, then for them to recite their preprogrammed platitudes, to tell him again never to change the course of human history or to remind him how different he was from them, then to send him on his way.

He didn't need to be told what he already knew. He needed only to talk, then to leave.

"Father," he called out, entering the Fortress. "It's been a long time since I've come to you. But I've never felt so alone."

The Fortress was dark, eerily so. The once-glistening crystal walls were like cold sheets of coal. He used his X-ray vision to guide him through the dark.

He approached the console and knew right away what had happened. The crystals, including Jor-El's father crystal, were gone. They had been removed from the Fortress.

He screamed, and his voice echoed through the Arctic like thunder.

"Father!"

He was gone, halfway back to Metropolis, before the echo faded.

Twenty-Six

Jimmy Olsen was shouting as he pushed his way through the office, carrying two long gowns on hangers as if they were vials of nitroglycerin seconds away from exploding. "Watch out, Pulitzer party dresses coming through." He circled around Anne from the City Desk, who peeked suddenly out of her cubicle to see what the noise was about, and almost trampled over Gil, who was hurrying to the bathroom. He finally made it to editorial, where he found Lois on the phone.

"Department of Water and Power, please," she said as she saw Jimmy hurrying to her. She gestured him closer.

He held up the two dresses, and she pointed to the gray beaded one, which he then hung on a coatrack behind her desk. He darted off again as she turned back to the phone.

"Hi, this is Lois Lane from the *Daily Planet*. I was wondering if . . ." After her Superman interview that morning she couldn't get out her name without someone interrupting her. "Yes, he is a very nice man. But I was wondering if I could ask you a few more questions about the black-out—"

Jimmy reappeared holding a dry erase board. On it he wrote: *Richard's late. Tux not ready at cleaners. Can you pick up Jason from school?*

She gave him a thumbs-up as the voice asked her about getting Superman's autograph. Jimmy ran off again. For once he was feeling needed.

She was impatient with the phone responses she'd been getting, but she tried to hide it. She knew this was the curse of working with middle management; they had a modicum of power and lived to wield it.

"I already spoke to the Technology and Energy Committee, and they sent me back to you, and now you're sending me back to them?" She forced herself to remain pleasant as she reached for her pad and pen. "The who? Okay? Can I get their number? Thank you." She wanted to add "You pompous bastard," but thought better of it.

She dialed the new number and waited. Voice mail sent her pressing '1' for English, then an abacus full of other numbers until she finally reached her new contact. "Metropolis Public Works? My name is Lois Lane. I'm calling from the—" She listened a moment. "Yes, I'll hold."

She heard four different movie themes before a human voice picked up the line again. This voice was female.

"Uh-huh," she said. "Stephen Jones. And he does what? Oh. Deputy Director of the Power Outage Task Force. Great. And you can forward me? Thanks so much. I appreciate it."

She found herself on a six-movie-theme hold this time. She used the time to change into her evening gown, making sure she was not seen by anyone else. She was slipping on her high heels when the music was finally cut off.

"Hi, Stephen, this is Lois Lane from the *Daily Planet*. I'm writing an investigative article on the blackout and just need a little info on a few outstanding power grids."

He put her on hold for two more movie themes. Just as "Tara's Theme" from *Gone With the Wind* began, she heard the phone make another click. The Deputy Director of *blahblahblah* had returned. This time with the information she needed. She could barely contain herself.

"So, let me get this straight. The uptown grid went dark at 12:36, and midtown ten seconds before. So which grid was hit first?"

"Grid J-12," Jones said, checking his chart. "Across the river. The Vanderworth property."

She wrote that down. "You're sure. Nothing before that?"

"That's it." Jones was certain.

"Thanks, Mr. Jones. I appreciate it." This time she actually meant it.

She hung up, then dialed 411 while staring at a map of Metropolis.

"Information please. I need a listing for Vanderworth." She waited just a few seconds. "Six Springwood Drive."

"Is that a business or a residence?" There was no delay. "A residence. Thank you."

She pulled the map off the bulletin board and traced a path to the Vanderworth property. Then she looked up and noticed the clock on the wall and panicked.

"Jason!" she screamed. She'd forgotten to pick him up from school.

She ignored half the street signs and twice as many lights as her Audi A3 sped to Jason's school, almost twenty miles away, in less than fifteen minutes, a new record for her. She saw Jason outside, standing by the stairs, holding the hand of one of his teachers. *Mrs. Morgan?*—she remembered. Lois pulled in front of him and honked.

"Get in," she called out. She was in a rush.

Jason toddled over and jumped into the back seat. Mrs. Morgan bent down and waved to Lois through the window. "Congratulations, Miss Lane. Say hi to Superman for me."

"Thanks. Will do," Lois replied, politely.

Jason was watching cartoons on the car's DVD system as Lois pulled to a stop just outside the Vanderworth Estate gates. She heard music, definitely opera, and it wasn't coming from the house but from behind it.

Jason looked around. "Mommy, where are we? Is this the Pulitzer?"

Lois opened the back door and unlocked his child-proofed seat-belt lock. "No. I just need to ask these people a few questions, then we can go."

She looked past the estate and saw a yacht moored to a pier behind it. The music was coming from there. *Good. Someone's home.*

"Can I stay in the car?"

Lois laughed. "Not on your life, you little monster." She hugged him tightly, wishing she didn't have to let go. He was clearly the one part of her life that had worked out better than she could have imagined.

She loved him without any reservations. It was complete and total, and it didn't matter what he gave her back—though in every little movement and smile and even in his pouting complaints, he gave her so much.

She watched him growing from that first prenatal sonogram to his troubled birth and right up to the present. He was ever-changing yet constant. His personality was set the moment he was born, although it was always a surprise when he did something so completely unexpected that it left Lois dumbfounded and helpless.

"This one's going to be a little fighter," Richard had warned her. He was right. Jason might have been physically weaker than the other kids, but no matter what was thrown at him, nothing ever fazed him.

She never thought she had the stuff to be a mother, or even the interest in ever becoming one. She used to watch other women doting over their babies, holding them, kissing them, hugging them, and thought, *I'm just not into that sort of thing.* Sometimes she felt horrible for feeling that, but she knew deep down that if she ever had a kid, she'd hire a nanny, let the help take care of him until he was, oh, eighteen, then ship him out into the world as her father had done to her and her sister, Lucy.

She had a life she cherished, she thought, and did not want it changed. She was free and independent and strong. She was going to win the Pulitzer Prize one day and prove that to everyone. She didn't need to be tied down to a husband and a kid for identity like everyone else she knew. She was Lois Lane, Ace Reporter, and that was all she ever wanted to be.

But something inside her changed when Dr. Mankiewicz handed Jason to her on that first early morning, just cleaned up, but all pruney and wrinkled like some kind of pitiful-looking shar-pei. And when she saw his eyes, those beautiful eyes, he became her world.

Any regrets she might have had, raising a child alone, not being married—not even being sure she wanted to be—were gone the moment he giggled at her the first time, or defiantly turned himself over in his crib at least six weeks before he should have been able to, or made his maiden voyage crawling across the floor.

She looked at him, all grown-up, and gave him another kiss, which he promptly wiped off his cheek with the back of his sleeve and an audible "Yuck."

"Let's go, kid," she said.

Her cell phone rang displaying the name DAILY PLANET on its screen. She thought about answering it for a second, then tossed the phone in the glove compartment. *No way Perry is talking me out of this.* She grinned at Jason. "Now we're going," she said, taking his hand.

They made their way to the yacht. The music was coming from somewhere belowdecks. She checked out the boat and whistled admiringly. The only time she'd been on a yacht bigger than this one was for that big party in Atlanta when the president of a cable news network tried to hire her away from the *Planet.* Although she turned him down, and the party, though grand, was ostentatious, she would never forget the boat.

Lois and Jason boarded the yacht and looked around. They stepped over empty beer bottles and pizza boxes.

Whoever lived here was a slob. Hardly the kind who would have a house like the Vanderworths'.

"Mom, are we trespassing?" Jason asked. She was impressed that he knew what the word *trespassing* meant. Not bad for a five-year-old.

"Yes," she said, then changed her mind. "No. I mean, 'shhhh.'"

They followed the music down a flight of stairs that led to a long corridor, where she saw a doorway just ahead, slightly ajar. Jason followed as she entered a large room filled with fine suits, shoes, jewelry, and other expensive items. This was a *closet?* Whoever lived here wasn't rich. They were fabulously rich.

"I like the curly one," Jason said. Lois turned to see him pointing at something on a shelf. Her eyes suddenly widened with fear. "Oh, my God."

She was looking at a mannequin's head. Sitting atop it was a toupee. Just one of many heads and hairpieces, all neatly lined up in rows. "Oh, no."

She grabbed Jason's hand and backed away. He could tell something bad had just happened. "Mommy, what's wrong?"

She was starting to panic. "Jason, don't argue, but keep quiet and run as fast as you can. This was a bad idea. We've got to get out of here."

The room rumbled as the ship's engine suddenly roared with life. She ran to a small window to see that they were pulling away from shore.

They hurried to the door. All they needed to do was make it to the deck and, if necessary, dive into the water. The shore wasn't that far away yet. She was a good swimmer, and if necessary, she could hold on to Jason while they made their way to safety.

She pulled open the door and shrieked when she saw him.

Lex Luthor was standing in the doorway, filling its small frame. He was bald—few people ever saw him that way—wearing a bathrobe with a monogrammed "V" on it, and he had a toothbrush stuck in his mouth.

"Lex Luthor!"

He narrowed his eyes at her and smiled. "Lois Lane."

As Jason played with the pool-table balls in the yacht's stateroom, ricocheting them off the various cushions, Lois impatiently marched back and forth, waiting for Luthor to reappear. She looked for a phone but couldn't find one. She cursed herself for not bringing her cell. Jason crossed the stateroom and sat down in front of the piano and played a few notes. "Heart and Soul" was his favorite, and he played it well. Or at least well enough.

Luthor walked in a few minutes later, joined by Stanford, Riley, and Brutus. Kitty entered beside him. He was now dressed and sporting one of his wigs. The curly one.

"And what's your name?" he asked Jason, who was hitting the piano keys with very little finesse.

Jason took his hands off the keys. "I'm not supposed to talk to strangers."

Luthor smiled at Lois. "Cute kid. Smart, too."

"Thanks," Lois said. *Stay calm. This will work out. There's no reason for him to kill us. Smile. Act nice. He'll let us go.*

Luthor walked around Jason again, teasingly mussing

his hair. Jason pushed his hand away. "But I'm not really a stranger, am I?" Luthor said. "I mean, this is like a little reunion."

Lois took Jason's hand, protectively.

"Hell," Luthor continued. "I'm a fan, Miss Lane. I love your writing." She didn't like the way he was leering at her. "And your dress."

"Well, I love your yacht," Lois said. No matter what he said, he was not going to get her to cower. "How'd you get it? Swindle some old widow out of her money?"

Kitty snorted a laugh, but Lex's eyes narrowed. "Didn't you just win the Pulitzer Prize for my favorite article ever, 'Why the World Doesn't Need Superman'?"

Lois glanced at her watch. "Not yet. Didn't you have a few more years to go on your double life sentence?"

Lex laughed, thinking about it. "Well, we can thank the Man of Steel for that. He's really good at swooping in and catching the bad guys. But he's not so hot on the little things. Like Miranda rights, due process—making your court date."

Lois checked her watch again. It was getting late. The banquet would be starting soon, and every second was taking them farther from shore. "Did you have anything to do with the blackout?" she asked outright.

She was surprised when she saw him laugh and his eyes light up. "Are you fishing for an interview, Miss Lane?"

She sat down in a chair. "Well, it's been a while since you were a headline. Maybe it's time people knew your name again, hmmm?"

Keep him talking, bragging about himself. It's what he loves the most.

She pulled Jason's chair closer. "So how about we turn

the boat around, call a cab for my son, and then you can do whatever you want with me."

Lex looked at her, thought about his schedule, then turned to Jason. "Do you know what posthumous means?"

Jason shook his head.

"Good," Luthor turned back to Lois. "Sorry we won't be turning around, but we do have some time to kill. So how about that interview?"

He saw a pad and pencil near the fax machine and handed them to her. "Your tools?" She felt her hand turn cold and clammy as she took them.

Luthor settled back into the chair. Kitty was behind them, pretending to read the newspaper. "Kitty. My martini. And an iced tea for Miss Lane and a glass of— *milk?*—for her son."

Lois saw Kitty put down the paper. Its cover showed Superman saving the bimbo from the runaway car. Lois suddenly realized Kitty was the "stripper." The whole thing had been a setup.

What is Luthor up to?

Jimmy Olsen was sitting at Lois's desk, staring at the photo of her and Jason on the cubicle wall. He was sighing when Clark entered, looking around the office for something.

"Jimmy, did you see the information Lois collected on the blackout? I need it for my story." Jimmy kept staring at the photo. Clark heard his sigh again. "What's wrong?"

"Lois and Jason are missing," he finally said.

"Missing?"

Jimmy pointed to Perry White's office. Perry and

Richard were both wearing their tuxedos. Richard was on the phone, while Perry was pacing around him, upset and nervous.

"What did the school say?" Perry asked, as Richard hung up the phone.

"She picked up Jason, but his teacher said she sounded like she was in a rush."

"I heard the news. What can I do?" Clark asked, entering.

Richard was staring out the window. "I don't know. This isn't like her. I don't know what to do. Her car's missing. She's missing."

Perry shook his head. "We've tried her cell, but there's no answer, and we're supposed to be at the ceremony in a half hour."

"When she's with Jason she always keeps the cell on. Hell, she keeps it on all the time anyway, even at night, in case one of her sources has something to report. She's never without it."

Clark was confused. "Okay, so understand I'm just being optimistic here, but maybe you're all jumping the gun. Maybe she got a flat tire somewhere. Maybe her cell phone ran out of juice. Or maybe she just wants a little bit of time to herself before the ceremony. I mean, I'd be nervous if I were her."

"He may be right, Richard." Perry said. "We were talking earlier. She was questioning whether she should even get the award, considering you-know-who's return."

"Yeah. See? There could be a hundred different explanations," Clark said. "Besides, I'm pretty sure she's not the type who'd ever put her son in any danger. I'm sure there's a reasonable explanation why she's late."

Richard continued pacing. "Look, I know you mean

well, Clark. You, too, Perry. But you don't know her like I do. What I'm getting is a feeling. Something's wrong."

Clark saw the emotions tearing at Richard. He was obviously in love with Lois. And even if she had some reservations, even if there was a Superman lurking somewhere in the background, they had had a child together. They were a couple.

"All right," Clark said. "Then we'll work together and find her."

Richard gave him a weak smile as he patted him on his back. "Jimmy was right. You're a good man, Clark."

Clark smiled, but he didn't feel that way.

Twenty-Seven

"What do you know about crystals?" asked Lex casually.

Lois shrugged, looking blank. "They make great chandeliers?" He laughed as he picked up a thick leather-bound book from his desk and dropped it into her lap. He gestured for her to open it. She flipped through the pages, filled with pictures of crystals and charts with complicated formulas.

When she looked up again, he was holding the white crystal he had stolen from the Fortress of Solitude.

"Miss Lane, this crystal may seem unremarkable, but so is the seed of a redwood tree." Lois thought she recognized it, that she had seen it before, but the memory was vague, like from a dream.

He stroked the crystal tenderly as if he was making love to it. "If you want to know the truth, it's how our mutual friend in tights made his arctic getaway retreat. Cute, but a little small for my taste."

He gestured with the crystal to the large antique nautical

map on the wall. He had modified it to show a new land-mass just off the coast of Metropolis.

She looked at the map, then at the book on her lap, *Make Your Own Crystals,* then back at the map. "You're building an island?"

He was grinning now, rubbing his hands together, glee-ful that he could show off his greatest plan yet to some-one who could appreciate it in all its dark, evil splendor. "You're not seeing the big picture, Miss Lane. Here, let me enlarge it for you."

He yanked down another nautical map that showed the landmass even larger than it was before. It was nearly the size of a continent.

"It's not just an island," he said. "It's an entirely new continent. Virtually indestructible and self-sustaining. For lack of a better name, it's Krypton. An extinct world, re-born on our own."

Lois kept staring at the map, understanding what he was saying, yet not comprehending it at the same time. "Why would anyone grow a continent?"

Luthor had been anticipating that question. It was the first one anyone of limited intellect would think of. Expla-nations would be so unnecessary if only they could see the world through his eyes.

"Land, Miss Lane." He turned to Kitty. "Kitty, what did my father once say to me?"

"Get out?"

"Before that. He said, 'You can print money, manufac-ture diamonds, and people are a dime a dozen, but they'll always need land.'" He turned back to Lois, pausing dra-matically before giving the punch line. "It's the one thing they don't make any more of."

"But the United States government," Lois started to say. Luthor was already yanking down another antique map for her to see. He had changed this one to show his new continent spreading over half of North America, with all the areas around it covered by water.

"The United States government, or what will be left of it, will be underwater. Simple logic, Miss Lane. Two objects simply can't occupy the same space."

He saw Lois staring at him as if he were insane. He was used to that. Small minds and people with eyes who didn't use them to see had always been the bane of his existence. "Go ahead. You have a question that is just waiting to be asked."

"You think the rest of the world will just let you keep it? They'll—" There was no reason to let her finish. The answer should have been obvious, but, of course, she couldn't hope to recognize it.

"They'll what? I have alien technology." He waited for her to react somehow, but she kept glaring at him.

"Advanced alien technology, thousands of years beyond what anyone else can throw at me. Weapons? Vehicles? You name it." He was hoping she would challenge him, but she just sat, silently staring at the maps.

"And eventually, the rest of the world will be begging me for a piece of this 'high-tech beachfront property.' In fact, they'll pay through the nose for it."

Lois looked again at the map of the US with Luthor's continent encroaching it. "But millions of people will die."

"Billions." Luthor laughed again. "Once again the press underestimates me. This is front-page news, Miss Lane."

Luthor looked at his audience and saw they were all speechless now. Kitty had never heard his full plan before, and she stood next to him, staring at the crystal in his hand, her mouth open, her eyes blank.

Lex could see that Lois was putting it together at last. Maybe she wasn't as hopeless as he thought. "Come on," he said, baiting her. "Say it."

"You're insane."

Luthor shook his head, disappointed. "No. Not that. Come on. It's just dangling off the tip of your tongue. Say it."

It came out without her even thinking about it. "Superman will never let you—"

"Wrong!" he shouted.

He picked up a metal box that had been sitting on the table. He opened it, and a green glow washed over his face.

"What is that?" Lois asked.

Luthor grinned. "I think you know exactly what this is." He tilted the open box for her to see its contents. Kryptonite. It had been sheared to a sleek arrow-shaped form, with a hole in the center. She reached for it, but Luthor snapped the box shut again.

"Mind over muscle, Miss Lane. Mind over muscle. Don't you agree?"

She looked at Luthor, then turned to Jason, who was staring in a daze at the nasty man in the wig.

"Miss Lane," Luthor said again. "Don't you agree?"

Although Lois wasn't listening, she nodded anyway. She was worried about Jason, and about how he would wrap his mind around what he was hearing. Until now, she and Richard had protected him from the madmen of the world. And in that small and selected pantheon of evil, Luthor was unquestionably the highest of the high.

But Luthor didn't care if she was listening or not. All he needed was to hear words of agreement, sincere or not. "Good," he said, triumphant.

Grant's voice crackled over the intercom. "Mr. Luthor, we're approaching the coordinates."

Lex thought about it for a moment. "You're sure. Absolutely sure we're there?"

"Yes, sir," Grant replied after a moment. "Latitude thirty-nine degrees north, and longitude seventy-one degrees west. Just like you said."

Luthor smiled as he picked up the box with the kryptonite and walked to the stairs. He paused, turning back to Brutus.

"Don't let them out of this room," he ordered.

Brutus nodded. As Luthor left, Lois scribbled quickly on her pad. 39N71W.

It was an overcast sky for as far as anyone could see. In the distance, Metropolis was a speck on the horizon. As Lex and Kitty stepped onto the deck, he heard the engines shut off. They were there.

Taking a deep breath, he approached Grant, who was setting up a modified rocket launcher. Riley was recording everything as usual.

He moved in for a close shot of Luthor removing the kryptonite from one box, and a crystal from another. "All right, watch carefully now. I'm only doing this once." He inserted the small crystal into the hole Stanford had drilled into the kryptonite. There was a brief pulse of light as the two Kryptonian objects were brought together. "This is gonna be so good."

• • •

Lois was nervous as she watched Jason at the piano, starting "Heart and Soul" over again. She almost smiled and started to enjoy his playing, then she remembered where she was.

Brutus came over and sat next to Jason, startling him. "You're pretty good," Brutus said. Jason kept playing. A few seconds later, Brutus joined in. He wasn't very good, but he and Jason both seemed to be enjoying themselves. Lois looked again at the fax machine sitting on the desk, then at the coordinates she had scrawled on her pad. She quietly pulled the sheet loose and wrote the words, "Help Us! Lois Lane" under the latitude and longitude coordinates.

Brutus and Jason were engrossed in their music as Lois backed toward Luthor's desk and casually sat on its edge. With her hands behind her, she slid the paper into the fax machine feeder and pressed a button on the dial pad. It beeped. Her heart skipped as she turned back to see Brutus still playing alongside Jason, oblivious to the world around him.

She waited for the music to grow louder again and she dialed the Daily Planet fax number, then pressed SEND. She could hear the machine dialing and connecting. She looked back to Jason and Brutus, but they were too busy playing to care.

As the machine began to feed the paper through its scanner, she sat back and pretended to enjoy the show.

The sky was darkening, and the wind was starting to blow again. The temperature dropped rapidly. Luthor hurried, securing the kryptonite crystal into the modified rocket, then inserting that into the launcher.

"Ready, boss," Stanford said.

Luthor stepped back and gave the signal, watching closely as Sanford pressed the firing button, igniting the rocket. It sailed for several hundred feet, then began its descent, finally smashing into the water, right on target, disappearing under the surface, with only a slight green glow to mark its presence.

Inside the stateroom the lights flickered, then went dark. Lois heard an electronic cough and saw that the fax machine had died just before the part of the paper with her message had gone through. She wanted to scream with frustration, but she held it in. *Damn!*

"Mommy?" Jason cried out. "What's happening?" He ran to her, frightened, and she held him close. "Just another blackout. It'll be okay, hon. Don't worry."

On *The Gertrude*'s deck, Luthor heard the yacht's power sputter and die. "It's beginning," he said, picking up his binoculars, staring out to the ocean.

Twenty-Eight

Clark was nervously pacing by Lois's desk as Richard turned on her computer and waited an interminable ninety seconds for the startup to finish its cycle. "It's taking forever. Why doesn't she keep this thing on?"

"Maybe she's at the burger shop on Mercer Street," Clark said as he stared out the window, focusing his eyes to begin a long-distance sweep of the city, block by block if need be.

"She's a vegetarian," Richard stated flatly. He was getting anxious. *C'mon, you stupid machine. Bring me to the damn desktop.*

Clark turned to Richard. "Well, where's Jason's school? And wait, she is? Since when?"

"Three years now. Lincoln Avenue and West Twenty-Fourth Street." Clark turned back to the window and focused on the Lincoln Street area, beginning with the school, then moving out in concentric circles from there.

"Oh, and what color is the car?"

"Gunmetal gray. It's an Audi A3. Clark, what are you going to do, mount an aerial search?" The desktop finally opened, and he started to type. "Damn."

Clark turned to him, worried. "What?"

"She has a password."

He typed in the password space. *Jason. Richard. Lucy. Pulitzer. Planet.* "Damn. C'mon, something's got to work."

Richard turned as he heard Clark sigh. "Try 'Superman.'"

Richard bit his lip, then typed it in. He hit ENTER and the computer clicked and clacked, opening her hard drive. "Got it." He double-clicked the file marked "Current stories," and waited. The file began to open just as the power went out.

He slammed his fist against the desk and buried his head in his arms. "This is wrong. This is so wrong."

"No. She's fine. You know her. Nothing stops her." Clark found himself next to Richard, consoling him. "But sometimes she's forgetful, and when she's on a story, you know, nothing else matters."

"Yeah. Right," Richard said. "That's Lois in a nutshell. Only sometimes I think the nut's still in there with her. So we know she's fine. But if she is, why am I so scared?"

Clark sat staring at the blank computer screen, both of them quiet. There was nothing to say.

From space, the planet Earth looked like a dark, lifeless orb, floating listlessly through the cosmos, lit only by the reflected light of the full moon. Then, slowly, sweeping across the planet, lights began to blink on again.

• • •

In *The Gertrude*'s stateroom, Lois watched as the lights flickered on. She heard the fax machine powering up. "Jason," she said quickly and loudly enough to drown out its sound. "Why don't you play that song again. You need to keep up your practice. And that's a lot better piano than our keyboard."

"I don't think I want to. Can we go home now?"

Lois looked at Brutus, then back at her son. She put on the best smile she could for him. "Not yet, hon. Soon. C'mon, maybe he'll play with you again, too," indicating Brutus.

Brutus shrugged his massive shoulders. "Sure."

Jason reluctantly began to play as Lois watched the paper begin to feed through the machine again. This time she crossed her fingers.

Jason's playing reverberated under the ocean, providing background music for the kryptonite-laced crystal as it plunged deeper into the dark waters. Its bright green glow intensified, seeping out of the rocket shell, lighting up the ocean floor.

It was then that the crystal grew, melding with the kryptonite, shooting off new branches that pushed outward with greater and greater force. It expanded until the rocket housing shattered.

The kryptonite/crystal amalgam continued to grow and change as it disappeared into a deep chasm, sinking into the black murkiness of the ocean bed. A sudden blast of light lit up the sea for miles.

On the surface the blast was so bright that Luthor, Kitty, and Stanford covered their eyes. But Luthor was also basking in its brilliance.

This was it, Lex knew. The culmination of everything he had worked for since he was a young man, watching as his father unwittingly destroyed LuthorCorp, the company *his* father had founded in the mid 1940s, right after World War II. He had managed to smuggle out Germany's greatest scientists even before the two superpowers, Russia and the United States, could grab whoever was left. *And they thought Von Braun was something special.*

Alexander Luthor had a dream that he passed on to his grandson: "There were always winners and losers," he'd say. "Those with vision and those who were blind to the obvious. The Luthors would always control, never be controlled. If knowledge was power, power was *everything,* and the pursuit of power was man's noblest goal."

Lex thought his granddad had a cliché for every purpose, a homespun homily that usually stated the obvious in the most simplistic way possible, but he knew though the old man was way beyond crazy, he was also right.

The goal, Lex was taught, was to accumulate power. His grandfather had done it by having his Germans create the consumer boom of the 1950s. Mass market merchandising that would build up the newly emerging middle class while simultaneously plunging them hopelessly in debt. When they tried to bail themselves out, at 26 percent interest, Alex bought up their property and their land.

"Land, Lex, always go for land. It's the one thing they ain't making anymore."

Lex's father, passing along that same advice, also did his best to accumulate *what they ain't making no more of.*

Early on Lex realized he was on his own in this world. Oh, his father had left him a few million, a nest egg starter at best, but dear Dad has squandered or lost the rest of their fortune, something Lex swore would never happen to him.

He studied both science and business in college, manipulating his grades by putting the pressure on some geek to turn B-minuses into A's. He could have gotten the A's himself if he had wanted to—his genius dwarfed everyone else's in those hallowed halls, but as he never attended classes or took tests, he began with several strikes already against him. *Why need to confirm what I already know?*

Graduating at the head of his class, he gave the valedictory speech, starting with the fact that one day they'd all be working for him.

"Not only that," he told them, proudly posed behind the podium, addressing the confused audience, "but when that happens, you're all going to be earning far less than minimum wage. And eventually, when you all need your jobs the most, that's when I'll export the work to India or Taiwan or Korea or someplace else where I can exploit the workers and where protest is verboten. Thank goodness for dictatorships, I always say."

While his audience sat silent, their mouths hanging open in shock, he turned, walked off the stage, and never turned back.

Lex realized very early on how to play the game. If you look like a hustler, talk like a hustler, or smell like a hustler, there's no way people will let you hustle them. Their giant red flags will be hoisted high. But if you're brilliant, and he was, his 180 IQ was documented when he was only seven, and if you gave everyone a big smile and acted like you were one of them, well, then they'd never see you coming.

He had accumulated his first hundred million before he was twenty-five by snookering seventy-five of *Fortune*'s Hundred Richest Businessmen out of 20 percent of their fortunes.

"Rule of thumb. The rich always want more, and they're the first ones who love a get-rich-quick scheme when they think it will actually work." The pyramid scheme did work, of course, but only for the stocky, bald man standing at the very top. He had been well on his way to a fortune that would make Bill Gates's billions look like loose change, when Superman made his first big splash, saving the president's plane, then following that up by saving Lois Lane.

It all went downhill from there.

He had fame and fortune, but it was all taken away from him in less than one second by that . . . *alien*.

He was staring at the ocean, waiting, his impatience wearing thin. He checked his watch. "We're there, kiddies." He laughed.

As the light blasted its way into *The Gertrude*'s stateroom Lois protectively turned Jason away from the window and covered his eyes. "Mommy? Why is everything so bright?"

"I don't know, hon. But keep your eyes closed and don't look, okay?" She hugged him again and kissed the back of his head.

Brutus stood and saw the light was fading. "It's getting dark again. Maybe it was a meteor or something."

Lois nodded. *Yeah. A meteor. At least that won't frighten Jason any more than he already is. A meteor.*

Brutus sat down at the piano and tapped the bench a few times. Jason slid in next to him, and they began to play.

The sky was suddenly on fire with flashes of wild lightning. Kitty grabbed Luthor as thunder shook the yacht. She counted the seconds between the flashes and the explosions as she'd been taught as a kid. Whatever was going on out there was close, too close. The sky was a sheet of gray and storm clouds were rumbling overhead. A minute ago it had been clear.

"Lex, this isn't like the train set," she said, afraid, holding him even tighter.

"I know," he replied, overjoyed as he watched the spectacular light show that he had provided for their evening's entertainment.

There was another booming explosion, followed by more flashes of light. Pulsing cracks etched a path through the ocean floor, pushing up the loamy bottom soil, releasing a sea of bubbles that spread for miles in all directions. The ocean rumbled as the chasms grew wider and deeper.

Then the crystal pillars began to grow.

At first they were only inches thick, but as they grew layer upon layer, they expanded quickly until pillars hundreds of feet tall shot up out of the water. There were thousands of shoots, screaming as they grew, crisscrossing each other, forming intricate patterns as they jutted up from the ocean.

Luthor observed that the crystals somehow seemed alive, a warm, green glow was burning inside them, its lifeblood flowing through them, giving them its strength, urging them to grow higher and stronger, and, he knew, more deadly than anyone could suspect.

Belowdecks, Brutus and Jason were playing "Heart And Soul" one more time. They were off-key, but as long as it kept them busy, Lois didn't care. She hit the REDIAL on the fax machine and heard it connect. The paper began to slide through the machine again, this time slowly moving past the written coordinates and the "help us" line. Lois's name was just below that. It was just about to accept the rest of the document when the power died again.

Lois was confused. The lights in the cabin were still on. Only the fax machine seemed to be affected. She heard a noise and saw Brutus standing in front of her, holding the power cord, looking very angry.

"Hi. I was just, uhh, faxing my interview. You know, on Luthor? The one he gave me. You were there, remember?" She was grinning as if she had no idea that what she was doing was remotely wrong.

He disagreed. He threw her against the wall, then slammed her into a banister. She slumped to the floor.

Jason had stopped playing before Brutus grabbed Lois by the arm. His heart was jumping as Brutus stormed past him, angrily tromping toward his mother.

• • •

As Gil Truman quickly made his way across the editorial floor, he felt another painful twinge stabbing his stomach, just below the beltline. Suddenly, he let out a loud belch. The taste of that street-vendor hot dog returned, filling his mouth, making him want to throw up all over again.

He sat down, his face cold and clammy, breathing in slowly until the sudden chill that ran along his arms and legs slowly disappeared. He wiped himself off with his handkerchief, shook himself alert again, and headed back to his desk. *Memo to self: No more hot dogs.*

As he passed the fax machine he saw a new piece of paper slide off the roller and into the bin.

It was handwritten, and all it said was, "Help Us! 39N71W." He was still trying to make sense of it as he walked back into the editorial room.

"Smile," Jimmy Olsen said as Noel Arthur, the pretty brunette from classifieds, passed his desk on her way to dinner. She turned and gave him a wide grin as he took her picture.

"Hey. Can you print me a copy of that?" She gave him a look that said she wanted him to ask her out, but Jimmy was oblivious.

"Sure, I'll get you an eight-by-ten and a couple of wallet-sized, too. Thanks, Noel." Disappointed, she got into the elevator.

Jimmy adjusted his telescopic lens and caught Gil in it, about fifty feet away, looking strangely at a piece of paper in his hand. He adjusted the lens to bring the note into focus.

The note only had a few words on it, but the handwriting caught his eye. "My God."

He grabbed the paper out of Gil's hands and ran to Lois's desk. Richard and Clark were still there, navigating their way through her computer.

"Richard, you have to see this. I can't believe it."

Richard took the paper. "Where did you get this?"

Jimmy pointed to Gil. "It came through the fax. It's Lois's handwriting. I'd recognize it anywhere. But I don't know what it means."

"They're coordinates," Clark and Richard said simultaneously. They looked at each other, then back at the note.

"It's twenty miles off the coast," Richard said. "Jimmy, call the Coast Guard and tell Perry that I'm taking the seaplane." He got up to leave, but then hesitated. "Clark? Coming?"

Clark was still staring at the numbers. He turned to Richard as his hand reached for his stomach. "No, planes make me sick. I'll stay here and keep an eye on things just in case."

Richard nodded and gave him a brief smile.

Clark waited until he was gone, then got up and made his way to the elevators. "Jimmy, I'm going to get some air," he said.

He stepped into the elevator and waited for the doors to slide shut. The elevator began to rise. His X-ray vision checked the next three floors and saw nobody had called for the car.

He pulled open his shirt, revealing the Kryptonian crest beneath it. In a single swift movement, his clothes seemed to fall off him. He pressed them into a paper thin sheet and tucked them into his cape pocket as he flew up through the elevator emergency roof hatch, into the shaft, and finally blasted out of the rooftop door and into the sky.

Twenty-Nine

The city passed under Superman like a blur. He could hear a million voices filling the streets, but they were a jumble of discordant sounds, noises without substance. His thoughts were elsewhere. Troubled.

He kept going over the fax in his mind. Lois wrote only two words. "Help us." She said "us." That meant she was probably with Jason. They were together. That was good.

But "Help." It meant wherever she was, she didn't want to be there. She had sent them a fax. That meant she hadn't found herself stranded on some deserted island somewhere. She was someplace that had a fax machine and electricity. Based on the coordinates she sent, that meant she had to be on a boat or ship.

He was soaring over the ocean, using his telescopic vision to search ahead. If she was out there, he knew he'd find her.

But he was still worried. If she was looking for help, it was obvious she didn't want to be wherever she was.

Had she and Jason been kidnapped? If so, by whom? And why?

He knew Richard was already on the way home, where the seaplane was gassed up and waiting for him. He knew Richard was nervous; his heartbeat was thumping wildly as he read the fax. Without powers, or even knowing exactly what he was heading into, Richard had gone off to rescue the family he loved.

Lois had found herself a new hero.

Richard was Perry's nephew, a good man with a good heart. He remembered the times when Perry mentioned his nephew, years before they met, years before Superman left for Krypton, leaving the Earth, and Lois, behind. Perry rarely if ever gushed, but he admired Richard, not because they were related but because of what Richard had made of his life.

He had seen them separately and he saw them together, and as painful as it was for him, he had to realize, he had to accept, that he no longer had a place in her life. That was asking a lot of him, more than he was sure he could handle.

He wondered what the past years of his life were about. What had gone so wrong that he was looking into space for a home? What should it have mattered to him that scientists believed Krypton was still alive? He had no real memories of that place. Everything he had known about it had come from Jor-El's lectures. It shouldn't have had any lure for him. So why did he forsake everything he had to reach for something he never thought he missed?

Below him dolphins were dancing across the waves, calling to each other, clinging together as they made their way to wherever they were going. Beneath the surface he could see schools of fish swimming close together for mutual protection as they made their way through the currents.

Suddenly, he saw them panic and scatter. It took a moment longer for him to hear the strange rumbling building deep under the brackish waters. There was a loud cracking explosion.

He saw that the ocean floor had ruptured as if on a fault line, releasing black dust that scattered into the icy cold. He watched as the rupture continued to spread, creating giant fissures in the floor. A great trench opened and expanded, pushing past Superman, heading toward Metropolis.

He stared toward the horizon; Lois was somewhere out there, in trouble, needing his help. But he saw the trench splintering the earth as it relentlessly cut its way toward the coastline. When it hit he knew it would be the most devastating earthquake the continent—any continent—had ever suffered.

He looked up again to the horizon. Torn.

Lois ran to the pool table, darting around it to keep it between her and Brutus. There was a dark rage burning in his dull eyes, and it scared her. She grabbed Jason and shoved him behind her.

"Mommy."

"Stay with me," she ordered. He had no intention of leaving.

Brutus clambered over the table. She grabbed the pool cue and slammed him hard with it across the face. He reacted for a moment, thought about whether it hurt or not, then shrugged it off. She swung again. It cut across his cheek, and blood began to trickle out. On the third swipe, he caught the cue and pulled it and her to him. He grabbed her neck with his free hand.

Out of the corner of her eyes, Lois could see Jason, cowering in the corner, frozen in fear, wheezing, trying to breathe as his nasal passageways shrank, slowing the flow of air to his lungs. *My God, his asthma.*

She kneed Brutus and slammed him with her fists, but like the cue, they had no effect. The man was a monster. She tried to squirm free, but he smashed his palm into her gut, and she collapsed, breathless, to her knees.

He stood over her, laughing as she tried to catch her breath. He picked her up and threw her across the room into a shelf of books. The books scattered as she slumped to the floor, barely conscious.

He stood over her, the cue high over his head, ready to come down hard on her.

She thrust her feet out again, but this time she wasn't trying to hurt him. She used his massive legs as the immovable post they were to push herself backward, closer to the bookcase. As he raised the cue over his head again, she grabbed the bookcase and pulled, tipping it over.

Brutus looked up just as it smashed down on top of him, cracking his neck. He fell to his knees, wobbled a few times, then fell face-first onto the polished wood floors.

Jason was staring at his mother, still paralyzed with fear, gasping for breath. He grabbed his inhaler, took a hit off it, then rushed to her as she was rising to her feet.

"Mommy," he cried, terrified.

"I'm okay. I'm fine," she said, cradling him, trying to calm him down so he could control his breath. "That man was so bad, and you were so brave, honey. I'm proud of you. And we're okay now."

She didn't believe it for a second, but she hoped he did.

Her legs were bruised and a little bloodied, and it was painful to stand. She took Jason by the hand and led him outside into the corridor. Somehow, she knew, they had to get off the boat.

She heard Riley and Grant heading down the stairs, and she ducked to the side. She turned to Jason and put a finger to her lips. *Shhhh*. Though frightened, he nodded. *Good boy*.

"Grant?" Riley said, pointing to Brutus's feet poking out from under the fallen bookcase. Grant turned and saw Lois and Jason cowering under the stairs.

"Big mistake, lady," Grant said, as Riley grabbed Jason and shoved him into a long, narrow pantry. A moment later Grant pushed Lois inside.

"Please. Let him go. He can't hurt you."

"Not gonna happen." She heard them lock the door. "Just a little suggestion. Stay put. Next time I see you, you're dead. And your brat, too."

"You can't do this. Let us out of here! Please." Lois was hammering on the door, shouting even as she heard them pounding up the stairs again.

"Can't you keep this stupid thing steady, Lex?" Kitty said as *The Gertrude* rocked back and forth, sending her falling port to starboard. Luthor ignored her as he continued to look at the sonar screen displaying the strange structures that were forming under the ocean.

He saw Riley and Grant step onto the deck. "Where's Brutus? I may need his muscles."

"There was a little problem downstairs. Brutus won't be joining us," said Grant.

Lex shrugged. *Easy come. Easy go.* "And where are they?"

"Locked up. In the pantry."

Luthor glanced down at the sonar image and saw that the structures were growing even larger and faster. His plans were almost complete, and the decision what to do with Lane and her son was made for him.

"Get the helicopter ready," he said.

He turned to the counter where Stanford had dismantled the missile, and opened a drawer and took something from it. He removed the monogrammed handkerchief from his pocket, placed the mysterious something into it, folded it over, then headed down the stairs toward the stateroom.

He saw his desk and the shattered bookcase with Brutus still lying underneath it. Luthor scooped up the remaining kryptonite crystals and made his way down the corridor. He unlocked the pantry door and greeted Lois and Jason, both cowering in the corner, her arms protectively around her son. Luthor winked at him.

"Catch," he said as he tossed the folded-over handkerchief to them. It fell to the floor and rolled to Jason's feet.

Lois tried to grab the door before Luthor slammed it shut, but she was seconds too late. She turned back to see Jason holding Lex's handkerchief. He had opened it, revealing the explosives Stanford had taken from the missiles.

Lois's eyes widened in terror. "Honey, don't move," she ordered. Jason didn't.

Luthor chuckled as he made his way back up the spiral

staircase. He saw the shadow of the helicopter blades spinning. "Like clockwork," he said to himself. He climbed inside the copter and buckled himself in.

"Home, James. My new home, that is."

As they rose, he took one last look at the beautiful yacht resting calmly in the sea below. "Gertrude, I hardly knew ye," he said, laughing.

The ocean floor was a bubbling black dust road map as the ground rupture continued to spiderweb in all directions. The crystals were regenerating, doubling in size nearly every five minutes, the structure's speed increasing even more as it entered the warm shallow waters of the Metropolis shoreline.

PART THREE

WORLDS IN COLLISION

Thirty

The city's day began pretty much like all the others. There were massive traffic jams on the 595 from the suburbs into the city. A twenty-minute weekend trip expanded as always into an hour-and-a-half endurance test. The Metro was packed before it left its first station, and the straphangers knew there would be no relief until it clattered its way to Center Square, only twenty miles away.

By early morning the city was crowded with workers, shoppers, and tourists. Restaurants had opened at six for the breakfast crowd and wouldn't close again until long after midnight, their workers alternating eight-hour shifts.

The museums opened at ten, while movie theaters would begin their first show at noon.

That was, at least, the plan.

By the time the first quake hit, more than 9 million people had packed themselves into a city that could comfortably fit only 4 million. But this was what living in Metropolis was all about.

There were, as always, complaints about the noise, about the traffic, about the sheer congestion of *everything;* but at the same time there was little talk of leaving. If you were born in Metropolis, you stayed there because you could never find another city that could rival it. If you were born elsewhere, moving to it was more than a lifestyle change. It was like a knight's knowing there was no reason to exist outside of Camelot.

The first indication of the impending disaster was the low rumble that seemed to be coming from everywhere at once. Most thought it was the subway system, the Metro trains speeding along underground, the sound of their wheels grinding along the tracks, escaping up through the street vents along with trails of smoke and the smell of things unholy.

But the rumbling continued to deepen instead of disappearing into the distance as the trains crawled toward their final destinations. Windows were rattling, then shattering, glass shards were showering the city streets.

Then the Wannamaker Building, built by those two eccentric brothers in 1937, John and Jonathan, began to sway.

Perry had been studying Lois's fax before the quake hit the Planet. "What are these, lottery numbers?" he wondered. The lights flickered, and Perry looked up, angry all over again. "Christ, not another blackout."

Jimmy heard a car alarm outside. He wasn't worried. Happened all the time. But within a matter of minutes the streets became a horrible chorus of alarms.

That was when the first rumble hit the Planet building,

shaking it like a kid spraying a soda can just to see what would come gushing out.

The awards in Perry's office pulled loose from the walls and fell to the floor, breaking. He screamed into the bullpen. "Someone better be covering this. Olsen, get out there and get pictures!"

But Jimmy had run under the doorway; he'd seen a documentary on earthquakes on the Discovery Channel and remembered the instructions. He held on to the jambs for support.

"Chief," he shouted. "I don't think this is just another blackout."

In the shaking, nobody noticed, but the lights had gone out again, and the computers were down.

Perry pulled himself up from his desk and, edging against the wall, made his way to the bullpen. The staff was nervously checking their areas, looking for damage.

He wondered if Lois had been right all along. Maybe the blackout was the story and Superman the sidebar, the under-the-fold item that was continued on page 98 in section C.

Jimmy kept his balance as he rushed to the window and looked out over the Metropolis skyline. He heard glass shattering across the city and saw chunks of debris falling everywhere.

Skyscrapers were shaking, first in the distance, by the piers, then fanning out from there, moving toward midtown, heading for them.

"Chief?" He turned to see Perry holding on to his desk as the room shook again. "I don't know how, but I think this is some kind of earthquake, and it's coming this way."

"Olsen, that's not the way earthquakes move."

"Yeah, I know. They also don't last this long, either."

Jimmy heard glass shatter. The family photos had fallen off Lois's desk.

"Oh, no. Lois is going to . . ." He stopped, wondering if Richard had found her yet.

He turned in time to see Polly swaying back and forth as her chair wheeled her across the floor, past Gil, who was hunkering under his desk. Jimmy wasn't sure, but he thought Gil was praying. He heard another crash behind him. The world time clocks had broken loose from their anchors.

That was when Jimmy Olsen saw the Wannamaker Building collapse.

The shock wave continued to spread. Building wreckage and broken glass exploded over the crowds.

Superman had just passed the Wannamaker Building when he saw a tower quiver, then collapse. He arced back toward the tower and flipped himself over, flying with his back to the ground.

He swooped under the falling debris and focused his eyes up at it. The air between them began to ripple and glow red as his heat vision created a light as bright as the sun. On the streets, people ran in fear, covering their eyes from the burning intensity.

The shower of steel and glass started to melt, becoming fiery liquid drops. He increased the heat, reducing them to harmless bits of ash and ember.

Suddenly, Superman was gone. He appeared halfway across town where the rope straps holding a construction worker safely to the side of a building snapped in half. Superman caught him in midair and brought him safely to the roof.

He heard screams coming from the street and saw passersby trying to pull a young man from a burning, overturned car. He flipped himself over again and streaked down, breathing in deeply, expanding his cheeks. As he streaked past the car, the people heard a sudden *WHOOSH* and saw that the fire had been extinguished, and the car was covered with a layer of frost.

Perry held on to the wall as he called his staff together. "Much as I hate to say it, Olsen's right. This isn't a blackout. So everyone stay down. Don't be a hero. Protect yourselves, and hopefully this will pass." The room shook again.

Perry followed his own advice and fell to the floor, then crawled under the closest desk. He thought of his wife, his children, and his grandchildren, and hoped that he would see them all again soon.

He had been working in newspapers, in one capacity or another, since he was nine. Back then it was in delivery, loading up his bike's basket with each morning edition and distributing the papers as he made his way to school. He got his first real job at fifteen by lying to George Taylor, editor of Cleveland's *Daily Star.* "Yessir!" he said. "I'm eighteen. Almost nineteen, sir. Next month. And I can do this job better than anyone else you can get for the money you're paying."

Perry wasn't sure if Taylor had believed him, but back

then nobody seemed to care much as long as he didn't get in the way. Taylor liked his writing samples and found him brash and capable, a good beginning. The kid had talent, and no matter how old he really was, was going to go far.

High blood pressure kept him out of the army, so once he was actually eighteen, he took a job with a London paper, which took him throughout Europe and Asia. He honed his skills working alongside some of the legendary foreign correspondents, all more than willing, at least after a drink or four, to help the new kid learn how to put together a story.

They taught him how to get the best answers during an interview, even with the most reticent interviewees. They showed him how to frame a story, to find its core, the nugget that made it special, then how to build on its theme. They explained how to lure the readers in, how to keep their attention, and, most importantly, how to end the piece.

Perry's descriptive writing brought him to the attention of several New York publishers. At twenty-two he wrote a book about his early correspondent days that made him a *New York Times* best-selling author. By thirty-four, with six more books to his name, married and with a kid about to enter second grade, and another on the way, he realized for his family's sake it was time to stop traveling. He accepted an assistant editor's job at the *Daily Planet*. Twelve years later he was named editor.

Perry saw Jimmy staring blankly out the window as a distant explosion shook him out of his reverie. He reached for his camera and began snapping photographs. *If the kid ever gets his head screwed on right, he might make it. He's got an eye, no doubt about it. What he needs is a brain to go with it.*

Jimmy wasn't certain if he'd survive the day or if there would be anyone left to download his pictures and print them, but as long as he could brace himself in front of the window, he was going to record the devastation as best he could.

He heard cries coming up from the street, and they broke his heart. Everyone was afraid, afraid of what was happening, afraid that there was no escape, afraid they wouldn't see their loved ones again.

Jimmy closed in on the faces of people. There was a scared middle-aged man standing in the street, not knowing what to do. A boy of twelve or so was helping an elderly woman. A young mother was sitting on the sidewalk, hugging her baby close to her. He heard his camera clicking away photo after photo until he had to reach into his shirt pocket and take out another memory card.

The people's faces told the story of Metropolis. They were afraid, of course, but they were determined, too, to make it back to their homes, to see their friends, their parents, their wives, their husbands, their children.

He snapped an uncountable number of photos of people helping others even as they were desperate to get out of the line of danger themselves. In that instant, when Hell seemed to be taking control, he saw the moments of kindness and caring that newspapers, yes, even the *Daily Planet,* all too often forgot to remind its readers was out there, still alive in people's hearts.

But the tragedy was overwhelming. He saw what

looked like a visual shock wave tearing through the streets, then traveling up the Planet building. As it rose higher it was shattering windows. First floor. Second floor. Third floor. Jimmy ducked as glass exploded all around him.

He waited, then repositioned himself in front of the window again. He heard screaming and saw the gas mains explode up and down Fifth Avenue. Electrical fires were sparking and exploding across the city. Green flares fireworked into the darkening sky as transmitter after transmitter fell and died.

Another wave struck the building and Jimmy fell. He wrapped his arms around his camera and let his back take the impact.

The shock wave moved up to their floor, cracking the Planet's ram's head gargoyles that had stood as silent protectors ever since this latest and last building was dedicated in June of 1938, 163 years after its founding. The wave continued past them, heading toward the roof.

He heard the crack of concrete and steel. It was the base the Daily Planet's art deco globe had perched on since that first day when Jack Mayer, then the *Planet*'s publisher, flipped the switch and turned on its lights. Since that day it had stood bravely against hurricanes and other disasters, but now the globe precariously teetered as the building swayed.

He saw shock waves ripple through the room, tearing up the flooring, knocking down cubicle walls, sending desk accessories flying in every direction.

The floor seemed to rise and fall like a wave. Monitors sparked and exploded. Overhead lights wrenched themselves loose from their ceiling brackets. Nothing was left standing.

And then, as Jimmy was struggling across the room toward Noel, who was trapped under a desk, calling for help, the rumbling stopped. For a long while, nothing moved. The room was quiet.

Jimmy pulled Noel out from under the desk, then ran back toward Perry's office.

Perry had struggled back to his feet and surveyed the damage. "Okay, everyone," he said. "Let's stay put and stay calm."

Jimmy saw one of the ram's heads outside the editorial office window crack. "Uhh, Chief . . . ?" he called.

Perry glared at him. "Olsen, don't call me—" He turned just in time to see the ram's head break loose and fall. He turned back to the bullpen.

"Okay, everyone, change of plans. Nice and orderly. Down the stairs. Move."

Superman was hovering unseen above the clouds as he sorted through the cries of the city. He was needed everywhere, and it was tearing him apart. He heard an explosive *WHUMPHHH* and with his telescopic vision saw a fifteen-foot geyser of flame gush up from a cracked gas main.

If anyone had been looking, they would have seen a red-and-blue blur streak across the city, flying no higher than ten feet off the ground, navigating through a tangle of buildings that he realized had been built in the five years since he'd been gone. *They've blocked off some of my best routes.*

The geyser exploded again, sending great gulps of fire into the sky. Superman heard another series of cries and screams and saw an apartment building, less than a mile away, on fire, nearly a dozen people trapped on its roof, pleading for help. He could see that the closest fire engine was only two miles away, but it had fallen into a crooked ravine that had suddenly split the road apart as it was responding to still another emergency.

He rocketed past the geyser, effortlessly blowing it out like a birthday candle.

He spun around and headed for the apartment building. "Grab onto whatever you can and don't let go." Concentrating on the blaze, Superman focused his superbreath. Eleven seconds later, the fire was gone.

He sighed, allowing himself a momentary respite. *This isn't going to stop, is it?* He swooped back to the fire engine he'd seen and pulled it onto the street. The firemen offered their thanks, but he was already gone.

He had heard a cracking sound coming from midtown. Already wary, he saw the Daily Planet globe teetering on its shattered base, then, suddenly, falling. It crashed onto the rooftop, rolled, then smashed into the water tower. It kept rolling toward the building edge.

He straightened himself, then used his arm like a swimmer to adjust his course. In less than a second he was speeding through the sky again, heading back to the Daily Planet.

Jimmy Olsen had run out ahead of the Planet staff streaming out of the building. He was already taking photos when they poured into the streets. He kept backing up and fell over one of the broken ram's heads.

He was looking up now, his eyes widening with horror.

Perry felt drops of water from above. *Don't tell me. On top of everything else, it's raining?* He looked up just in time to see the Planet's globe tumble over the side of the building. "Great Caesar's Ghost," he said quietly to himself.

The globe slammed into the side of the building as it made its way toward the ground.

Superman was less than a half mile away, keeping his eyes on the globe. It had fallen out of view.

He whipped around buildings, winding his way through the city, flying faster than he ever had.

He crashed through a window and, without stopping, continued through the empty office—smashing his way through walls without pause.

The globe was only seconds away from crashing into the crowd. He saw Jimmy, on his back, taking more photos when he should have been running to safety. He was directly under the falling globe. *SNAP SNAP SNAP.*

Superman swooped down to just below the globe. He was hovering a dozen feet above Jimmy as he caught it. The momentum tried to push him down, but he struggled, holding his position.

He lowered the globe on his shoulders; *Atlas holding the Earth,* Jimmy thought. Superman was perfectly framed in his viewfinder, looking every inch the hero he was. He snapped the picture.

Superman set down the globe and allowed himself a moment to exhale, exhausted and spent.

Perry White pushed through the gawking crowd. "Superman, Perry White, *Daily Planet.* What the hell just happened?"

He was still trying to catch his breath when he heard more rumbling in the distance. It was something much larger than the shock wave that had just hit Metropolis. He realized this wasn't over.

"I'm not sure, but I'm going to find out."

He began to rise when Perry called to him again. "Wait. Lois is missing."

Superman looked at him for only a second. "I know."

And then he was gone.

The crystals kept growing. They filled in the original rupture heading for the coastline, and Metropolis.

From his helicopter, Luthor watched as they rose from the ocean floor, adding new layers, increasing its mass, feeding its own growth. Like an insatiable predator, it would soon destroy anything it came across.

The crystal superstructure broke the ocean surface, growing larger and larger by the second.

Thirty-One

The waves had slammed into *The Gertrude,* nearly overturning it. But Lois held Jason until the ship finally settled
into an eerily calming rocking motion.

"Mommy, is it over? Are we okay?"

"You're doing great, honey. I can't believe how brave
you were." She saw him nervously smile at her, then she
kissed his cheeks and blew into them, making a terribly
rude noise. He laughed, and she relaxed her grip as his
breathing slowly returned to normal.

And now to deal with Luthor's explosives.

"Okay, sweetie, you know that thing in the handkerchief you're holding? Well, it's very bad, and we have to
get rid of it. So while you keep standing still, not moving,
I'm going to keep hitting that porthole—you see it?—
until it breaks. Then we'll throw the bad thing away. You
understand?"

"Yeah," he said, nervous but willing to go along.

"Great. So here's what I'm going to do, honey. I'm

going to pretend it's like the *Whack-a-Wabbit* at the county fair Daddy and I took you to. You remember that?" He nodded, smiling.

"Great. But instead of using a hammer, I'm going to hit it with my hands as hard as I can."

He was staring earnestly at her as she pounded at the glass, over and over.

"It's not breaking," he said after a while.

She stopped. The porthole didn't even have the courtesy of scratching. "Yeah, you're right. Okay, we've got to find something else."

"Mommy, what's that?" Jason was looking at an air conditioner grating on the floor, partially hidden under some boxes.

"Good eyes, sweetie," Lois said as she knelt and pulled at the vent cover. It was bolted firmly in place and wouldn't loosen. She looked around the small room. *I'm in a kitchen pantry. There's got to be tools here.* She saw a large metal soup ladle hanging from one of a series of hooks on the far wall.

Jason watched, amazed, as his mother used the ladle like a crowbar, jamming it into the vent. He could see the panic on her face and wanted to help. "Mommy," he called, moving to her.

"Jason. Don't," she screamed, quickly regaining control. "Just stay where you are, okay, honey?" he nodded, knowing what he had to do.

"Sorry, Mom."

"Don't be. You were just trying to help. I love you, sweetie. I love you so much."

It still amazed her when she thought about how much he had changed her. She looked at him, thinking how beautiful he was and how, in such a very short time, he had become the most important thing in her life.

She strained to pry the vent loose. The ladle began to bend under the pressure, but then, as she was about to quit, the cover popped off. She looked back at her son, obviously afraid, but still not moving. *God, what he's going through, and it's all my fault.*

She wanted to cry, but knew she couldn't. There'd be plenty of time for that later.

"Remember, honey, I need you to stay still. Don't move," she said, as he started to step toward her again. She saw him freeze like in a game of "Red Light, Green Light." *Good kid. The best.* "I'm going to take it from you now. So be ready to run to the other side of the room."

She stared at the explosive in her hands as if taking her eyes away from it now, even for an instant, would cause it to detonate.

She leaned over the duct and threw it inside. Then she jumped, grabbed Jason, and pushed him to the other side of the pantry, her back to the vent, shielding him from the explosion she knew was coming.

She began counting quietly to herself. *One. Two. Three . . .*

There was a series of dull clanging sounds as it dropped through the air duct. The noise gradually faded as it fell farther and farther away.

Eight. Nine. Ten . . .

Then there was silence.

Eighteen. Nineteen. Twenty.

She waited, still holding on to him, a prize more precious than anything she had ever had before.

Twenty-seven. Twenty-eight.

Silence.

Twenty-nine.

She opened her eyes as he opened his. She let out a heavy sigh . . .

Thirty.

. . . just as they both heard the terrifying explosion.

The yacht jerked upward, throwing them both across the small room. Boxes and utensils, cans of food and cleaning supplies, bottles of water and miscellaneous nonsense that was stored there for years and long since forgotten, exploded off their shelves like so much kitchen shrapnel.

The Gertrude wouldn't stop rocking as the hull ruptured, creating a huge gaping hole in the ship's belly.

A burst of flame shot up from the vent. Lois grabbed Jason again and pushed him down protectively.

"Mommy," he cried. She held on to him tighter now, afraid to let go. "Are we going to die?"

"No. That's not going to happen. I've got you, Jason. And you've got to know I won't let anything happen to you. I promise."

She knew she was lying, but she was his mother, and her only thoughts were of him, about keeping him calm, about finding a way, any way, to help him survive this insanity.

The flames quickly subsided, but then a geyser of seawater crashed through the vent. The ship was half-submerged and sinking fast. She tried to open the door again, thinking its lock might have been damaged in the blast. But it was still locked from the outside and wouldn't budge.

Then the lights went out.

"Mommy, what's happening?" She heard his breath beginning to labor again.

"It's just the lights, sweetie. It's okay. Just stay with me. We're going to get through this, you trust me, don't you?"

He nodded. "I do."

"Right, so just do everything I say, and we'll be fine." She took his hand and made little swirls in his palm with her finger. It tickled him and he laughed and she heard his breathing return to normal again.

The yacht suddenly tipped over, sending them falling against the wall again. The loose supplies cannoned into them. Water streamed up through the vent and threw Lois back, away from Jason. She saw him floundering, then he grabbed on to a cabinet shelf bolted to the wall. "Jason, hang on to that, honey. Don't let go," she screamed.

She saw him begin to cry. He fought away the tears.

She tried to crawl to him but she couldn't move. Her leg was tangled in the rope of a life preserver. *Talk about irony.* "Honey, my foot's stuck. So stay put while I try to free myself, okay?"

"Hurry, Mommy," he pleaded.

The water was up to her chest. She kept pulling at her leg but was unable to untangle it.

She heard him starting to hyperventilate again. *Oh, no, not now.* "Honey, find your inhaler. It should be in your pocket. Use it now."

He struggled to find it, checking his pockets, then frantically checking them again. "Mommy, it's not there." He began to breathe harder, wheezing uncontrollably.

"I know how scary this is, Jason, but try to calm yourself down. Everything's going to be okay. We're going to be fine. Jason. Look at me. Don't think of anything else.

Just look at me." She had to distract him, to get his mind off his breathing. *He's being so brave, but I don't know what to do.*

The seawater kept rising as it flooded through the vent and into the pantry.

He saw her fighting to stay above water. She was shouting for help. He saw the water flooding into her mouth a moment before she disappeared under the surface. He started to panic but then realized he had to help her.

Jason tried to swim for her, but *The Gertrude* shook again, and he fell back. He grabbed the shelf, steadying himself. He felt his throat tighten, and he knew he was going to have another attack unless he helped himself.

He concentrated on finding his mother, lost in the dark water. He looked for bubbles rising to the surface. He saw her, a shadow under the water, her arms frantically waving, trying to pull herself up but still stuck below.

Then he heard something from outside and saw the pantry door rip open. There was a man standing there, in the dark, but Jason couldn't see who it was. The man stepped into the room, then dived underwater.

The man saw Lois struggling, panicking, her face filled with fear. He dived lower and pulled the rope from around her legs. He grabbed her by the waist and hoisted her up into the air, pushing her back to the dry side of the pantry.

Lois was gulping in air as she saw the dark silhouette in front of her. She couldn't see him clearly yet, but she knew who it had to be.

He was holding a flashlight, and its light caught his face.

Richard White grinned at her, then saw Jason clinging desperately to the shelf on the other side of the room. The water was up to his neck.

"Hang on, Jason. I'm here."

"Daddy." He saw his father reach out a hand, and he grabbed it tightly. Richard tugged him in, holding him firmly.

Lois stared at him, not fully comprehending what she was looking at. "How? How did you get here?"

He looked at her with a curious smile. "I flew."

As they heard another rumble, the ship shook again. The water under the yacht was churning and bubbling. And something dark under that was moving.

"Can you walk?" Richard asked her. She nodded, still not sure where she was or what was happening. *It's Richard, but how can he be here? How did he find us? I'm dreaming, aren't I?*

"Good," he said. "I've got Jason. The seaplane's just outside. Let's go." But Lois was staring back into the pantry, listening to the growing rumble that seemed to be coming closer and closer.

Richard saw her hesitating. "I can't let you alone for five minutes. What have you gotten yourself into now?" he asked lightly.

She turned back to him. "Don't blame me. This is Lex Luthor's mess."

"Luthor?"

They heard a heavy metallic groan, then the ship lurched again. But this time it was moving up.

"What in hell?"

Lois knew what was happening. "Richard, grab on to something. Hurry."

She held on to Jason as a huge crystal column wrenched

itself up out of the water, then impaled the bottom of the yacht, piercing the hull, pushing up to the ceiling, then through it.

The pantry tipped upward as Lois, Richard, and Jason clung to each other. "Luthor? My God. What did he do?" Richard shouted over the groaning rumble.

Lois stared at him, shaking her head. "Trust me, right now you don't want to know. Let's get out of here. Please."

The crystal shaft easily lifted *The Gertrude* up out of the water. Lois gripped Richard's arm as he held on to both her and Jason. The yacht shook again, and the seawater that had nearly swallowed her seconds before, poured out the door.

"C'mon," Richard shouted. "We can make it to the plane." He turned to Jason, smiling encouragingly. "You're doing great. I'm so proud of you." Jason held on tight and tried to smile back.

Lois held on to Richard's hand. "You should have seen him, Richard. You wouldn't believe how good he was."

She heard a shrill cracking as the yacht's bow snapped and broke away from its crystal perch, then sank back under the water.

They held on as the ship's stern tumbled off the spike and landed flat on the ocean surface. It floated, but just barely. They fell to the back of the room as the pantry tipped under the surface and seawater rushed into it again.

Through the open door she could see the yacht had been sheared in half. The water was quickly filling the small room, crashing against the door, shoving it closed. "Richard!" she shouted. "Get the door."

She struggled to keep it open, pushing with all her

strength against the crashing waves that kept pouring over her.

"Lois, wait. Don't." Richard tried to yank her back, but the door slammed into her, smashing her head. She fell back, unconscious, next to Richard and Jason.

Richard was suddenly afraid. He grabbed her with one hand and held Jason with the other as water poured in around them, filling the room. There was only a foot or so of air above their heads, and the sea was quickly rushing in to fill that already slender gap.

The broken hull sank into the ocean, joining the other chunks of debris. The only sign of life was the beam of light from Richard's flashlight shining through one of the portholes.

Water filled the room to the ceiling. Richard held Lois and Jason close to him. He kissed Lois on the forehead, then did the same with Jason as he waited for the end to come.

He heard a booming sound from just outside the room but knew he was fantasizing. Then he saw two shafts of red moving outside the porthole. Through the murky water he tried to make sense of what he was seeing. *Are they feet? Red feet?* He knew he was dreaming. *Is this what people see before they die. But why red feet?*

Then he saw a face peeking through the small window. Superman.

He felt Superman's hands grab hold of the pantry, then water began to pour out of the porthole. They were rising as murky water gave way to gray clouds. Through the porthole Richard could see a stormy, dark sky.

He heard the door pulled off its hinges and saw Superman lean inside, his left hand extended.

"Give her to me, then take my hand," he said calmly.

Superman cradled Lois in his arms as Richard smiled at Jason. "We're safe now." With his free hand, Richard grabbed Superman's arm.

"Got us?"

"Got you," Superman said.

Superman opened his right hand and let go of the broken hull. It slid back, silently disappearing into its watery grave.

The seaplane bobbed on the surface. Superman was still cradling Lois as he landed on one of its pontoons. He saw Richard set Jason down inside it, then quickly placed her next to him.

She wasn't moving. Richard looked up at Superman, panicking. "Is she—?"

Superman's eyes were already focusing on her. After a few moments he looked up and shook his head. "No. She'll be fine."

The seaplane shook as a blast of wind hit them. Richard grabbed Jason again.

"What the hell's going on?"

Superman was concentrating, staring into the ocean. "That's what I'm hoping to find out. Take her. Hold on to them both," he shouted. Richard grabbed Lois as Jason held on to him.

"Superman," Richard shouted. "Lois said Lex Luthor did this. But how? How is any of this possible?"

Superman grimaced. "Luthor? I should have known. He just won't go away, will he?"

"What does it mean?"

"He's sick and twisted. Whatever he's up to is worse than anything we could imagine."

Superman was trying to steady the seaplane when the ocean started to bubble. Without warning, waves smashed at them, tossing the plane.

"Don't let go," Superman shouted, staring into the water. "In about two seconds it's going to get a lot worse."

Crystal shoots tore through the waves. As they hit the open air they began to grow even faster. Hundreds of immense crystal columns, each one larger than any man-made tower, wrenched their way into the sky, displacing the water, forcing waves that crashed over the seaplane, then continued on toward Metropolis.

Superman struggled but held the plane steady.

They stared, awestruck, as even more crystal columns roared their way up through the turbulent waters.

Jason held on to his mother as he looked again at Superman. His face, lean and taut, looked familiar. "Hey, you know, you look just like—"

"Can you fly?" Superman said to Richard, cutting Jason off.

Richard remembered where he was. "What?"

"Can you fly Lois and Jason out of here?"

The waves kept smashing at the plane, nearly overturning it. "I can't take off in this."

"I'll help." Another wave crashed into them. Superman pushed against the seaplane, steadying it. "Just promise me you won't come back."

"I won't. I promise."

Jason scrambled into the backseat as Superman buckled Lois in.

Richard took the controls. "We're ready," he said.

Superman stepped off the seaplane and floated in front of it. "Hey. Wait." Richard called to him. Superman turned back as Richard gestured toward Jason and Lois, still unconscious. "Thank you."

Superman nodded, then dived into the water.

Richard started the engine as he called back to Jason. "You strapped in?"

"Yeah," Jason said, holding on to his mother.

"Good boy."

The seaplane started to rise. Richard couldn't see him, but he knew Superman was under them, lifting them out of the water, above the waves. They kept rising until the crystal columns were below them. All they could see now was a dark sky.

The seaplane jerked forward, dropped for an instant, then rose again. Richard was now in control.

He saw Superman hovering behind him and gave him a quick salute, then took off through the maze of rising crystals. *Metropolis is only twenty miles away,* he thought. *But what do we do when we get there?*

Lois was still unconscious in the backseat. Richard saw Jason staring at the columns that were forming all around them, creating a glowing gateway to the city.

"Jason, you helped Mommy when you were both in trouble, and you were so good when Superman saved us. You should be proud of yourself."

"Superman didn't save us, Daddy. You did. I was so scared, then I saw you in the water. I love you."

Richard didn't want to cry, but he couldn't help himself.

Thirty-Two

Superman waited until the seaplane disappeared into the clouds. Lois belonged there on the plane, he knew, as he belonged here.

He was staring at the crystals as they kept growing, covering the ocean, expanding toward the coastline. They had begun as a latticework of interlocking shafts that crisscrossed each other, constructing its basic frame. Then more crystals grew, filling in the gaps between the openings. Other crystals jutted upward, forming spires and peaks to give the base size and depth. Somehow Luthor was creating a terraformed topography that was eerily familiar.

He saw more crystals thrust up from the expanding framework, growing over each other, layering and forming into vast mountainous chains. What once took countless millennia to accomplish was now happening over a span of minutes.

Superman was horrified. He was watching the birth of an island. No, he realized, suddenly very aware that this crystal landmass was going to be larger than any island. It was almost the size of a continent. If it didn't stop growing, he was afraid it could become an entire world, crushing and superseding everything that existed before it.

Is that madman trying to destroy the Earth?

A vast vertical mountain suddenly erupted, pushing up thousands of feet from its base, its cliff walls tall and sheer, its peak leveling into a wide, flat plain. Below it a deep chasm was forming, as if its crystals were fleeing the gorge only to feed the growing mountain.

Then he realized where he was.

He was hovering beside Mount Argo, above the mist-covered Xan Chasm, just as he had on his return to Krypton. But there were no buildings here or any other signs of life; it was barren and stark, waiting for a Sor-El, Kol-Ar, or Pol-Us to transform it into something great.

But he saw more than just Mount Argo spreading over the ocean like Atlantis rising from its watery grave. The crystals were constantly growing new shoots, spreading into the distance, creating more land, more of Krypton.

Superman was flying over his home planet again, but this time not in some life-preserving ship. The world he'd visited was a devastated ruin, a mockery of what had been, but this *planet in progress* was different, this was what he imagined Krypton must have looked like before the birth of man—unsullied. Unshaped. Unspoiled.

For a brief moment he let himself forget where he was, and transported himself back in time, to before Sor-El and the others brought peace to the planet, to before the first Kryptonians thought to reshape their future. He was transfixed, awestruck by its radiance.

He allowed himself to feel a part of this place as if it

was his past, his heritage. The great crystal columns rose high above him, dwarfing him. It would be impossible to walk these planes without being humbled in their presence.

He was looking at what Jor-El must have seen, what Lara must have felt, and he understood how impossible it would have been for them to forsake their world. They had given him the chance for life, across the endless void, but for them there could be no question that they had to stay behind. Their memories were of a world that would never die, and they would be part of it always.

He saw a low valley just ahead of him, the size of an arena. Immense pillars shot up from the ground, arranging themselves in a large circle.

He was hovering above the Valley of the Elders, watching as those great monoliths were forming in front of him; perfect replicas of the original, with only the family crests missing. But they were unmistakable; ahead of him he saw Sor-El's tower, standing proud and powerful, as if to say it had returned from the grave, now better than ever.

Next to it Pol-Us's and Kol-Ar's towers rose toward the sky. He realized this was probably how the original towers were grown, but these were instantaneous creations, not the labor of years.

"Krypton," Superman said softly. "Luthor is rebuilding Krypton."

The realization snapped him out of his daydream. This wasn't Krypton. There was not even a tangible connection between it and the planetary shard he had flown over. That was a world long dead, long gone. The people who had lived on that planet, who had built it and grown it, crystal by crystal, atom by atom, were gone, too.

Krypton might have been dead, but as horrible as that

was, he knew this wasn't any world that had nurtured his parents or his grandparents or any of his ancestors. This was a loathsome travesty, a product of insanity, a blasphemous echo of a once-great civilization, and Superman was sickened by it.

"We yearned to touch the impossible, and more often than not we succeeded."

He knew that worlds were not the ground one walked upon, but the flesh and blood of those who lived on it, who took its crude form, who toiled in its fields and built its wonders. Until its ground was walked on, until some intelligence looked at it and said *I can make it better,* all it was was rock and mud. No matter what this *thing* looked like, it could not nor ever be the planet of his birth.

He flew over the monuments and saw, in the middle of the circle, part of the ocean surrounding a new latticework of crystals that was just beginning to emerge from it, forming a peak hundreds of feet high. Atop it, its slanted columns reshaped themselves into what looked like a great temple, like something else he had seen growing in front of him a long time ago, exactly as it was now.

Seventeen years old. Alone. In the Arctic. In his hand was Jor-El's father crystal. He threw it over lakes and mountains until it finally crashed into the ice and sank into the Arctic Ocean.

It was the crystal that gave birth to his Fortress, provided the explanation of who he was and where he came from, and allowed him to understand his life and his destiny.

He stared—afraid, silent, and bewildered—as a new Fortress of Solitude grew in front of him just as it had before. He saw Luthor's helicopter parked next to it, but there was no one inside.

Luthor had stolen the crystals from the Fortress. He used them to create this nightmare. That madman had taken Jor-El's dream and corrupted it.

And now he's going to answer to me.

As he flew up the cliff side to the Fortress, he felt the winds rising, and in the howling he heard what sounded like ghostly voices. For a brief instant he stood at the entrance, transfixed, unnerved, as echoes of voices called to him as if they were Jor-El and Lara welcoming back their long-lost errant son.

"See anything familiar?" Lex Luthor asked, chuckling. Superman had heard that maniacal laugh too many times before, and in his heart, in his anger, he wanted to strangle it out of existence once and for all.

Luthor was standing atop the staircase that led into the new Fortress. Beside him was Kitty. She smiled at Superman, waving at him.

Superman glared at him. "I see a twisted man's sick joke."

He made his way up the stairs and saw Riley's camcorder pointed at him. He turned and focused his eyes. Nothing happened. He concentrated, then, finally, they burned red, and the camera melted in Riley's hand.

Superman continued up the steps, but he was suddenly feeling weak. His face was cold. He touched it with the back of his hand, and it was moist and clammy. He was beginning to sweat.

Luthor was enjoying himself. "Really? Just a twisted man's sick joke? Because I see my new apartment. And a space for Kitty and my friends, and that one there, I'll rent out," he said, pointing to the Fortress's south wall.

He looked at it again and grimaced as if seeing it in a new light. "No, you're right. It is a little cold. A little . . . *alien*. It needs that human touch.

Superman struggled his way to Luthor's side. They were face-to-face, staring at each other.

"I don't have time for this, Luthor. You have something that belongs to me. I'm getting it back, then I'll deal with you."

Superman pushed past Luthor to head inside this damned crystal copy. But if it was anything like his fortress, he knew that Jor-El's father crystal would be in the main chamber, fitting comfortably in its holder.

"I got a better idea, Superman. Why don't you deal with me first?" Luthor said as he suddenly punched him in the face. Superman fell to the ground, reeling in shock and pain, blood spilling from his mouth.

"How?"

He saw Luthor standing over him, a twisted grin on his face. "Or maybe it's me dealing with you."

Then he kicked Superman in the face, and the Man of Steel groaned and collapsed.

Lois moaned as Jason touched her gently. "Wake up, Mommy, wake up." He looked up at Richard. "She's making noises." Then he saw her eyes open and look around, startled.

"Where am—? Jason?" She saw Richard in the front seat. "Richard?" She remembered the water flooding into the pantry. There was no way they could have survived. "Are we—?"

He turned back to her, smiling. "It's all right. We're safe."

She then realized she was in the seaplane. She looked out the window onto a mountainous terrain that seemed to be made of glass. *Dammit. Luthor succeeded.*

"How did we get here?" she asked, trying to sort it out in her mind.

"Superman. He really came through for us. I can understand why you . . ." He didn't finish.

"Superman? What happened to him? Where is he?"

"It's okay, hon. He went back to stop Luthor."

He saw her eyes widen in horror.

"No. We've got to stop him. Luthor has kryptonite! Superman doesn't know it. Richard, we have to turn around."

"What?"

Lois was adamant. "We haven't got time to argue about this. Turn the plane around. *Please.*"

He looked at her, then at Jason, nodding in agreement. The decision was made by the three of them.

"You got it."

Superman tried to roll over, but Luthor had a foot pressed against his back, pinning him to the floor. His saw that his hands were turning green.

Luthor chuckled again. "Kryptonite. You're asking yourself 'how?' Well, didn't your dad ever tell you to look before you leap?"

Superman felt his head nearly explode as he struggled to aim his X-ray vision at the crystal. The back of his skull was throbbing, and he could barely see what was directly in front of him. But slowly, an out-of-focus image began to come together. In the ground and walls of this Fortress replica were pockets and veins of kryptonite which had somehow fused with the crystal, becoming one.

"How?"

"Crystals are amazing, aren't they?" Luthor laughed, then smashed his foot into Superman's back. He laughed again as Superman recoiled in pain.

Luthor hunkered down and looked him in the eyes. "They inherit the traits of the minerals around them. Sort of like a son inheriting the traits of his father."

Luthor stood up again and smashed his heel into Superman's side. He thought he heard a bone break, and he laughed out loud. "Oh, this is good. This is so good."

Superman was in Smallville now, getting out of his dad's truck and heading up the stairs to school. Before he joined the others on their way to homeroom, he noticed Jonathan Kent pull the truck around the corner, where, Clark knew, he'd park at Leo Hamilton's Feed & Grain and buy supplies for the upcoming winter.

Superman groaned again as a foot smashed into the side of his head.

Clark saw Lana across the crowded corridor, taking math books out of her locker, talking and laughing with Pete. Before Lana's dad moved them into an apartment in town, they owned the farm next to the Kents, not that Professor

Lang ever farmed it. His wife's family had inherited the place, and they lived there until Lana's mom died, when Lana was only nine.

Luthor's elbow crashed down on his side. Superman heard several ribs crack.

As far as Clark was concerned, there was nobody more beautiful in Smallville than Lana Lang. Nobody Clark cared about more and nobody he had more trouble talking to. He could chat to her about class work, or about sports, and certainly gossip about mutual friends; but the only way he could suggest going to a movie with her was by asking all their friends to go at the same time.

He was so timid then, as shy as Clark later needed to be. There was safety in numbers, he thought, and if she turned him down she wasn't turning *him* down, she was turning down the group.

A foot smashed into his face. He felt blood spill from his broken nose.

Despite his trepidations and fears, those Smallville days were his favorites. He knew his powers were growing and that he was changing, yet he had the freedom to be himself, perhaps for the last time in his life. There were no disguises then. Almost no pretense or lies to cover up an identity no one then suspected he was keeping.

But then, after Jonathan's death, as his powers emerged stronger and faster than before, Martha suggested he prepare for the day when there would be a Clark Kent as well as a Superman.

But those days were long before he learned to hunch over, to shorten himself by several inches, and to raise the timbre of his voice so that Clark spoke at least an octave higher than his future alter ego.

As he understood the need to create a facade, a persona to separate his two identities, he also realized his life was changing. It would never be as innocent as it had been 'til then. Never quite as carefree.

But that was all right, he thought. His friends, all living in town, were hoping for a future where they might move from Smallville, but no farther than fifty or a hundred miles away. Most would live their lives within two hours of home. Many would never get on an airplane or visit other states, much less other countries. Most of them would have very happy, fulfilling lives.

Luthor kicked him again, but this time Superman didn't feel it.

He knew he couldn't stay in Smallville even if he had wanted to. To him, his world *was* the world, not just some 127 square miles of farmland, no matter how special or wonderful that farmland may have been. Because of who he was and the amazing things he could do, his horizon began where the cornfields ended.

• • •

Luthor kicked him again, reveling in his anger, living for the violence, crude and barbaric. "Look, Superman, you've got no one to blame but yourself. We sent you there to die, but you had to come back!"

Superman could feel blood smearing his face and hands.

"Don't you know where you're wanted and where you're not?"

Superman forced his eyes to look up, his expression turning from agony to realization. Luthor laughed at his dumbfounded look.

"Oh, yeah. All those photos? Those stories about Krypton still existing." He pointed to himself with glee. "It was me. And, oh yes, him," he said, gesturing to Stanford. "Thankfully, the press doesn't check facts like they used to."

Superman tried to speak, but blood was filling his mouth. Luthor glared at him again as he kicked him once more in his side. This time Superman yelped in pain. Blood spattered across the glittering crystal.

"You took away five years of my life. I just returned the favor."

Thirty-Three

Luthor watched Superman squirming on the ground, red welts spotting him, blood seeping out of open wounds. A couple more good, swift kicks, he thought, and the costumed fool will bite the big one. And not a second too soon.

"Do you have any idea how long I've been waiting for this day? Probably from the very moment you made your first big splash rescuing that Lane woman. By the way, did you know she's dead? I killed her and her little brat, too."

Superman glared at him. "You're sick."

Luthor leaned over Superman and swiped a finger through the blood smearing his face. "Sick? Maybe. But tomorrow you'll be dead!"

He slammed his foot into Superman's side again and laughed as his victim groaned in pain.

"But that day, Superman, that awful moment when all of Metropolis looked up to you, you never-lying bastard, and proclaimed you a hero, well, that's when it began. In that single instant you went from an unknown to the object of worship."

"I was just doing what was right."

"Oh, *'I didn't ask to be a hero.'* You idiot. What did you think was going to happen? They'd all suddenly forget a man could fly? You want to know what rankled me? *I* was the one who should have been worshipped. I should have gotten the adulation and the headlines."

Luthor leaned over him again, their faces nearly touching. Everything he had ever wanted to tell Superman was spilling out faster than he realized.

"Look at all the crimes of the century that I'd already committed in my short, wondrous life. And I did it without your pesky alien powers. I've earned everything I've ever gotten through an off-the-charts IQ and the idiocy of others. So what's so wrong in having the world worship me?"

"You're not a god, Lex. No more than I am." Superman was staring at him. *Keep him talking. I need time to regain my strength.*

"Oh, really? Gods create and destroy worlds, and you know what? I was nearly there. If it weren't for guess-who?—California would have not so quietly sunk into the Pacific. I would have ruled the new West Coast. And no government could have stopped me."

"They would have found a way."

"No they wouldn't. I had them stymied. But then you had to show up, all tall and pretty, with muscles bulging and your ridiculous blue-and-red circus costume that cried out, 'Look at me!' But why should they be looking at you when they should have been on their hands and knees praying to me!"

Kitty tried to pull him away. "Lex, you don't have to do this." He pushed her aside, then slammed his fist into Superman's stomach for effect.

"Don't do that ever again, Kitty. This is my moment. This is what I thought about every day I wasted behind those bars."

He turned back to Superman, angrier than he'd ever been. "You stand for everything I despise. 'Truth?' Be honest now, what does the truth ever get you? 'Justice?' If there was real justice, I would already have been Earth's ruler. 'The American Way?' Well, soon there won't be an American Way because there won't be an America."

He smiled at Superman one more time. "You know, pal, whether you call it fate, or kismet, or destiny, it always had to come down to this. You and me. Alone. A fight to the finish that ends with you dead and me, well, me finally achieving my greatest triumph."

Lex stood up again and kicked Superman as hard as he could. This was the kick that was going to break the last of Superman's ribs. The kick that would crush his heart.

Kitty turned and covered her eyes, unable to watch the brutality. "Lex, stop it! This is wrong. Just kill him. He doesn't deserve this."

Luthor blew Kitty a kiss as he smashed his foot into Superman's face. "Sorry, pumpkin, this is only the beginning."

"Lex. Please." Kitty grabbed him. "For me."

Luthor watched quietly as Superman pulled himself to the edge of cliff. He walked over to him, his hands in his pocket.

He leaned down, grinning at Superman. "Why don't you

get up and walk? Oh, right. Your once-invulnerable legs are broken. I guess the Man of Steel's a little rusty, eh?

Superman struggled to look over the cliff's edge; the drop was steep, almost endless. A cold, hungry ocean was waiting below.

He saw a blur of motion to his side, and then he screamed out in pain, arching backward, blood spitting from his mouth. Luthor had taken the kryptonite shard he had chipped from the meteor from his pocket, and plunged it deep into Superman's back, a glowing, green dagger.

The poison quickly began to insinuate itself into Superman. He tried to pull out the shard, but Luthor shoved him back to the ground and snapped the shard at the base, leaving most of it inside the deep wound.

A sickly-looking green pulse flowed through Superman's body. He shivered as the poison made its way through his system.

Luthor leaned in close and whispered in his ears. "Now, fly." Then he stepped back, watching his adversary die.

Superman looked down off the edge of the cliff again. He closed his eyes.

And fell.

Thirty-Four

He plunged into the water, sinking quickly, tumbling and spinning. The cold sent a shock through him, forcing his eyes open. He was dizzy and disoriented, not at all certain where he was or what he was seeing, but realizing parts of his body were growing numb.

He noticed his hands floating in the water. They were green. He felt the stabbing pain in his back, then he remembered the kryptonite dagger.

He saw the crystals edging their way toward him. Smaller shards were floating freely in the water. They all looked so beautiful, with their bright green glow, their kryptonite shine.

He tried to swim back to the surface, but his arms wouldn't move. They hung at his sides like dead meat on a rack. He tried to reach for the kryptonite shard, but Luthor had left him no exposed hilt to grab.

He opened his mouth in a silent scream, struggling to

stay alive in the mesh of crystal that was closing in around him, over him, surrounding him like a tomb.

Maybe it is time, he thought. *Maybe it's time to go back to Krypton.*

Richard's seaplane banked toward the massive, growing continent. Jason looked down and pointed at the ocean. "Mommy. Daddy. There."

The seaplane was flying just above the water. Lois looked, but couldn't see anything. "You're sure, honey?" She saw Jason nodding, certain.

She unbuckled her seat belt and threw the seaplane door open.

"What are you doing?" Richard asked.

She didn't answer. Instead, she jumped into the water.

Superman was floating, his eyes rolled up into their sockets, not moving. A single bubble escaped his mouth. He was sinking quickly, disappearing into the darkness.

He thought about Luthor. Without him, that madman would finally get his way. He thought of his fathers. It would be so easy to take their hand and surrender to the cold. It would take the pain away. It would bring him peace. After everything he'd been through, surely he deserved at least that.

But no.

He wasn't ready. Not yet. Someday he would proudly walk with them again, talk over their lives, rekindle lost memories, but not today. Today he wanted to live. Today, he knew his mission was not yet accomplished. Today, there was still a world to save.

But it was so cold. He thought, maybe he was too late, maybe he was already dead. He saw a beautiful woman moving through the water toward him.

He was sinking as his arms listlessly floated upward, his fingers were like grasping claws, trying to grab at the beautiful woman, trying to grab a thing he knew could not be there. He saw his red cape floating upward, above him, pulled by the ocean current.

The woman's hand reached out and touched his cape, as if ready to take him. He tried to resist, there was still so much to do. The woman looked into his eyes and smiled at him. And he smiled back.

As the seaplane hovered above the surface, Richard and Jason were anxiously staring into the water. *Where was she?*

Jason gasped, pointing. "It's Mommy. I see her. I see her."

Richard held his breath as Lois surfaced, gasping for air. Another figure bobbed to the surface beside her. Superman.

"I need help," she shouted. "He's unconscious."

Without hesitation, Richard landed the plane on the water and dived in.

He was lying in her arms, unconscious, his skin green. She frantically searched for a pulse but couldn't find one. "Come on. Wake up! Come on!"

She was shouting at him, but he didn't move. She slapped his face, but his eyes were rolled back, staring at nothing.

She turned to Richard. "What are you waiting for? We've got to get out of here."

"I'm trying. But I can't gain altitude." Richard pushed the controls, desperately trying to get the seaplane back into the air, but it wasn't cooperating. Instead, it cruised through the choppy waters like a motorboat.

"Daddy!" Jason screamed. Richard swerved as a crystal mountain suddenly appeared in front of him. The seaplane jerked to the side as more and more crystals rose from the sea.

"Richard!"

He pushed again, but the seaplane wasn't responding. "Honey, I'm doing my best. How is he?"

Her hands were caressing his face. He wasn't responding. "You can't die," she whispered to him. "You can't leave me . . . leave us again. Please . . . please . . . you can't die."

His eyes were moving under their closed lids. Slowly, they began to open. She remembered they had been blue. Now they were green.

"Kryptonite," he said, his voice weak and coarse. "There's kryptonite in the crystals."

She turned back to Richard. "We have to get him away from here."

"I'm trying."

He saw that the crystals in front of him were expanding even faster than they had been. He was surrounded by dozens of columns that were blocking his path. He saw an opening, already narrow, but filling in quickly.

"Seat belts!" he shouted. He heard Jason's click into place.

Richard gunned the gas, and the plane jerked forward,

pushing through the narrow pass a second before it closed up. He heard Jason scream. *"Daddy!"*

"What?"

Jason was staring out the windows, his eyes wide with fear. Richard saw they were on top of a giant waterfall. Without their even realizing it, the crystals had pushed them up thousands of feet.

He turned back, frantic, and all he could do before the seaplane fell off the edge and plummeted down to the ocean, was to call out Lois's name.

They were falling. He looked back to see Jason holding on to the edge of his seat just like he did on the rollercoaster ride at the amusement park. He saw Lois holding Superman in her arms. He turned back to the controls and gunned the engine one more time.

As the engine revved, he felt the plane catch the air. They were pulling up, higher, over a crystal obelisk that appeared suddenly in front of them. They were flying again. They were safe.

Richard looked back and smiled at Lois. "We did it."

She reached out and tenderly touched his hand. "I love you," she said. There were tears in her eyes as she turned back to Superman.

She pushed his cape away as she felt something sticking out of Superman's back. She pulled up his shirt and saw the stab wound. It was glowing green just below the surface.

"Oh, my God. He was stabbed with kryptonite." She saw part of the broken shard embedded near his spine.

"It's too deep. I can't grab it. Richard, I need pliers."

"There's a toolbox under the seat."

She pulled it out and fumbled it open. Tools spilled

over the floor, including a pair of needle-nose pliers. "Got it."

She stared at the wound, afraid to do anything, but knowing she had no choice.

She wiped the tears from her eyes and inserted the pliers inside. The seaplane was dark, and it was hard to see, but she used the green kryptonite glow as her bull's-eye.

She shifted the pliers back and forth until she felt the shard. She clamped down on the kryptonite and tugged. She felt something move. *She had it.* Slowly, she pulled the pliers out, revealing the small, glowing shard. There was no blood on it. She looked at his back and saw the scar was more like a burn.

She stared at the kryptonite for what seemed forever, then opened the seaplane door and threw it out. She watched as if fell into the ocean, disappearing from view.

"We did it, honey," she said. "We did it." Richard looked back and saw she was speaking to him.

He saw Superman lying in Lois's arms. Superman opened his eyes slowly and saw everyone staring at him. He was weak, but he was quickly regaining his strength.

"How did you find me?" he asked.

Lois held on to him. "Quiet. Just take it easy. You're hurt."

He pushed himself up a bit and felt the stabbing pain in his back. It hurt, but not as it had before. "It's okay. I'll be all right."

He looked at Richard. "You promised you wouldn't come back. You lied."

Richard turned to him and smiled. "I'm not you. I can do that."

Superman looked at him quizzically and grinned. He

turned to Lois. "I have to go back." He felt the pain again as he reached over to open the seaplane door.

Lois held on to him, refusing to let go. "No. You'll die if you go back."

He wasn't smiling as he looked into her eyes. They were filled with longing and uncertainty. She thought for just an instant that he also looked frightened.

"Good-bye, Lois," he said as he flew away.

Thirty-Five

Floating high above the Atlantic, he saw that Luthor's island was still growing in size. He kept rising, high into the air, past the almost-black storm clouds, into the stratosphere.

As the clouds parted, he saw the sun, Earth's bright yellow sun. He stretched out his arms and let its warm, invigorating light wash over him. Under Krypton's red sun he would have been normal, unable to help anyone. But Earth's sun gave him his strength, allowed him his powers, and he knew he needed to embrace them now.

Superman arced back down and reentered the atmosphere with such renewed speed and power that the air around him ignited. He was a brightly glowing comet streaking through the sky.

His eyes focused and a ripple of heat vision blasted outward and vaporized a cloud bank. Superman continued down as his heat vision struck the ocean's surface. The frigid waters bubbled and misted just as he plunged into them.

He was underwater, swimming at the speed of sound toward the ocean floor. He increased the intensity of his heat vision, and the rocky ground turned to liquid magma. He disappeared into it as a huge cloud of sand and dirt flew up, then just as quickly, was sucked back into the hole Superman had left behind.

He could see massive rifts appear in the ground around the base of the crystal structure. Geysers were bubbling and gas was exploding from the crevices as the ocean floor continued to split.

Lex Luthor sat in the main chamber of his new Fortress, hunched over a table, staring at Grant and Riley. He had a twisted gleam in his eyes as he looked back at the cards in his hand and laid them down one at a time. "Full boat, suckers."

He took a Cuban from his pocket and clipped its end. He was about to light it when he heard Kitty complaining behind him.

"It's leaking," she said. He was beginning to hate that whine.

He turned to see her standing under an umbrella, protecting herself from the small drops of water falling from the ceiling.

"Leaking?" He glared at her. "Kitty. I kill Superman and create all of this, and the only thing you can say to me is, 'It's leaking'?"

She was looking at the Fortress's crystal walls, not liking what she was seeing. "Are billions of people really going to die?"

He lit the cigar and took a long drag on it. "Yes," he said, matter-of-factly, a point of extreme pride, in fact.

He saw his cigar smoke tremble, then disperse suddenly. He fell back as the Fortress shook and tilted, and a huge crystal lump plummeted onto the table, smashing through it. Grant and Riley jumped back, falling out of their seats.

"Boss, what the hell's going on?" Grant shouted, confused and frightened. "Are we having an earthquake?"

"You want me to record this, boss?" Riley asked.

"I want you to shut up, both of you," Luthor snapped. He touched the wall and felt it vibrate under his hands. "Can't you feel it? Don't ask me how, but this place is moving." The Fortress shook again, harder now. Crystals were falling from the ceiling, shattering on the ground. Grant and Riley ducked under the table for protection.

Luthor felt the vibrations increasing. He grabbed a small metal box sitting on a ledge and tucked it under his arm. "Come on. What are you waiting for?" He was already halfway toward the Fortress exit.

He held on to the wall as he stepped outside, staring at the horizon. It was moving, getting lower.

"We're going up? How is that possible?" He scrambled back inside the Fortress, grabbing the wall for support.

He felt fingers digging into his arms. Kitty was holding on to him. "Lex, what's happening?"

He didn't know, but he couldn't tell her that.

Close behind them, in the Valley of the Elders, he saw one of the monoliths begin to crack. It seemed to scream, then fall over, crashing into the Fortress. Had there been a family crest, Luthor would have known this tower stood as a warning against the return of dishonesty and violence.

Sor-El's monolith rumbled as it tore through the false Fortress, crushing it to dust.

"Get to the helicopter! Now!" Luthor screamed.

Kitty was wavering, not sure what she should do. "But our stuff?"

"Leave it. Leave everything."

Stanford, Grant, and Riley were running when they felt the ground beneath them vibrate again. They pushed their way over the moving crystal toward the waiting helicopter. They heard another cracking sound and looked up to see a second monolith begin to sway. Suddenly, Kol-Ar's tower shook loose from its foundations. The open hand of justice fell on them with a deafening crash.

Luthor scrambled into the helicopter and took the pilot's seat. He saw Kitty climb in next to him and strap herself in. He passed the metal box to her. It was filled with crystals. "Here, you hold. I'm flying."

As he started the engines she stared at the box. This was the cause of everything bad. This was the stuff of nightmares, not dreams as Luthor had promised.

She thought of Andrew, her ex, probably still sitting in his cell, waiting for his parole in eight months, staring at the picture of her in that little thong she had sent to him for Christmas last year when she and Lex vacationed in Maui for a week. *Yeah, he was small-time. A penny-ante jerk mostly. But he never wanted to kill billions.* She missed kissing his crooked smile and fingering his tattoos at night when he was asleep.

She looked back at the case of crystals with uncertainty and apprehension. Her eyes focused on the Metropolis skyline. She had made a decision.

She saw Luthor working the controls, and dumped the crystals out the door. Luthor turned and saw them tumbling outside.

She gave him a large, innocent smile. "Oops."

Luthor raised a fist, but then started to climb outside to retrieve them instead. *I'll deal with her later. At ten thousand feet.*

Suddenly, he saw fissures and cracks forming under the chopper, threatening to swallow them. He scrambled back inside and gunned the engines. The copter lurched, then dropped.

The crystals beneath them had crumbled away, falling into a gaping chasm that was growing wider every second. The copter plummeted, then it began to rise, flying up and over the collapsing crystal mountain.

Luthor stared out the chopper window in a forlorn daze, not yet understanding what had happened. The crystals were structurally sound. He had made sure of that. They shouldn't have broken apart as they had. The Fortress shouldn't have shook or collapsed. The monoliths were supposed to be eternal. *What had gone wrong?*

He felt the island still rising, and heard a great roar as its base broke the ocean surface, revealing an underside of brown, rocky earth. The island was floating upward, higher and higher.

He kept staring until the island—*his island*—was at eye level. And below it, a mere speck in its massive underside, was Superman, straining with all his strength, pushing it from below.

"No. No. Nononono. NO! It's impossible. He's dead. I killed him. He can't be doing this. He's not real."

Kitty smiled at him. "No. I see him. He's not a ghost, Lex. Not a dream. Not an imaginary hero."

Luthor growled at her, then pointed the chopper out to sea. It was time to regroup.

The continent was growing even as he carried it higher. He was drawing in all his power to push it spaceward, away from his home. Away from Earth.

Everything that was Krypton was here; the valleys, the cliffs, the vast and great mountains. Everything except, of course, for the people. But they were the ones who mattered, the only ones who did.

He knew Earth's beautiful golden sun would imbue him with the strength to continue.

Great chunks of earth began to break apart, plummeting into the ocean. He felt a wave of nausea grip him as the falling dirt and crystals exposed the poisonous veins deep inside it. The pain cut through him like that kryptonite dagger. He was crying in agony, almost losing his grip, but he kept pushing the island higher into the storm clouds.

He had traveled half a galaxy to find his home, but now that it was here all he wanted was to get it as far away from him as he could.

Miles below, the Earth was floating in a speckled sea of black; drifting wisps of clouds circled a pristine blue-and-green planet teeming with life.

Superman felt as if a lightning bolt had pierced his chest. He doubled over as a terrible pain lanced through him. His arms had become heavy and leaden, and he could barely move them. More dirt and crystal had fallen from the island, exposing even more kryptonite.

He thought he heard his father's voice, his Kryptonian father. "Kal-El, my son, you are all that remains of a once-proud people. And in you Krypton's glory will live on."

The Last Son of Krypton.

Everything was dark, even the green-glowing island. He was in space. Endless. Immutable space. And he let out a primal scream that would have shattered worlds if sound could be heard.

But in that scream he summoned all his strength, and all his power, into one last action, and he hurled the mountain into the black.

After a moment, he closed his eyes and leaned back. He wasn't flying back to Earth. He was falling, unconscious.

He couldn't feel the cold of space or, just moments later, the air around him heat up as he reentered Earth's atmosphere, then, finally, igniting into a bright orange ball of fire.

In the Metropolis streets below, people saw the glowing streak tear through the clouds. They stared at it, terrified at what they somehow knew they were seeing.

It soared over their heads, this flaming comet, crossing the city, heading toward the city center.

He crashed into Metropolis's Centennial Park, and the massive explosion shattered trees and sent debris flying hundreds of feet into the air.

And then there was silence, and smoke and steam rose from the scorched crater.

Thirty-Six

The sirens hadn't yet trailed off when the doors burst open and two paramedics, flanked by an escort of police, pushed the gurney into Metropolis General, rushing toward the emergency ward at the end of the corridor. Everyone had been warned, and they had had time to prepare. Doctors had been called in. Others, who had been driving home to the suburbs after their shifts, were helicoptered back to work. They were all ready.

The paramedics were running alongside the gurney when they were met by a doctor and two nurses. "Breathing became shallow in transit. Can't get a blood pressure reading, but his heart rate's less than thirty.

"Get him inside, quickly."

A nurse removed Superman's shirt and pulled off his cape, revealing the deep stab wound on Superman's back.

A bright halogen bulb spotlighted it. "Penetrating stab wound to right side of back. No hemorrhage."

The nurse attached the EKGs. She checked the waveform oscillating across the screen. "Code blue. Flatline," she called.

"Give him an epinephrine one milligram. IV push," the doctor snapped.

The nurse tried to insert the needle into Superman's arm. It broke. "Can't."

The doctor shook his head. *Okay, let's try something else.* "Shock at two hundred."

The nurse turned to him, worried. "Is that enough? He's not . . . human."

He nodded, understanding, then took a long breath, pausing, thinking. "All right, charge to three-sixty."

The doctor placed the defibrillator paddles on Superman's chest. "Clear." The paddles crackled with electricity. The nurse saw the lights flicker, then the defibrillator sparked and smoked.

No good. Even half-dead he's invulnerable.

He turned to the heart monitor but was greeted by silence. He turned away, trying to phrase his words carefully.

Then he heard a single beep.

Thirty-Seven

The Daily Planet headline said "Superman Is Dead." Beneath it was Jimmy's photo of Superman holding up the Daily Planet globe.

"What do you think," Perry White asked.

Richard looked at the other mock-up. "Superman Lives." Beneath it was the same photo. "It's kind of gruesome, Perry."

White nodded solemnly. "Always be prepared." He put aside the paper, then sat down, saying nothing.

Richard looked out to the bullpen and saw Lois at her desk. She was playing with a pencil, spinning it, finding ways to keep herself distracted. He looked back at his uncle, just as quiet, just as somber. Noticing Lois, Perry gave him a weak smile.

"How is she?" he asked.

Richard made his way slowly through the bullpen. Work crews were cleaning up the debris. Aside from the TVs and phones, there was little noise. Everyone was joylessly going about their day. *A job of work* he once heard it called.

He saw Jason sitting across from Lois's desk, quietly looking at a book, his handheld video game sitting next to him, turned off.

She was sitting in her chair, her face blank and emotionless. A new document was opened on her computer, but aside from the toolbar, the screen was blank, the cursor blinking. She heard the staff murmuring in the background and looked up. The TV was blaring.

"And the city is still reeling from the shock of a geologic disturbance in the mid-Atlantic. Federal authorities on scene have promised to issue statements before the day is out. In his press conference, the president said . . ."

Lois closed her eyes, trying with all her heart to shut out all the noise. *Why won't they stop talking?* A hand gently touched her. It was Jason. She wrapped her arms around him, hugging him tenderly.

She saw Richard approaching and quickly wiped away her tears.

"Lois?"

"Yeah," she said, not even trying to smile.

"We can leave whenever you're ready. I mean, you don't have to be here."

She kissed Jason on the top of the head, continuing to hold him close. "Where else would I be?"

He looked up to the TV and saw Jimmy's photo of Superman. The newscaster was still gibbering on. It was like this on every channel: nonstop talk, twenty-four/seven. "And the world waits as Superman remains in critical condition at Metropolis General. Police have surrounded the area . . ."

"I could drive," Richard said.

She looked at him, uncertain, as Perry walked out of his office and called to Gil. "Hey, what's the story on that big chunk of whatever-it-was Superman pulled out of the ocean?"

Gil checked his notes. "Well, astronomers say it settled into orbit somewhere between Mars and Jupiter. Supposedly, it's laced with kryptonite, and it's still growing."

Perry nodded. "But what are we calling it? It needs a name. Something splashy. Something big."

"Planet ten?" Gil suggested, lamely.

Perry shook his head, making a face. "Well, that's a terrible idea." He saw Lois sitting across the aisle. "Lois, what do you think?"

She looked up at Richard, then got up and grabbed her coat. She took Jason's hand, then turned back to Perry. "I don't know Perry. Call it . . . New Krypton."

Perry smiled. "New Krypton. Gil, run with it." He saw Lois and Richard leaving. "Where are you two going?"

"To the hospital," Lois answered.

Jimmy walked by. "I'd be careful down there, Miss Lane. It's a madhouse."

"We will, Jimmy. Thanks."

"Tell him I . . . tell him we're all thinking about him."

She gave him a slight smile as she and Richard and Jason headed for the elevator.

Metropolis General was surrounded by a wall of people filling the streets west to Broadway, east to Jefferson, north to Forty-fifth and south to Thirty-ninth. They had come there, some holding plates with lit candles, others just standing and waving placards, since the news had first hit. The police, many on horseback, moved through the crowd to keep it under control, but there were no disturbances, no problems. They had come only to honor the man who meant so much to them.

Lois, Richard, and Jason were staring at the throngs of people blocking the roads. The hospital was only a block away, but their car hadn't moved for almost an hour.

"So much for parking," Richard complained.

Lois was already out the door. "It's okay. I can walk. Think I can get in?"

Richard smiled at her. "You're Lois Lane. They'll let you in."

Jason held on to her hand. "I want to go with Mommy," he said. She looked back at Richard. "It's okay. If that's what you want." He gave her a hug, then sat back in the car.

"We did everything we could."

She looked at Richard, sitting patiently behind the wheel. *A wonderful man. A loving man.*

"I'll be there as soon as I can, hon," he said.

Lois and Jason made their way through the crowd, toward the hospital entrance. The guards recognized her and let her in, calling ahead.

They were met by a doctor, who accompanied her down the long corridor. The walk seemed endless. She kept her eyes focused ahead, but saw the people staring at her as she passed.

They entered the reception area, and Lois saw it was being guarded by two police officers. The doctor ushered her past. "This way, Miss Lane."

She started to move forward, but then realized the

doctor was gesturing to his right, toward a simple hospital room. She paused for a moment then opened the door.

He was lying there, unconscious, in a small hospital bed, hooked up only to a heart monitor. She gasped, trying to hold it all together.

She'd seen him struggling, seen him bleed, seen his face torn in pain, but now, lying there, eyes closed, his breathing shallow but constant, he looked so calm and peaceful.

She turned to the doctor. "Could we have a minute, please?"

"Of course," the doctor said as he stepped out of the room. The door closed behind him, leaving Lois and Jason standing across from his bed. They were all alone.

"Is he going to get better?" Jason asked.

"I don't know."

"I want him to. I like him."

"Me, too." The words choked in her throat.

She stepped closer, trying to find the words she had wanted to say, but nothing was coming.

She thought of that first day, in the helicopter, when he had saved her so unexpectedly. *You've got me? Who's got you?* Thought of that first night when she saw him descend like a god from the heavens. He was smiling at her as he stepped onto her patio.

That smile changed her life.

Pink.

She blushed at the memory, so long ago.

She had had so many questions.

I'm from pretty far away. From another galaxy, as a matter of fact. I come from a planet called Krypton.

I like pink very much, Lois.
I'm here to fight for truth, justice, and the American Way.
I never lie.
He never did.

"Can you hear me?" she said, softly. "They say, sometimes when people are . . ." She stopped and turned away.
"Never mind."

The room was silent again. Just the slow beeping from the
heart monitor kept her rooted to the moment, to the place.

She walked to his side and took his hand. "There's
something . . . something I need to tell you."

She bent low, whispering in Superman's ears, her eyes
filled with tears which she tried, fruitlessly, to wipe away.

On the other side of the half-drawn curtain, Jason ran
his finger over the emblem of Superman's neatly folded
costume. He was trying to be brave, but he was crying.

Lois looked at Superman again and leaned in closer.
She shut her eyes and kissed him. It was tender, everything she remembered.

Tears streaming, she pulled away and looked again at
the heart monitor, perhaps hoping, impossibly, that the
kiss would bring her sleeping beauty back to life.

But there was no change. No magic awakening. No
fairy-tale ending.

Only the beep of the heart monitor.

She stood up and wiped away her tears again, composing herself. She slid open the curtain and gently took Jason's hand.

"Come on, honey."

They were at the door when Jason squirmed his hand free. He ran back to the bed and kissed Superman on the forehead. Lois's tears were flowing again, but this time she did nothing to push them away. She felt a terrible pain in her heart and a dryness in her throat. Jason ran back to her and guided her out of the room.

The reporters were waiting as she and Jason stepped into the waiting room. A wall of cameras were taking her picture, microphones were shoved in her face. Voices were shouting at her from everywhere. She held Jason close.

"Miss Lane, what did he look like?"

"Did he say anything?"

"Is he going to make it?"

"What did you say to him?

"Do you still love him, Miss Lane?"

"Does he still love you?"

The police cleared a path for her as she and Jason hurried from the hospital. There were thousands more people crowding the streets.

Martha Kent and Ben Hubbard watched as Lois made her way through the crowd toward the waiting car. Martha saw Lois's son, so handsome and so proud as he walked just ahead of her, holding her hand, protecting her from harm.

She wanted to say something to Lois, but knew she couldn't. *Nobody can know the truth, Ma. Not as long as any of my loved ones are alive.*

She wanted to go into the hospital, to tell them who she was, to sit at the side of her son, to hold his hand, but nobody would believe her.

But Martha saw his window, knew it was his even with the shades drawn, and she saw him in her heart. She felt Ben's hands holding her, and as her tears flowed freely she whispered to her son.

A thousand miles away, a small, tired figure stood up on a small, rocky beach. Kitty Kowalski stared out at the ocean. It was almost peaceful.

Behind her she heard the furious shriek pierce the quiet calm—*again.* Luthor screamed again as he furiously hurled a coconut into the water.

"You've got to stop that, Lex. We only have six of those."

Luthor stomped over the sand, angrily kicking it in all directions. "Six? SIX? I'd trade three hundred thousand coconuts, and every drop of your blood, for one quart—of gasoline!"

The helicopter was halfway across the beach, lying on its side, probably laughing at him for bringing them to this godforsaken stump of nothing.

"Least you have your island, Lex," Kitty said, drawing a large "S" emblem in the sand. "It's what you always wanted, right?" She watched as a large wave washed over it, erasing it from sight.

She heard him growl. "Lex?" she said.

He glared at her. "What, Kitty? What now?"

He saw the worried look on her face. How could it get any worse than this?

"I think the tide's coming in."

Thirty-Eight

A nurse was on her rounds at Metropolis General as she approached Superman's door. A guard opened it for her. She picked up his chart and checked it. She approached the bed and froze in her tracks.

It was empty. She looked at the chair. The costume, his costume, was gone.

She hurried to the window and pulled open the blinds. The window was open.

She gasped, shouted, and fainted.

The clock on Richard's nightstand read 5:00 A.M. He was sleeping soundly, but the other side of the bed was empty.

Lois was in the kitchen, typing on her laptop, a mug of steaming coffee by her side. She looked at the computer screen.

"Why the World Needs Superman" by Lois Lane, it began. She had already written three pages when she stopped.

She stared at the framed photo of her with Richard and Jason, hit the save key, and got up, frustrated.

She walked to the back porch, looked out at the river, and put a cigarette to her lips. She flicked the lighter, but the flame died. She looked around, puzzled, then flicked it again. This time the flame held. She stared at it for several seconds, then she snapped the cover closed. She dropped the cigarette and stomped it out.

The voice behind her was quiet, yet powerful. "Thank you, Lois."

He was there, in front of her, floating over the water.

"I—I wanted . . . I'm . . ." She struggled so hard but couldn't find the words.

"It's all right." He smiled at her the same way he had on that first night. *I never lie.*

It was what she had wanted and needed to hear for years, and she began to cry again.

Superman looked to the house. Lois followed his gaze and saw Jason watching them from the window. She turned back to see Superman looking at her.

So handsome. So perfect. What a . . . super man.

"Will   *we* . . . still see you . . . *around?*"

He smiled again. He looked so strong, so alive. "I'm always around. Good night, Lois."

She smiled sweetly, watching as he rose and disappeared into the clouds.

She stood watching the skies long after he was gone. After all, she knew where he was, swimming through the heavens, the Earth below him, highlighted by the dawning sun casting its warm glow over the planet.

She knew he would be smiling.
The Earth was safe again.
His home was safe.

She looked back at the house and Jason still watching her.
She waved at him, then went back inside and walked up
the stairs to his room.

They sat together on his bed, his small hand in hers,
looking out the window, toward the stars.

Beautiful.

Twinkling.

Eternal.

Acknowledgments

There are so many people to thank when you novelize a movie script. Everyone at DC Comics and Warner Bros. has been great and incredibly helpful. A special thank you to my DC Comics editor, Chris Cerasi and to my Warner Book's editor, Devi Pillai. Another extra thanks goes to my Warner Bros.'s folk, Maureen Squillace, who had to put up with a ton of really picayune questions like: What exactly are the names of the two teams playing baseball? And Emma Rodgers for setting up meetings, getting the movie script to me when it almost looked like that wasn't going to happen, plus a slew of other help along the way.

Again, I want to thank the screenwriters, Michael Dougherty and Dan Harris, for their time and advice. And, of course, Bryan Singer for making it possible for me to work on this project.

I also want to thank the people at Electronic Arts, especially Chris Gray, Sam Clifford, and, of course, Sergio Bustamante, for making it almost easy for me to work on both this and the Superman video game at the same time. A really special thanks to Flint Dille for all his understanding, help, and his immeasurably invaluable guidance. I can't even begin to say how much it was appreciated.

To David Abrams of Warner Interactive and to Paul Levitz, John Nee, and Dan Didio at DC Comics.

A thank you and a special tip of the hat to Dr. Michael Watkins for his help on understanding exactly how supernovas work. Without him I would probably have written, "It was a big, hot gassy thingie." And to Marina Stern for her medical knowledge.

To Elle Dee for curling up under my desk as I wrote the book. And when I was stressed by the crushing deadlines, for letting me pet her. Oh, did I mention L.D.'s my beautiful keeshond puppy?

And, as always, to Noel for understanding when I had to stay in the office working Saturdays and Sundays instead of going out and having fun.

If I left out anyone, I apologize and thank you, too.

—Marv Wolfman
12/15/05

About the Author

Marv Wolfman has created more characters that have gone on to television, animation, movies and toys than any other comics creator since Stan Lee. The multi-award winning writer is the writer-creator of *Blade, the Vampire Hunter* which has been turned into three hit movies starring Wesley Snipes, and a TV series. Marv also created Bullseye, the prime villian in the 2003 movie *Daredevil*, and co-created the *New Teen Titans*, which has become a runaway hit show on the Cartoon Network. Marv's character Cat Grant was a regular on the *Lois and Clark: The New Adventures of Superman* TV series.

Marv has also been editor-in-chief at Marvel Comics, senior editor at DC Comics, and founding editor of *Disney Adventures* magazine. He has also edited and produced educational comics and was given a special commendation by the White House for his work on three anti-drug comics for the "Just Say No" program.

Marv has written and story-edited TV animation, movies, theme park shows, video games, and of course, comics. His 1985 series, *Crisis on Infinite Earths*, was voted by fans and professionals as the 2nd best comic series of the 20th century and is still in print 20 years later. His work at Marvel and DC has earned continuing praise and has been reprinted not only in the United States but across the world.

Most recently, Marv has written a direct-to-video animated movie, *The Condor*, for POW Entertainment as well as co-writing the video game version of *Superman Returns* for Electronic Arts. He is also working on *Homeland*, the graphic history of Israel. His last novel, *Crisis on Infinite Earths*, was published in April, 2005. His first novel, *The Oz Encounter*, written some 27 years ago, has just been republished in a deluxe hardcover edition. Marv is also producing 15 graphic albums for the educational market.

Marv is married to his lovely wife, Noel, and has a wonderful daughter, Jessica, from his first marriage. Marv and Noel also have a brand new puppy name Elle Dee Deux (L.D.) who is currently chewing on everything that is and isn't nailed down. You can reach Marv through his website, www.marvwolfman.com.

LAST SONS

ISBN: 0-446-61656-7

By Alan Grant

SUPERMAN. MARTIAN MANHUNTER. LOBO.

Interplanetary bounty hunter Lobo is a notorious maverick. Happily wreaking havoc as he brings in his prey, he cares little who his clients or targets are—even when his latest quarry is J'onn J'onnzz, Martian Manhunter of the Justice League of America. Suddenly Lobo finds himself confronting . . . Superman. Cogs in the machinations of a powerful artificial life-form, these three aliens, the sole survivors of the planets Krypton, Mars, and Czarnia, have only one thing in common—they are the last of their kind. . . .

LAST SONS

Available wherever books are sold.

INHERITANCE

ISBN: 0-446-61657-5

By Devin Grayson

BATMAN. AQUAMAN. GREEN ARROW. NIGHTWING. ARSENAL. TEMPEST.

A gunshot shatters the Gotham night as Slade Wilson, the superhuman killer-for-hire Deathstroke, fails to assassinate the young son of a visiting Quarac dignitary. Now three legendary crime fighters, Batman, Green Arrow, and Aquaman—and the three young heroes who had once been their loyal sidekicks—join forces to stop Slade and those who hired him. But as the hunt stretches across continents, opening lost memories and old wounds, it turns into a desperate race against time: for Deathstroke is but one player in a plot to destroy all of Gotham . . .

Available wherever books are sold.

HELLTOWN

ISBN: 0-446-61658-3

By Dennis O'Neil

BATMAN. LADY SHIVA. RICHARD DRAGON. THE QUESTION.

There are a lot of unanswered questions about Vic Sage, the Question: how he spent—or misspent—his youth; and how he came to be a journalist in the country's worst city. This story will solve these mysteries, retell and embellish some tales already told, and tell a new tale of how Vic, with a bit of help, brought some measure of serenity to a truly dreadful place. From his first meeting with Lady Shiva, where he was almost killed. To training with Richard Dragon, the best martial artist in the world (except perhaps for Lady Shiva and Batgirl). And how Batman, while threatening his life, also saved him, this story will finally provide answers about the Question. Who he is and what hc did.

Available November 2006.